MARKED BY MOONLIGHT

MATELESS SHIFTERS BOOK 1

ELLA MILES

CHAPTER I

LUMI

"On the count of three. One, two—"

"No."

"No?" I ask.

Kael chuckles nervously. "We're not going to kiss on the count of three."

"Why not?"

"Because it's weird. It's not how it's done. It's not romantic. Kissing is supposed to be more spontaneous than that. You kiss someone because you can't not kiss them. The draw to them is so strong that it overpowers any other senses, and all you can think about is kissing them."

"Hmmm," I say, thinking about what he said, and sit back on my heels as we kneel in the forest before the full moon.

"What are you doing?" he asks after a moment.

"Apparently waiting for you to be so drawn to me that it overpowers you, and you kiss me."

Kael chuckles again.

"What now?" I snap. *This isn't going how I hoped this would go.*

"Nothing—you're just funny, Lumi."

"No, I'm not your funny friend. I'm the attractive woman you want to kiss and go all beast man on."

My words make him laugh harder.

I sigh. *This is never going to work.*

No, it has to work. We are all out of options.

"You take the lead if you don't like how I'm handling this then!"

Kael goes silent for a second. "I've never kissed anyone either. I don't know how this is supposed to go."

We both stare up at the moon—the one thing to which we are both drawn. The one thing that should be our salvation, and yet we can never tap into its full power. We've never felt what it's like to unleash our wolf selves and run free through the woods, letting our instincts take over. And it's all because of the curse.

Kael pulls his eyes down from the moon, and I can feel him looking at me. It's dark, so I'm not sure how well he can see me, even with the moonlight slipping down through the branches of the trees. He only has normal human eyesight, while the one wolf trait I possess is enhanced vision at night. The wolf vision allows me to make him out perfectly.

Kael is a good-looking man. Even if he can't shift either, he keeps himself in shape. His biceps bulge against the fabric of his black T-shirt, and his legs are long and lean. He's stronger than most humans, even if he isn't in wolf shape. But the man looks like a beast of thick, shaggy brown hair that hangs over his hazel eyes. He's desperately in need of a haircut, but it does make him look younger than his thirty years and closer to my twenty-one.

He smiles softly at me with his boy next door charm. As the only member of the pack who's even close in age to me, we've grown close over the years. Now it's time to see how close.

I reach out to his chest in the darkness and run my finger down his thick muscles. My lips part as I imagine what lies beneath his shirt. I've seen him shirtless plenty of times, and I conjure up a memory in my head that leaves me drooling and needing to lick his swollen pecs. My eyes begin to hood, and a single word escapes my barely parted lips. "Please..."

"Lumi, I—" he begins the same speech of how we shouldn't do this, the one he's given me a million times before.

But I'm tired of it.

I close the space between us and press my lips against his, as if I'm drawn to him as much as I'm drawn to the full moon.

But I miss, or he moves. I'm not sure, but my kiss lands on the side of his jaw.

He freezes.

I blush bright red, my entire body on fire as I quickly pull away.

He puts his hands on my shoulders, and I can feel the power beneath his hands begging to break free. There's a caged wolf inside of him that can't escape, thanks to the curse our pack triggered.

His broad hands stay on my shoulders. He doesn't break the connection. But his lips don't come crashing down on mine either.

My breath catches in my throat as I wait with unbridled anticipation. Kael is close, but it appears he needs more convincing.

"I know you find me attractive. I can see it in the way you look at me when you think I'm not looking. Your body is hard, and your breath is heavy with need," I say.

He doesn't deny any of my words, but they still aren't enough.

"We're perfect for each other. You're my growly beast-man, and I'm your clumsy silver beauty. We know everything there is to know about each other—the good and the bad." I take my hand in his, marveling at how our hands seem to fit together. I don't need wolf super hearing to notice our heartbeats matching at a rapid pace.

His other hand reaches up, tucking a strand of my long silvery-white locks behind my ear. He stares into my crystal blue eyes.

I smile and lick my lips. *We're so close, so close to breaking the curse; I can feel it.*

For twenty-one years our pack has been blamed for the curse that descended on all the wolves after our female alpha, my aunt Elara, rejected her true mate—the alpha from the Moonlight pack, the strongest of us all. No one had ever rejected a mate before, and it cost each of them their life. They couldn't survive without the other, dying soon after.

From that moment on, the packs were cursed for rejecting what the gods had offered us. The mating bond that had served us so well for centuries shattered. No wolf could feel the pull to their mate. The magic that held it together disintegrated into nothing.

Mates lost their ability to communicate with each other. Fights broke out between couples that had loved each other for decades. All love, connection, and trust was lost. Replaced by hate and rage.

Slowly, one by one, at least one of the mating pairs would die. Oftentimes at the hands of their former mate.

Those who hadn't found their mates yet became incapable of finding them. No wolf pups were born to replace the quickly dying population. Only mated couples are able to bear children.

The Wintermoon pack we belong to is the weakest of all—punishment from the shifter gods for rejecting the mating bond they gifted us, after the curse they created wasn't enough punishment in their eyes. I'm the youngest in our pack—born just before the curse swept through the packs. Kael is the next youngest. With only seven of us left in the entire pack, there hasn't been enough power for Kael and me to get our wolf forms.

As outcasts, we don't know how the other wolf packs are fairing. Hopefully, better than we are.

But things are about to turn around. There's a prophecy that Thalia, the most powerful seer of all the witches, has told. According to her, when a wolf finds their true mate, the curse will be broken for every wolf. Then, we will be able to have pups again and regain our natural powers as wolves.

Tonight is the night we break the curse. Even if Kael isn't so sure, I am.

"You're my mate, Kael. I can feel it all the way to my bones." In the dream I had last night, it felt like the gods were speaking directly to me, telling me I'm going to be the one to break the curse.

He wets his lips. "I'm going to try, Lumi, but nothing changes between us if this doesn't work. We remain friends."

"Yes, friends. But this will work. It's you. It has to be you."

He nods.

"Kiss me," I demand.

He lowers his lips, and this time, our lips meet.

As his lips press against mine, I close my eyes, letting me lose myself in the moment. His lips part, and his tongue gently coaxes my lips open and slips into my mouth.

Oh.

His tongue skims over mine in a hesitant kiss. My toes curl and flex as if waiting for the butterflies floating in my stomach feeling to turn into flaming hot desire. And then suddenly, he's not so hesitant anymore. His kiss is aggressive as he captures me, filling my mouth with his tongue.

Kael pushes me back, his hands gripping my arm and waist as he lays me onto the soft moss.

My heart thuds to a stop. Vibrations rumble through my body at his intrusive touch. A brush of his hand against my bare stomach has my skin crawling. I was wrong. This isn't right.

Kael doesn't seem to notice any of it. Either he feels something I don't, or he's forcing himself to push through it to find out the truth. We have to see if, once and for all, I'm his mate or not—even if that means ruining our friendship in the process.

A sharp sting scrapes my neck. My eyes widen in horror as I realize his fingers have turned into sharp claws. It's the only part of him that reveals his wolf form, and only then, rarely. He can't control that part of him.

Fear radiates through me in a flash. *This is wrong. We aren't mates. I can't lose Kael's friendship. He's all I have. Why did I push us to do this?*

His claws dig deeper into my skin as his lips clamp down on me.

I begin to push against his chest, trying to stop him. It's no use, though. He's twice my size and far stronger than I am. I open my eyes to find his hazel eyes staring back at me, glossed over in a lust-filled haze. The Kael I know isn't the man on top of me. He hasn't shifted into his wolf form; this is his animalistic side. He's still human in every way other than his claws, but he's not Kael anymore.

There's a frenzy in his movements, making it clear that he's not thinking clearly and that he won't stop until he gets what the beast inside of him wants—me.

"Kael!" I scream at him, but it's muffled with his mouth over mine.

I have to stop this. This isn't Kael making decisions anymore. And he's never going to forgive himself once he realizes what he did.

Think! What do I do?

This is my fault. I suggested it. I just didn't think Kael's wolf side would come out. Or if it did, I thought I would want it. I thought fucking under the full moon would help us feel the bond the curse dulled. I didn't think it would turn Kael's mind into a monster.

"Kael!" I try again, pushing harder. He doesn't budge, as his claws now dig into my jean shorts, ripping the waistband.

I'm running out of time. Soon, he'll rip my clothes completely from my body.

I gulp.

My body is hot and sweaty as the fear takes hold of me completely.

I close my eyes and try to tap into my own wolf—it's

the only way I'll have the strength to get him off of me. Father says that turning is like coaxing an old friend to the surface. One that's lived caged and afraid all their life. You have to be gentle and not give her a choice but to come forward.

Come on, wolf. There is nothing to be afraid of. Come forward.

Nothing.

I open my eyes as Kael rips through my shorts entirely and begins pushing them off.

No, no, no.

"Kael!" I scream at the top of my lungs as he breaks the kiss.

His hazel eyes have turned a bright yellow as he stares down at me.

Fuck.

I ball my hand into a fist and try the only option that comes to mind. My fist flies into his jaw, but his head barely twitches. No blood spews. No crack of a bone. He's completely unaffected, while my hand feels like I broke every bone in it.

Tears threaten to fall from my eyes as his body presses against me, and I can feel how hard he is. Even through his jeans, I can feel his thick cock between my legs.

"No!" I say fiercely. I'm the alpha's daughter. My father has the ability to command anyone in the pack with a single command. Maybe I have that power, too.

Kael stops, his ears twitching as if he's hearing something for the first time.

Yes, oh my gods, yes! It worked.

Then suddenly, Kael's body isn't on mine anymore as I see a whoosh of fur and teeth whiz past me.

I scramble up, looking to see who my savior is. The

gray-colored fur tells me it's not a wolf from our pack, and the wolf isn't stopping.

"Kael!" I scream now for very different reasons.

Kael seems to come to, his claws returning to hands and the glow leaving his eyes. His gaze is now wide-eyed terror as the large gray wolf rips into his side.

"No!"

I reach for a weapon—anything I can use to stop the attack long enough for Kael to make a run for it.

I grab a rock and throw it at the gray wolf's head. It hits him hard enough that he turns his attention back on me.

"Run!" I yell at Kael as I begin running in the direction of our home, hoping that Father or one of the other Wintermoon wolves will be there to save us.

"Help!" I shout at the top of my lungs, hoping some of their superior wolf listening kicks in enough to hear me.

I feel the wolf's breath hot on my heels. His teeth snap too close for comfort as I jump over a fallen branch.

I don't know which pack this wolf is from, but he's clearly messing with me and enjoying the chase. He could have taken me down in one leap the second he saw me. He's much faster, stronger, and has far more power than I do.

Suddenly, I see the clearing that leads to our home. I feel guilty for bringing danger to our home, but I don't have a choice if I want to stay alive.

I run faster, needing all of my speed, but it's an error. My foot catches on a rock, and I fall hard onto the ground. A stabbing throb shoots through my wrists as I catch the weight of my body on the ground. I prepare to be ripped to pieces—slowly and painfully. *This is how I die.*

A familiar growl echoes through the forest, and my

heart eases as a comforting smile reaches my cheeks—Father.

Before I can stand up, I hear teeth ripping into fur and the familiar clash of claws battling it out above me. I have no doubt that my father will win. He's an alpha, and as far as I could tell, the gray wolf was a lone wolf without any position of power.

I sit up and begin scanning the woods for Kael as two more members of our pack join my father. My father howls, drawing my attention back to him as he stands over the fallen wolf. The fight is over in seconds.

I sit on the grass, wrapping my arms around my legs, and take a deep breath.

I'm safe.

I quickly stumble to my feet, needing to ensure that Kael is okay.

"He's fine," Tavian, our beta, says.

I stop dead in my tracks as I see Kael in his arms with a deep gash on his side.

"He doesn't look fine."

"Maybe if you hadn't left the safety of the pack, then he wouldn't have gotten attacked," Tavian says.

I open my mouth to respond when I feel my father's eyes on me. He's shifted back into a human, and he stands naked before me. I keep my eyes focused on his face—something I've honed over the years. I refuse to see anything I don't want to see on a family member or friend. His jet-black hair is peppered with grays, and his eyes are a deep brown. I have no clue who I inherited my ivory tresses or my blue eyes from. I look nothing like my father, and my mother died in childbirth. But from what my father told me, she had blonde hair and green eyes.

My father always said it was because I was born in the

middle of a snow storm and so the gods gifted me with the beauty of the color of snow. It's where my name comes from anyway. But I'm not a believer in the gods gifting us anything after the curse they bestowed on us.

I wait for his disappointment to befall me. I'm not supposed to leave the safety of our home at night, especially not during a full moon when the other shifters's strength will be at their highest. We are most vulnerable to an attack on nights like these, and this isn't the first attack we've had.

He sighs and offers his hand to me. He pulls me into a gentle hug; his gaze is filled with a sad determination. He's decided something tonight under the full moon, and I know it will be final. I'll have to accept whatever he says, as he's the alpha and I'm not.

"You and Kael are going to leave the pack. You're going to live as humans. You're going to forget about us—about the curse. You're going to be happy."

CHAPTER 2
LUMI

"What?" My heart stops as I look at my stone-faced father. There is no wavering in his eyes, no emotion. He's clearly been considering this for a while. Tonight, he made his decision, and it's final.

I still can't believe I heard him correctly. This can't be true. He's never even hinted at wanting me and Kael to leave. Surely, he's simply sending me to get help, to find a way to break the curse. He doesn't really want me to leave and never return.

But my father doesn't repeat himself. He ignores my question and starts heading back toward our house through the clearing. I follow, hot on his heels. I need a lot more answers from him as he opens and shuts the door to our small two-bedroom, two-bathroom cabin.

It has a small, rustic feel with large windows—designed to let as much of the nature surrounding us into our home. It doesn't provide much protection against an outside attack.

But it's home with its warm fireplace, basic oversized furniture, and modern appliances. It's peaceful here despite the times we live in and the turmoil all around us.

The small cabin in the heart of the woods is one of five that were built after the curse took out most of our pack and we fled after the other packs continued to seek retribution against us. We are in the most remote part of northern Alaska where only a handful of packs live in the harsh conditions. Most prefer to live closer to civilization, where they can enjoy more human comforts.

Only three of the cabins are currently occupied. I'm afraid of how few will be left if Kael and I leave. There will be no more hope. Only the eldest will remain, and I doubt they will continue to put up much of a fight against the surrounding packs trying to take our land. The pack won't survive until winter, which is the only time we have the advantage. Our pack has grown accustomed to the harsh winters, unlike the surrounding packs that prefer their luxuries and warm heat.

I throw the wooden door open and step inside after Father, determined to change his mind now that we aren't in front of the rest of the pack.

"I'm not leaving."

"You are." He hunches over the kitchen counter. I can't tell what he's making, but he's pulled several items out of the fridge, and his broad shoulders block my view.

"You need me! You need me here to help stop the curse. To help rebuild the pack. To—"

Father turns with a growl. "There is no pack left!"

His growl sends shivers down my body and forces me to stop and listen. He hasn't used a growl like that on me in a long time. I'm not even sure I ever recall him getting this worked up around me. He's always been a calm, gentle giant. He's a firm leader who never needs to raise his voice or show his strength to get others to follow. He's never even been questioned as alpha. No one has ever fought him for the title.

My mouth slams shut as if on its own accord. I don't know if he gave an alpha command or just raised his voice so loud that my basic instinct is to snap it shut.

"There is nothing left for you here, Lumi. *Nothing*. And you have to accept that you will never get your wolf. Your heightened wolf eyesight isn't enough to live in a pack, risking your life every day pretending you'll someday be something else. By every indication, you are human..."

I open my mouth to speak, but nothing comes out.

"You're not a wolf shifter. You're not one of us. You're human. And you will learn to live as a human."

My eyes water as my mouth gapes open. *But I'm not a human. It doesn't matter that I'm only showing a single wolf strength. I'm more than a human. I'm...*

Father looks down at me with a cold expression I've never felt from him before. This isn't up for discussion.

He turns back around, and I'm left trying to figure out how to convince him. I need to talk to Kael. I need to talk to the others. They will be on my side. They'd never kick a member out of the pack. There would be a revolt.

Before I can speak, I see what Father was making. Four sandwiches sit on the counter in ziplock bags. He begins loading them into a backpack—*my* backpack.

I look around the living room behind me until I spot it —my packed duffel bag.

He really has put thought into this. There is nothing I can say that will change his mind.

He turns, holding my backpack out to me.

I take it.

"There's all the cash I have on hand and enough food for you to survive the week. Take the car, take Kael, and head south. Leave Alaska. Go find a job. You're smart. You could go to college or open your own business. There are credit cards in there. Use them to pay for everything. The pack and I will pay them off. Use them to start a new life, a better life."

I shake my head, desperately trying to hold back the tears swelling in my eyes. A drop of sweat from my brow sinks down into my eyes, burning them and forcing the tears to finally fall.

Father doesn't react. He doesn't come and hold me like he used to when I was younger. He just stares at me with a dark shadow of indifference I've never seen before.

"Look," he says, nodding toward the window behind me.

I turn and see Kael being bandaged by his aunt. As she wraps a large bandage around his upper chest, I see he has a nasty cut on his forehead as well.

"You almost got him killed tonight."

"That wasn't my fault—"

"Enough." He silences me once again. "I know you care about the boy. He hasn't gotten his wolf either and likely never will—you can both live as humans. You can both escape this tortured fate. Take him and leave."

I wipe my tears, looking at Kael. He does deserve better than this. He deserves so much more. I don't want to sacrifice everything—my family, my life, my pack—for him. But I can help him get out if he wants.

"No," I finally break free enough of the alpha command he has on me to speak.

Father ignores my outburst and picks up my duffel bag on the floor. He carries it outside to the Jeep parked at the side of the cabin. There's just one road that leads back here, and it isn't well-kept. Our Jeep usually gets stuck multiple times on the drive into the closest town.

After putting my duffel bag into the back of the Jeep, he walks over to Kael. I notice Kael's uncle carrying his bags to the back of the Jeep next.

I stare into each pack member's face. Not one of them speaks up on our behalf. No one is on our side, and everyone agrees we should leave.

"Go south. Go to the border. Go somewhere warm," Kael's uncle says to him.

Kael looks at him with a wide stare, and I know he can't believe what Theron is saying either. Then Kael looks to me.

"I'm trusting my daughter in your hands. Take care of her," Father says to Kael.

I frown. I don't need anyone to take care of me, especially not Kael.

There's a low growl from the woods, followed by several howls. It's our only warning before wolves jump through the lining of the forest and into the clearing where we've made our homes.

The wolf shifters of our pack, who still possess the ability to shift, begin to take their wolf form. Fur and claws and muscles begin appearing from where human skin and bones just were. But it takes our pack too long. The intruders have already shifted and are attacking—their claws slice through skin mid-shift.

No!

I have to do something. I can't let them take the last of my family and pack.

Father doesn't give me a chance. He knows me well enough to know that I will stay and fight—even if it means certain death.

"Run! Run away, take the Jeep and drive until you run out of gas, then get another tank and drive some more. Live as humans, be happy, and never return," he says, giving an alpha command that I feel deep in my bones. "Both of you." He says, commanding Kael as well.

We both run to the Jeep. I jump into the driver's side as Kael jumps into the passenger's. Before I can think of what I'm doing, my foot is pressed all the way down on the gas, and we're driving full speed away from the carnage, away from my home.

We don't speak as the clearing turns to woods. The Jeep bounces roughly over dried mud and small fallen branches on the road.

All I can think about is my pack—my father, Kael's aunt and uncle, Akela, Tavian, and Aire. *How many are left? Did any of them survive? And who was the wolf pack that attacked us? Most likely, the Nightshade or Frostbite packs. Both live near us and have made it their mission to end our pack in hopes that it ends the curse.*

We drive through the night until the Jeep is almost out of gas before I finally stop. I'm out of breath, and my heart is racing rapidly. I turn to Kael, who hasn't blinked in a while. He seems to be in shock.

"Are you okay?"

He nods.

And then I feel it—I can breathe again. I look over at Kael as he sucks in big lungfuls of air. The magic my father used on us suddenly disappeared—the alpha command gone.

"Does it mean…?" I ask, but I can't finish my sentence out loud. *Does it mean that my father was killed?*

Kael shakes his head. "With how weak our pack is, the command probably just wore off the further away we drove."

"What now? We could go back," I say, blinking back my tears, trying to remain strong. *He's not dead. He's not dead. He's not dead. None of them are.*

He shakes his head. "What good would that do? We can't help the pack, and your father would just command us to leave again."

I nod and swallow the lump in my throat. Anxiety races through my chest. I need to know if they're still alive, but going back would only devastate me. I'd either realize they are all dead or have my own father banish me all over again.

I yawn, and my heightened eyesight begins to strain as I stare out at the endless road. It's after four in the morning, and neither of us has slept. We need to find a hotel to regroup before driving onward in the morning.

Where will we go? And are we really going to forget about the pack and live as humans?

No.

I can't.

I can't just leave and forget about them.

Kael can if he wants to, but I can't.

Kael notices the shift in me. "Tell me. Tell me what you're thinking."

"I'm thinking that I will drop you off wherever you want to go, but I'm not going to live as a human. I'm not giving up on my family. I'm going to find the Moonlight pack. The Moonlight wolves and Wintermoon wolves were what caused the curse. My best guess is that someone from both packs is the way to break the curse."

He looks at me in shock, wide-eyed.

"I'm going to find them, and I'm going to break the curse."

CHAPTER 3

LUMI

"Finally, a motel. Stop here. We need to sleep tonight," Kael says. We've been driving all night and all day after not being able to find a hotel the night before.

A yawn overtakes my entire body as I blink through my dry eyes, trying desperately to moisturize them. I don't want to stop. I need to find the Moonlight wolves as soon as possible. It's the only way to save my father and the rest of our pack.

That is, if they aren't already dead, that brutal voice in my head says.

They're not dead. I would feel something if they were, wouldn't I?

Still, Kael is probably right, so I pull off the highway and up to the single-story lodge just off the road.

"Wait here; I'll see if they have any rooms." Kael jumps out before I respond.

Tapping my finger against the leather of the steering wheel, I watch him run inside. The lodge has maybe a dozen rooms and is the only building we've seen in hours.

If there aren't any rooms available, I don't know how much longer we will have to drive until we find another place to stay.

Kael jogs back to the Jeep. "One room left."

"Thank gods."

We grab our bags and head into the lobby. The second I step into the lodge, my nose is assaulted by stale cigarette smoke and a damp, musky scent.

"Maybe the car would be a better place to sleep," I mumble to Kael.

He shakes his head. "I know this place isn't great." He walks two doors down the hallway and then stops in front of a moldy door. After three failed swipes of the room key, the door finally unlocks, and Kael opens the door. He holds the door open with his duffle bag over his shoulder. "But this place has a bed and bathroom. It's better than sleeping in the car."

I step inside and see the single bed in the corner, a damp spot on the floor, and a stench coming from the bathroom that smells like something died in there. It's obvious this place has barely been cleaned, if it has ever been cleaned at all.

With a raised brow, I say, "I'm not sure I agree."

Kael sighs. "We really can't get any luck, can we?"

"We are the cause of a curse that stretched across all the wolf shifter packs. We are the definition of bad luck."

He smiles as I drop my bags on the floor and then fall onto the bed. One of the springs in the bed snaps, and the bed lurches.

I jump up as Kael laughs at me. The sound is rich and hearty, the likes of which I haven't heard since before my father ordered us to leave.

I hit him playfully on the shoulder, but the sound of his laughter warms my heart. "Don't laugh at me."

"Maybe we can put the mattress on the floor. Then, if it breaks, we won't have far to fall."

"Do you think we'll both fit on it?"

Kael's pupils dilate in an intense and piercing blackness, and I think for a second I see the flicker of lust I saw when we were kissing in the woods.

But that can't be. He doesn't like me. He doesn't want me. We aren't mates. We're just friends.

He yawns. It's contagious, and I yawn again.

"Do you want to shower first or just go to bed?" he asks with another yawn.

I stifle my own yawn as I say, "Bed. I don't think I can keep my eyes open for another second."

Kael grabs the mattress and slides it off the creaky bed frame and onto the floor. I still don't see how we are both going to fit, but Kael kicks off his shoes and jeans until he's standing in his boxers and a dark gray t-shirt. The dressing from his wound is thick enough to see under his shirt.

"Undress," he says.

I raise an eyebrow and grip my midsection with a blush.

He lets out a boisterous laugh as he yanks off his shirt and then climbs under the covers. "I just meant take your shoes and jeans off."

I kick my shoes off easily enough. But I'm only wearing a thong, so I'm not sure I want to take my jeans off.

"Really? You were willing to kiss me and let me have sex with you in the woods if the bond shone between us, but you aren't willing to take your jeans off so we can sleep."

"Close your eyes."

He rolls his hazel eyes before snapping them shut.

I yank my jeans down and then hurry to the spot on the mattress next to Kael, my heart racing as I slide under the covers.

"Okay."

Kael opens his eyes with a soft grin. "Come here." He holds his arm out, and I slowly lower my head onto his shoulder.

"See? I'm not going to bite."

"Doesn't it feel strange, though?"

With a rough exhale, he stares down at a spot on the comforter like it's the most interesting thing. His shaggy brown tendrils fall into his eyes. "Yes. I should have told you earlier, but you were so convinced that we were mates, that we'd discover a bond between us. I couldn't deny you that chance. But I only think of you as my annoying little sister."

His hazel eyes finally look at me in the protective way they always do. I can't be mad at him. He loves me—he's just not in love with me.

Maybe it's because we grew up together as the only two young members of our pack. Maybe it's because even if we were mates, we'd never feel anything until the curse is lifted.

I let my eyes drag down his bare chest and bandage, then over the taught skin of his thick muscles before his narrow waist disappears beneath the covers. I've imagined his muscles contracting over me countless times. I've imagined how his tongue would taste against mine and how his hard length would feel pushed between my legs.

But after that kiss, after feeling him, it felt wrong—so fucking wrong. It must have just been a silly crush. Now that I'm here in this bed next to him and he's shared his feelings, I'm beginning to see him as what he's always been—my protective older brother.

"Thank you for telling me. I feel the same."

He grins, and his eyes light up with relief. "Good. Now, let's sleep. We can discuss our next move in the morning."

"You mean you're not going to argue with me about finding the Moonlight wolves?"

He narrows his eyes. "No. Why would I when I plan on coming with you?"

A soft smile spreads across my face, and the uneasiness in my belly disappears instantly. I would have searched for the pack on my own, but having my best and only friend with me gives me more courage to face whatever dangers we will encounter.

CHAPTER 4
LUMI

I stare at the maps pulled up on my phone, clueless as to where to search next. It's been over a month, and we are still no closer to finding the Moonlight wolves. All we've done is find a whole bunch of places they aren't.

We've searched southern British Columbia near Vancouver, Seattle, most of Washington, and Portland. We haven't found so much as a paw print to tell me we're searching in the right places. No fearful whispers at the local stores about the wolves that run through the woods at night. No sign of a wolf pack nearby or anywhere.

And as Kael and I are the only ones searching, it could take us months or years to find even a trace of them existing at all. Unless, they want us to find them.

But why would they? Why would any of the packs want to be found by us or know who we are?

In their eyes, we're just members of the lowly Wintermoon wolves—the outcasts, better off dead than alive.

Tears well in my eyes at the thought of my pack. For all we know, we might be the only two surviving members. But I can't accept that, not until I know for sure. I have to believe they are alive. I have to believe that when I break the curse, I'll have a pack to come back to.

There is no way for us to know if the pack survived unless we go back. My messages have gone unread, but that doesn't mean they are dead. It could just be that my father was absolute in his decision to cut us off from the pack.

Kael looks across the room at me from where he's sitting on the tiny, full-sized bed we've been sharing in this Seattle motel. He flips mindlessly through the channels while his eyes never leave me. I beg the maps to give me some clue, some gut feeling that will tell me where the other wolf packs are. Finding them and breaking the curse is the only way I'll be able to go back and find out the truth of what happened when we left.

I quickly wipe my tears before I think he notices. We haven't talked about our pack, our family, since we left. It wouldn't do us any good—we can't go back.

Unfortunately, I know very little of the other wolf packs. The things I do know feel more like fairytales my father told me to get me to sleep than reality. The Silvercrest wolves are the only other pack I've met in real life, and their customs were mostly hidden from me. I don't know what is normal for the other wolf shifters.

Do they live as humans most of the time and travel into the forest when they want to be in their wolf forms? Do they have cabins or tents and live in the woods full-time like we do? Are there markers or scents I should be picking up to find them?

There is so much I don't know, so much I realize now that my father hid from me.

As I search for some hidden clue in the maps of the

vast forests near Seattle, my frustration grows, and I start muttering. "The Moonlight pack has to be here. And if not them, then some pack that would know where they are. We have to keep searching here in Seattle until we find them."

I say the words more for myself than for Kael. He's been mostly silent this whole time. He started off very supportive, making it clear he'd follow me anywhere. He went along with me when we traveled long days and spent our nights wandering dark forests, but I can tell he's getting antsy.

"I think we should go back," he says solemnly.

"What?" I drop my phone on the couch I'm sitting on and lift my head to stare at him. He slouches against the headboard, his long legs stretched out. His wound has finally healed, but now there's a darkness that shades his features I'm not used to seeing on him. His shaggy hair has grown longer over his hazel eyes, which also have changed. His hazel eyes now glow with a soft streak of silver as he stares at me. It's a glow I've only ever seen in the shifters in our pack.

"Kael...?" I whisper in a warning. A warning of what exactly I'm not sure, but something is changing in him.

He sweeps his muscled legs over the edge of the bed, and then he's staring at me down, a mere five feet from each other.

"This is pointless. We'll never find the Moonlight wolves, that is, if they even exist at all. For all we know, they were killed off when the curse swept through our kind."

"We can't go back," I whisper even softer.

He stands.

I rise, not liking the power imbalance if I were to stay

seated. Still, Kael towers over me, and a thick tension fills the air.

"We need to go back. There is nothing for us here. At least back home, we have family. We have our way of life. We have a chance to learn how to shift into our wolves."

"They're dead!" I scream, releasing the truth I know deep down inside me. The truth that I've been desperate to ignore.

He blinks, the hazel in his eyes vanishing with a blink until all that remains is a bright silver. "No."

"They're dead," I say, calmer, the reality hitting me like a freight train. We have to both accept it. "They're dead. They were weak before we left and under relentless attacks. We've tried contacting them time and time again, and they don't answer. The alpha command is gone. Our alpha, my father, is gone. Your aunt and uncle are gone. We can't go back. It would be a waste of time. There is nothing to go back to."

He shakes his head, and his hands grip my shoulders, shaking me. "No, no, no..."

"Kael." I reach my hand up to brush his scruffy cheek. I don't know why he's reacting so strongly. He's been fine with our mission to this point but suddenly has this urge to go home.

I whisper so softly and gently, "It doesn't matter if they are alive or dead; we can't go back. They don't want us to."

"No, they want us to move on. To live as humans. To get jobs. To buy a three-bedroom house. To fuck. To have human babies that won't even have the tiniest spark left of their true heritage. I can't do that!" His eyes turn bright silver now, the glow filling the room as his grip on my arm tightens. Still, he continues to yell.

"I'm not a human! I don't have any skills. I can't just get a job. I can't play the part of your live-in boyfriend. And I sure as hell can't keep following you around endlessly, living out of cheap motels, searching for something that doesn't exist."

"Kael." I try to move my arms, but I can't. His strength is far superior to my own, especially when he's angry. Although, I've never seen him this upset. The anger doesn't even make sense. It's like a rage has been building uncontrollably inside him, and he has no choice but to unleash it to survive.

For a moment, I think this is what is going to finally set his wolf free. My father said strong emotions are a common way that we shift for the first time. A strong tantrum at three years old. An unrequited crush at thirteen. An encounter with a bear in the woods. A nightmare. A first love. Any strong, heavy emotion can unleash the wolf.

It's almost unheard of not to have had a strong enough emotion to unleash your wolf by our age. Teenagers are usually the oldest to receive their wolf. Maybe this emotion Kael is feeling is his body's way of forcing a strong enough emotion to unlock his wolf. Maybe this isn't really how he feels.

Whatever the reason, it doesn't matter. If he shifts, while I'll be incredibly happy for him, I'm a goner. Shifting in this hotel room is less than ideal. He'll tear me apart, along with the rest of the room, and threaten human authorities trying to tame him.

As it is, with his strong grip on my arm, I fear for my life. He's not in control of himself.

I have to think fast and find a way out of this. I do the

only thing I can think of that might knock him off balance enough to free myself.

I slam my mouth over his, and he gasps. A second later, I feel his claws forming where his fingers once were, digging his razor-sharp tips into my bicep. This time, I won't get away completely unscathed.

I deepen the kiss, trying to lock into his primal urges or at least dampen his rage.

I lean into him like I'm enjoying kissing a man who I now think of as a brother. His reaction isn't the real him. I've already forgiven him for this moment, but I still have to find a way to survive.

When I kiss him harder, he pushes me away. A small sliver of consciousness returns to his body, and his claws loosen on me.

"Run," he croaks out. "Now!"

CHAPTER 5
LUMI

For a split second, I consider staying. I don't know what's about to happen to Kael. And if he is going to turn, I need to help him find a safe place for it to happen.

"Please," he groans.

I turn and run—out of the motel room, through the open-aired hallway, down the open staircase, and toward our Jeep. I'm not sure where I'll drive, but seeing as the sun is setting and the moon will soon begin to rise, making his shift more likely, I'm going to have to spend the night away, hoping Kael survives.

Panting, I make it to the door, but the handle doesn't budge.

Shit, I didn't grab the keys.

I can't go back.

I hear a door thrown open and footsteps pad down the hallway above the parking lot.

Fuck, I don't have time to hesitate.

I start running again, but I don't know where I'm

going to go. There's a busy highway to my left. I can't lead Kael there; too many witnesses.

Woods—there's a forest behind the motel. We've searched it before and found no wolf packs. There also aren't any hiking trails, so we shouldn't run into any humans.

Kael will be safe if I can lead him far enough away.

And what of me?

I should have spent my time learning how to fight, how to wield a weapon, anything to defend myself. Instead, I put my energy into trying to shift. I thought once I could shift into a wolf, I'd be safe—so foolish.

Maybe I'll climb a tree or something once I lead Kael far enough in the woods?

I don't know; I just run.

I hit the edge of the forest just as the sun begins to dip down beneath the horizon. The faint glow of the sky is all that lights my path as I jump into the thick underbrush— branches and leaves cut into my skin as I dart between trees and bushes.

Growing up in a forest comes in handy, as I know exactly where to step and how to make a path for myself where none exists. I keep running, even as I hear his footsteps behind me. I don't glance back. I don't look to see if he's shifted—I know he hasn't yet. His footsteps would be heavier, he'd howl, and he'd be screaming in pain. My father said it can take a while to shift the first time. If he shifted now, I might have enough time to run and hide.

Sweating and panting, my lungs and thighs are burning from how quickly I run. If I stop, I'll never escape again. I have to keep running.

But I don't know how much longer I can go on like this. I need to find a place to hide and catch my breath.

Even though he'll be able to sniff me out if he turns, hiding in the darkness is my best chance. My eyesight is far better than his, at least at the moment.

I need a dark spot to hide.

The lingering sunlight is almost gone. It's still not dark enough for me to have the advantage.

A howl streaks through the air from behind me.

I stumble at the sound, almost losing my footing, but somehow manage to stay on my feet.

Did Kael turn?

I can't help myself. I glance back.

It costs me.

My legs stop moving, and I gasp.

Brown fur and bright silver eyes stare back at me. A large brown wolf is running toward me, his fur shaggy, just like his human hair. He doesn't seem to hesitate in his body. He runs like he's shifted into a wolf hundreds of times already.

It's beautiful watching him run so elegantly. He's majestic and too fucking close.

How did he shift so quickly?

He growls, baring his sharp canines at me—as if he's trying to tell me to run. Maybe he still has some control of his thoughts but hasn't figured out how to control his wolf instincts yet.

Gods, I turn and take off again. I run faster than I've ever run before.

My heart sings for Kael, and I can't help the grin that spreads wide on my face. *He did it! He finally shifted!*

My heart shutters faster—*his shifting might kill me.*

It might be a better fate than living with the fact that he can shift and I can't. He's finally grown into who he's always been, while I might as well be a normal human.

I'm so in my head while I run that I don't see the dip in the forest floor. My feet give out from underneath me, and I slide onto my ass.

Suddenly, a hot breath flames my neck. He's right here.

This is it—the end.

A ball of fur lands on top of me as I squeeze my eyes shut, preparing for the end. But I don't feel the claws, the teeth, the sharpness of my flesh tearing. All I feel is his heavy weight on top of me.

I peek open one eye, hoping that Kael has figured out how to control his primal urges. The sun has completely set now. Darkness covers the forest like a thick blanket, but I can see as clearly as ever.

The fur on top of me is not the same muddy brown color I saw before. This shade is midnight black. When the wolf's head turns to me, its eyes are bright red.

I gasp.

The wolf gives me a harsh look devoid of any softness, and even though I can't hear what he's saying, I know the meaning deep in my bones.

Stay here and hide.

And then the weight of him is gone, and I hear a deep howl that trembles through me. The howl is much louder than Kael's earlier. It's a howl that can be heard for miles and miles, meant as a command to be followed.

I shudder.

Growls shortly follow. I arch my head back, peering over the top of the small ridge I fell between, and see flashes of teeth and fur.

Kael.

Fuck, Kael is going to be hurt. He's not ready to fight another wolf, especially not one as massive as this one.

I'm guessing the midnight black wolf is an alpha, and a strong one at that. He's far larger than my father, and his howl is louder, deeper, and fiercer.

"Stop!" I shout, my voice cracking, dry, and barely audible.

I scramble up as a high-pitched whining sound cuts through my heart.

Kael—no.

I'm on my feet, running toward the two wolves as if I'm strong enough to stop them. I have to be.

"Stop!" I shout again as the much bigger, black-haired wolf's bite clamps down around Kael's neck.

Kael whimpers; there's no telling how much he's hurt.

The wolf releases Kael. For a moment, I think Kael is going to run. He needs to get away from this wolf. We can't both survive, but now that Kael can shift, he has to leave. Maybe now Kael has a chance at stopping the curse.

Kael takes a deep breath through his long snout, breathing in my scent. His head snaps to me, and he growls low and deep. The rumbling courses through me, and my legs freeze to the spot where I'm standing.

He thinks I'm prey.

"Kael, it's me. It's Lumi. Stop."

He doesn't hesitate. His front legs move toward me, eyes locked on me as he drops low like he's ready to pounce.

"It's Lumi. It's your best friend."

He leaps, and I squeeze my eyes shut again. I'm tackled to the ground as his incredible weight lands on me. I wait for my head to hit the ground, for the ripping and tearing of my body to begin. But one deep, commanding howl later, there is nothing.

I open my eyes. To my surprise, I'm staring into the

same red eyes as before, but this time, they're attached to a man. I study them closely, watching as the red fades and blackness engulfs them. Deep black hair sweeps across his forehead in long tendrils over flawlessly tanned skin. My eyes trail down his high cheekbones and over the dark five o'clock shadow of his sharp jawline.

He's incredibly handsome. The way he's staring at me so intensely makes me squirm beneath him. That's when I realize how naked he is—so incredibly naked.

"I would stop doing that if I were you," he says, his voice deep and growly.

I freeze. "Stop doing what? And why?"

"Squirming. You're rubbing your hot body all over my naked one. I won't be responsible for my actions if you keep doing that."

I stop immediately and swallow the hard lump in my throat. *Hot? Did he say I was hot?* I must have imagined it.

Kael.

What happened to Kael? Where is he?

"Don't worry, your boyfriend's safe."

This man is hot, yes, which causes my heart to do a little flip. But my stomach also grows uneasy with the fact that his naked body is still pressed against me. Something stirs inside my gut that tells me not to trust him. Even if he did save me, there is something off about this man.

"He's not my boyfriend."

He raises a cocky eyebrow, and a sinister smirk crosses his lips. "Interesting."

"What's interesting?"

"You; both of you." He drags his eyes down what he can see of my body. It unsettles me, and I squirm, feeling his hardness press against my lower stomach.

"I warned you," he says.

"Where is Kael?"

"I have some questions for you first."

"No, tell me where Kael is. And get off of me—now."

He chuckles. "Such a bold and strong snow wolf, aren't you?"

I glare. "I'm not a..." I almost say I'm not a wolf, but I snap my mouth shut. *And how does he know my name means snow? How does he know the winter and cold flakes of snow are where I feel at home?*

He tilts his head, causing his dark hair to fall across his forehead. "So very, very interesting. Tsk, tsk, tsk..." He stares at me, his body growing even harder against my stomach until I can feel the entire hard length of him.

I shake my head. "Stop that."

He grins. "It's your fault I'm hard."

"No, it's not. And it's your fault you're still pressing your heavy body on mine."

"Ouch," he chuckles, not the least bit offended. "I prefer 'strong, muscled, handsome body.'"

I roll my eyes. "Get off of me and tell me where Kael is."

His eyes lock on mine, trying to figure me out. "If I get off of you, do you promise not to do something stupid that will get you killed?"

"No, I wasn't doing anything stupid."

"Facing a wolf who has just shifted for the first time, isn't in control, is alpha-less, and has the hots for you is stupid."

"How do you know that? And Kael doesn't have the hots for me; we've established that."

He laughs. "Every man who sees you has the hots for you, Lumi."

"Where is Kael?"

He ignores me, staring deep into my eyes with a forceful persuasion. Luckily, wolf shifters don't have the power to force the truth out of another.

"What pack do you belong to? And what are you doing here?" he demands.

"If I answer, will you get off of me and tell me where Kael is?" I push against his hard chest, but it's a mistake. There is no moving him. His skin is cool to my touch, and it feels like I'm trying to move a stone wall.

"Possibly."

"Thank you for your honesty," I say sarcastically.

He snickers.

My eyes sear into him. He takes a deep breath, sniffing my platinum locks. When he pulls back, I see he has gathered some knowledge, and it changes his expression from flirty to devious.

"Never mind."

"Never mind what?" I ask.

"Are you going to question everything I say?"

"Are you not going to explain anything you say?"

He pauses. "I don't need you to answer me anymore. I know what pack you're from."

"How?"

"Your scent. I can't always tell. Most wolves wouldn't let me get close enough for long enough to be able to scent them in this way. But I know now. You're Wintermoon."

I freeze, unsure how he's going to react to that information. When he doesn't immediately kill me after a minute, I try to explain. "Kael and I are looking for the Moonlight wolves. We're here to help break the curse."

He stills, my words landing, but he doesn't say anything.

"Kael is running north through the woods to an area where there are no human trails, no pack territories, and little chance he can harm anyone. He'll keep running until morning, when he's most likely to shift back into his human form."

I stare at him, unblinking.

"I gave him a command, and since he's alpha-less, he followed it," he says.

"You're an alpha?"

He doesn't answer me.

"Does that mean Kael belongs to your pack now?"

Again, he doesn't answer my question.

"I have one more question for you. When Kael was attacking you, why didn't you turn?" he asks.

I blush bright red and look away, unable to tell him the truth. Now that Kael can, I'm probably the only wolf shifter on the planet who has grown to adulthood and not figured out how to shift. I'm an outlier. There's something very, very wrong with me.

But I can't tell this stranger any of these things.

I turn back to this nameless man with rippling muscles, a thick cock, and a hint of evil in his eyes. He may have saved me, but I don't trust him. He's told me practically nothing, and his effect on my body is strange. But I trust my gut, and it's telling me that he's up to no good.

"Thank you for saving me," I say.

That wicked grin creeps up his face again.

"Oh, my naive snow wolf, I'm not saving you. I'm taking you."

My eyes widen, and I struggle beneath his hold. Something sharp sinks into my neck, and everything goes black.

CHAPTER 6
LUMI

Startling awake, I find myself sliding off the muscled surface I'm lying on. I dig my fingers in to keep myself from falling and get a fistful of midnight black fur.

It's then that I realize where I am or, rather, who I'm on top of. I'm riding the back of the wolf who rescued me. I try to pull my hands apart, but they're stuck together by rough vines roped tightly around my hands and ankles. It's a miracle I've managed to stay on top of the wolf the entire time I've been passed out.

How long have I been out?

Minutes, hours, days? I have no way of knowing.

Kael?

"Kael?! Where's Kael?" I scan the forest, and that's when I see them—at least a dozen other wolves jogging beside us. None are as large as the alpha I'm riding on, but the others look healthy. Their numbers are good too, not dwindling like our pack.

My eyes dart from wolf to wolf. There are several wolves whose fur is a similar brown shade to Kael's, but none seem quite right. And when I look at them, none look back at me with the recognition I would expect from Kael.

The alpha doesn't answer my question, and neither do any of the other wolves. They'd have to shift back into human form to answer me, but it doesn't stop me from asking everything that's racing through my mind.

"Where are you taking me?

"What happened to Kael?

"Is he safe?

"What are you going to do with me?"

All of my questions go unanswered and completely ignored.

"You could at least tell me your name," I snap.

He answers with a lift of his shoulders that has me bouncing on his back.

"Hey, that wasn't very nice!" I dig my nails deeper into his fur, cutting into his skin with my nails. I get no indication that it hurt him, or that he even noticed.

His head looks back at me, and I swear I see him smirking at me.

I glare back. "You could at least untie me if you're going to make me ride on your back. You asshole!"

He bounces me again, and I fly through the air. I flail and manage to get my legs free as I land on his back, straddling him like a horse.

Did he mean to set my legs free?

I take a deep breath, calming my heart before saying, "Thank you."

A loud howl rips through the forest, and his ears perk up. Everyone stops moving as they listen, deciphering the meaning. I have no idea if they really can or not. The howl sends shivers through me and begs my body to move toward the sound, but my instincts tell me to run in the opposite direction.

The other wolves all look toward the alpha, toward us, waiting for his command.

He howls back in equal length and volume. My body trembles at the sound, wanting to bow down to him to show him respect even though he's not my alpha.

Suddenly, we're all running again toward the first howl, and it takes all of my energy to stay on his back. My thighs clench over his fur, and my white-knuckle grip tugs at his skin as we sprint through the forest.

There are more howls and growls throughout the trees. Each one lights a spark deep in my chest. My heart pounds louder, hoping I can turn. I pray any part of my body will answer the call and prove that I will one day be able to shift just like Kael did. It will take time, but maybe being with another pack will help me learn to shift faster.

That is, if I live that long.

I don't know what this alpha or pack has planned for me. They tied me up but haven't harmed me—yet. *But what did they do with Kael? Where is he?*

This alpha with the midnight black fur saved me and then took me as his captive. I'm not sure if I should trust or fear him.

The howls quickly grow in volume and number. Goosebumps pepper my arms and legs as my body tenses in anticipation.

The cacophony of wolf vocal cords ramps louder and louder and louder...

And then, suddenly, we all stop.

I look down and realize the pack is standing at the edge of a cliff, looking down into a valley.

I gasp.

There are hundreds of wolf shifters below. Most are in wolf form, but some remain as human.

Suddenly, I'm thrown into the air and falling.

Strong arms catch me, and I stare up into red eyes, shifting to black. His body is once again naked as he cradles me against his bare chest. My wrists are still tied together, preventing me from fighting back.

A shudder works through my body as I stare up at this man as we still stand on the cliff.

"Good job not falling to your death, my clingy snow wolf." His eyes snap into the blackness that matches his hair, completely vanishing the red-eyed wolf within him.

"I'm not *your* anything."

"Not for much longer, you aren't. But for a few hours, you were mine." He says it in a melancholy whisper that doesn't make sense to me.

I open my mouth to speak, but before I can say anything, he straightens and peers out at the vastness beyond the cliff. I look down at the array of wolf shifters gathered in one place. *Why didn't Father bring us here? Why couldn't we have come here and found help?*

We are the traitors, the reason everyone is cursed, my mind reminds me.

But there had to be at least one pack here that would have helped us. If only my father had been willing to seek help instead of accepting his fate. Then maybe he would still be alive, and our pack would be, too. And Kael and I wouldn't have had to search them out ourselves.

No, it's not too late. They are not dead. He's not dead…

"Ambrose," the alpha's voice booms in my ear and through the forest, so loud that everyone moving around in the valley stops and looks up. I don't know who this Ambrose is, but there is no doubt that he heard him.

"The Bloodmoon wolves are ready to present our offering," the alpha says.

Chills race over my skin, and my heart thuds to a stop. I was foolish to trust this man at all, foolish to think he cared about me when he saved me.

I'm their offering.

CHAPTER 7
LUMI

"Where's Ambrose?" the alpha carrying me says in his deep, commanding voice. He's not messing around. He'll bite anyone's head off that doesn't do what he wants.

A man walks forward from the hustle and bustle of the packs. Most of the wolf shifters have stopped paying attention to us and resumed their own activities.

My mouth gapes as I stare at the man walking toward us. He's just as handsome as the man holding me. Sandy blonde hair frames his face, and sparkling blue eyes shimmer in my direction. He smiles, and it's not the least bit intimidating, even when he flashes a bit of the canines that I know could tear into my throat and end me in a single breath.

His muscles glide under his skin with every step he takes. They're muscles that have been honed after his wolf shifter abilities emerged, no doubt. These muscles aren't naturally human but something more. He's wearing nothing but a pair of loose shorts that hang low on his waist, letting me ogle almost every part of him.

Warmth spreads through my body as I stare at him and then again when I remember I'm in the arms of another very attractive, very naked man. Wolf shifters are used to nudity. It's not something they even waste a breath thinking about, but I've never been used to it, and I doubt I ever will. Coming from a small pack that was mostly my family and Kael, it's weird to see strangers strutting around like being half-naked is nothing.

The man's grin naturally has me smiling back. My heart goes from a speeding freight train to a light simmer. For a moment, I feel safe with this man here. *Who knows what this psycho holding me is going to do?* But this other man standing here—he won't let him hurt me, that much I know. Even if he isn't an alpha, he's high enough up in the chain of command to hold some power here.

"Emeric, where is Ambrose?" My skin vibrates as my carrier speaks.

Emeric cocks his head as he stares at us, his gaze skimming over me, the dark alpha, and his pack members, who are still in wolf form. Amusement dances in his eyes as a chill spreads from the alpha holding me.

"Nice to see you after so long, Nyx. You, of all people, know how busy Ambrose is tonight."

Nyx.

I glance up to be reminded the alpha is as dark as the night itself. It fits.

"And you, of all people, know what I'll do to you unless you're a good little puppy and get Ambrose, now," his growl demands. There is no way Emeric could ignore it.

To his credit, Emeric stands taller, his smile never faltering. He waits as if pausing for Nyx to figure something out.

"Talking to me is as good as talking to Ambrose," Emeric finally says when Nyx seems to have calmed. Nyx doesn't seem to like it, but he doesn't make any more demands to see Ambrose.

"Our offering," Nyx says, holding me out like a lamb to be slaughtered. My chest squeezes tight as my breathing increases. *Offering—that can't be good.*

Emeric stares at me, quickly assessing the situation, and then turns back to Nyx. "You're sure?"

"Yes," Nyx says without another word.

Emeric nods, stepping forward, arms outstretched. Then I'm transferred from Nyx's arms to Emeric's as easily as I would hand a light backpack to Kael. I weigh practically nothing to them.

The cool chill I felt in Nyx's arms transforms into warmth in Emeric's. The unsettled feeling I had before morphs into ease. As Emeric starts carrying me away, I look back to see Nyx and his pack are completely gone.

I gape. *How did they disappear so fast? Did I imagine it all? I wouldn't put it past myself.*

"You can put me down; I'm not going to run." Not when I need to find Kael. Not when I need to talk to the Moonlight wolves and help them find a way to break the curse. Not when I have nothing to run back to.

Emeric grins wider. "I know, but what fun is that? I'd rather carry you."

He bounces me joyfully in his arms, and somehow I laugh. I freaking laugh. I'm still being carried like a sacrificial lamb with my wrists still tied together. I'll most likely end up with my neck slit on some alter by the end of the night, and yet I freaking laugh.

But that word 'offering'...

"Hey, you have nothing to worry about. Nyx can't hurt you now."

"What makes you think he hurt me?" I ask.

Emeric's smile drops. "Nyx hurts people. His pack has been forced to live outside of the rest of us for years now. But..."

"But not anymore?"

Emeric shakes his head, not really explaining anything to me.

I sigh, knowing that I have more important questions to ask than about Nyx and the Bloodmoon pack. My questions could mean my survival or death.

"What's your name?" he asks.

"Lumi," I say, not bothering with my last name. I'm not sure he would take too kindly to realizing that I'm from the Wintermoon pack any more than thinking I'm a Bloodmoon. My guess is if they despise the Bloodmoon, they hate the Wintermoon worse. The other packs are willing to at least have a conversation with the Bloodmoon, something they won't do with the Wintermoon.

"That's a beautiful name."

"Thanks," I blush.

Emeric's eyes light up when he sees my smile. He stares at me as if I'm the answer to all his prayers.

Heat fills my body as an undeniable attraction spreads through me. *Gods, is every wolf shifter this attractive? Am I going to go crazy with an unquenchable need for every man here?* No wonder no one can find their mates—every male is gorgeous. I can't tell which man I'm more attracted to; I want them all.

I swallow, trying to hide my obvious attraction to him.

"You're not from the Bloodmoon pack," Emeric says as a statement, not a question.

I don't know how to respond. I can't tell him I'm Wintermoon, but I can't persuade him that I'm from Bloodmoon, either.

"Packless," I answer, realizing I speak the truth. Wintermoon is gone. Even if any of the other members survived the latest attack, my father is dead. I know it deep in my core. Without an alpha, the pack is gone, so I am packless.

"I'm sorry. Nyx is an ass, but you won't be packless again, not now."

I glance around at the hundreds of shifters walking around us as Emeric continues to carry me nonchalantly. It feels like we have all the time in the world and are just going for an evening stroll after a first date, getting to know each other better.

"What's going to happen? I'm—" I swallow. "I'm an 'offering.' What does that mean?"

Emeric chuckles. "It's Nyx being dramatic is what it is."

I narrow my eyes, even as a blanket of calm sweeps over my body.

Emeric sets me down on my own two feet, surprising me. He lifts my wrists up and breaks the vines in one quick motion of his hands.

"Thank you," I say sincerely.

He shrugs and then takes my hand in his. Tingles shoot from my hand through my body. I wonder what it would feel like to kiss him. I know that without even trying it, that it would feel far better than any kiss with Kael.

Could Emeric be my mate, the one I've been looking for? I trust him inherently. I barely know him, but the only person I've ever trusted more in my life is Kael.

Kael, where is he? Is he here somewhere? Or is he still following Nyx's alpha command and running as far away from here as possible?

We walk a bit further, past tent after tent filled with glowing eyes from the other wolf shifters staring at us as we pass. But Emeric puts me at ease by distracting me with his charming smile, calming touch, and a quick history of the different packs here. But I barely register anything after he tells me he's the beta of the Moonlight wolves. I found them, finally.

I can break the curse. I can restore the Wintermoon pack name into one that is worthy of being remembered for saving the packs instead of destroying them.

We stop on the other side of a clearing where the edge of the forest starts again. Emeric is still holding my hand in his casual way, and then I see what appears to be an opening to a cave.

My heart thunders in my chest, telling me not to enter.

"What's the offering, again?" I ask him, knowing he's not telling me everything. My trust in him vanishes as my instincts kick back in and alarm bells sound in my head.

"There's nothing to worry about, Lumi. Trust me."

"Well, what should I be worried about?"

Emeric doesn't answer me. Instead, he continues guiding me to the entrance of the cave.

"No!" I shout, trying to break free of his hold, trying to run. I try to turn into my wolf form, but I don't feel so much as a tingle in my body. I scream for help from Kael if he's nearby or from anyone willing to help me. But I barely get a solid scream out. Emeric is infinitely stronger than me. I'm powerless.

He shoves me into the cave as easily as if he were batting a fly off his shoulder.

I immediately turn and try to run out of the cave, but I slam into an invisible wall.

What the hell?

"It's spelled by a witch. You can't get out, so don't waste your strength trying." Emeric looks at me with a deep sadness, as if he truly wishes things were different. A second later, the look is gone, replaced by a determined gaze.

"Liar. You're worse than Nyx."

He shakes his head. "No one is worse than Nyx, but I'm sure you'll figure that out soon enough." He pauses. "I'm truly sorry. I know you don't understand, and unfortunately, I don't have time to explain everything. But you really don't have anything to worry about. You'll survive —I can feel it."

"What does that mean? Survive what?"

But Emeric's gone, and I'm left alone in this damn spelled cave.

"Survive the offering," a feminine voice sounds from behind me.

I turn and see more than a dozen other young women in the cave with me. Fear marks several of their faces, but excitement is plain across the others. *What could make some of them terrified and others excited?*

"You're a true offering, it seems. I'm sorry that your choice was taken from you—most of us chose this," a woman with auburn hair and warm honey-brown eyes says.

"Chose what exactly? What is the offering? What's about to happen?" I ask.

The woman smiles as she looks from the others to me. Most are smiling now, with a relaxed, fated look.

"We're being offered to the alphas of the packs in hopes that one of us will become their mate and break the curse," she says.

I stare at them, and my heart rate speeds. That isn't the whole story. There's definitely something they are leaving out. What they said is what I came here to do. I shouldn't be afraid of being offered to the other male alphas to see if I can be mated to any of them.

"So what exactly happens?" I ask.

"One by one, we stand before all the alphas for their review. If any of the alphas feel the tug of the mating bond pulling them to you, they mark you as their mate."

"Mark you? What does it mean to be marked?"

"They sink their canines deep into our flesh, severing the carotid artery. If you're really mates, the mating bond will appear and heal your wound, keeping you alive. It will be clear to everyone. Once a mated couple is found, the curse will vanish."

There's a stillness in me, a calmness that shouldn't be there. But I ask the next question anyway.

"And if I'm marked by someone who isn't my true mate?"

"You die."

CHAPTER 8
LUMI

"It's almost time," a woman to my left says with long, golden blonde hair. I jump at the sound of her voice, and she chuckles at my response.

"Don't pay any mind to Kaida. She was just being dramatic. Most don't die at the offering."

"So they find mates?" I ask.

Her laugh deepens. "No, none have since the curse began. Only those foolish enough to think they can actually find their mates die." She looks me up and down. "But you're not going to be foolish, so you have nothing to worry about. You won't die tonight." She pauses. "I'm Rowena."

"Lumi," I say, sucking in a deep breath, trying to believe this kind stranger.

Rowena is the most beautiful woman I've ever seen. She's tall—at least half a foot taller than me with piercing yellow eyes and thick, peachy lips. There's almost an unnatural glow about her that none of the others here possess.

"I'm Moonlight pack—that's what the glow is about,"

she states matter of factly, like she's explained a hundred times. For her, it's completely normal. Then she raises her eyebrows, waiting for me to respond with my own pack.

"I'm the Bloodmoon offering," I reply.

Her eyes widen for only a millisecond, as the shock spreads through her body. She blinks it away a second later.

She takes my hand and squeezes it hard, in what I assume she thinks is a reassuring gesture. Instead, it feels like she's cracking every bone in my hand as her strength far outweighs mine.

I swallow back my wince.

"All you have to do is say none of them is your mate. That's how you survive. You say you don't feel a bond with any of them, no matter what happens. They won't force you to mate with anyone if you say you don't feel a bond. Stay alive; I like you," she winks at me.

I smile softly back as she shoves something into my hands. My stomach does somersaults despite her intended calming words.

"Change into this. Nothing but this," Rowena says firmly.

I stare at the thin white fabric in my hand. Before I can ask Rowena what it is, she's already walked away. I unravel it to discover a sheer white gown.

This can't be what I'm expected to wear. But as I look all around me, the rest of the women are already changing into similar gowns.

"Hurry, she's coming," a woman with dark ringlets and brown skin to my left says.

I strip out of my clothes and into the white gown, moving as quickly as I can. The others finish dressing almost instantly, the speed of a wolf shifter on their side.

Somehow, I manage to get the gown on quick enough. My hand runs over the thin fabric on my body, my eyesight seeing straight through it to my darkened nipples pebbling in the cold. I might as well be naked.

I scan the shadows of the cave, looking at the other women. None of them try to cover their bodies or fidget with embarrassment. As wolf shifters, this doesn't feel strange to them.

"Line up single file, starting with the Moonlight pack and ending with Bloodmoon," a woman from outside of the cave says.

I jump as her voice somehow carries throughout the cave, as loud as if she were standing right next to me.

"That's Isolde—a witch from the Moonfire coven," Rowena says before she walks to the entrance of the cave. Women start lining up behind her before I can question what a witch is doing getting involved in wolf shifter business.

I don't know much beyond my own pack's lifestyle, but I do know that witches are our enemies and not to be trusted. *Or was that a lie my father told me to not seek their help in unlocking my wolf?*

Isolde chants something in an ancient language as she waves her hand in front of the cave, lifting the spell that keeps us caged inside here. A tightness I didn't realize was pressing against my chest lifts, and I take a deep breath.

Chills race up my spine, as our line of women in white gowns starts walking out of the cave. Rowena said there was nothing to be worried about. Emeric said the same. *But why else would they have a witch cast a spell keeping us trapped in a cave if there's nothing to worry about? Why are we called offerings?*

On a narrow trail, we walk single file through a dense green forest with nothing but moonlight guiding our path. My shoulders brush against the branches of the trees next to me as I lift my feet high to avoid tripping over a tree root, rock, or fallen branch.

I stop for a second, looking up at the full moon almost at its peak. Despite never having turned, I feel a pull to it.

Everything I'm feeling is heightened—my fear, my excitement, my anticipation. All of it beckons me forward. And the growing thrill of the group sweeps through me.

If there was ever a time I wish I could shift, this would be it. But I feel nothing more than the usual tingle and joy that comes with existing under a full moon.

I count the heads in front of me—fifteen of us in total, and I am the last. There are no guards keeping us in line. Isolde could be using magic to ensure that we follow her, but I don't feel any coercion.

This might be my last opportunity to escape. I should run into the forest, find Kael, and do what my father said —live my life as a human and give up hope of ever shifting into a wolf.

But now that Kael has shifted—has felt his full power, felt what it's like to run through the forest in his beast form—he won't want the life of a human. He won't be able to resist this life or hide who he is.

And I don't want to run away. I don't know why my fear has been dampened as I walk behind the other women, the other offerings. I don't know if my confidence is too high or if it's the pull of the moon giving me the courage to keep walking. Despite Rowena's warning, maybe I'll find my mate tonight and be the one to break the curse.

Whatever the reason, I don't try to escape. I don't run; I follow.

Isolde leads us down a path from the cave to the top of a hillside.

I gasp at the sight in front of me. From the top, there is a panoramic view of the forest that stretches for miles and miles.

My heart soars at the picture in front of me. Hundreds and hundreds of our kind are gathered, sitting on a massive sloped hill as if in rows of an amphitheater. Conversations and laughter fill the air in excited anticipation. It's amazing to see so many of us here.

My eyes focus on the bottom of the hill. I'm a mile up, but I can clearly count the massive male figures standing in a group below, waiting for us—the alphas.

Time slows as a yearning I've never felt before slams into me. I need to go down there. Someone is waiting for me. My mate is waiting for me.

I swallow hard, focusing on the women in front of me as we begin climbing down the sloped hillside to the males waiting below.

Silence falls across the crowd as we walk. All eyes of the hundreds here are on me and the other women—the other offerings. With a thrumming pulse, I keep my head level and force myself to remain calm, to keep a blush from striking over my cheek.

The closer we get to the waiting males, the more my yearning for them intensifies. I try to look past the woman in front of me to once again look at the males below, but even from the higher ground I stand on, I'm too short to see over her.

I make the mistake of looking to the left, to get a better look at the ones gathered. Male eyes look at me with lust and a soft howl of appreciation finally forces a blush to my cheeks.

I glance down, and the moonlight shines through the material of the gown, giving them all an unobstructed view of my body.

I fold my arms over my chest, trying to hide out of instinct. Distracted, I don't pay attention to where my feet are, and I trip on a rock, falling forward into the back of the woman in front of me.

She turns swiftly and manages to catch me before I slam into her back—her wolf instincts kicking in. Her hands grip my biceps as she stares at me curiously.

"Thank you," I whisper.

Her hazel eyes stare into me, as if she's trying to read my mind. She turns back around without a word.

Well, okay then.

I focus on my feet to ensure I don't fall again, while butterflies flutter in my belly.

I'll survive it, whatever it is. I have to. It's my destiny. I can feel it in my bones.

I'm so focused on my feet that it takes a minute to realize we've made it to the bottom of the hill.

Isolde walks over to me, and with a wave of her hand, my head lifts. Her power pulses through me, and her voice rings in my head, "Sit."

I've never felt such power before, never experienced a witch using their magic to control another. Mindlessly, I walk to the rows of chairs where the other women are already sitting and take the last seat.

Once seated, I feel the power lift and my self-control return.

I take a deep breath, afraid it will be my last. Looking up, the stare of fifteen handsome alphas devour us like dinner. If Isolde's power scared me, the power they wield is absolutely terrifying.

Say you don't feel a bond with any of them, Rowena's words pop into my head.

I don't know how I could deny any of them. A warm tingling spreads through my core, my lips part, and my body aches as if I need one of these males to live. My mind spins with desire, and I can barely think through the flaming heat beating in my body.

"Welcome," Isolde says, her voice carrying through the crowd. "Welcome wolves, witches, and vampires to this month's offering."

CHAPTER 9

LUMI

Isolde's words cause my stomach to twist in on itself as I stare up at the people gathered on the hillside in a different light. There aren't just shifters here—there are also witches and vampires. Staring around the hillside, I have no idea who is what.

I thought witches and vampires were our enemies. Or at least, I thought they didn't care to interact with us. I was told we all keep to our own kind. *Why would they care if we broke our curse or not?*

There's so much I don't know, so much my father kept from me. Or our separation from the other packs kept the truth from all of us, including my father, this whole time.

"Three curses plague our different species. Three curses we have all suffered under for twenty-one years. But they will all be broken soon—starting with the shifter curse," she continues.

I hang onto her every word, as it's all brand new information to me. *Three curses? How did I not know that? Are they all tied together? If one is broken, are they all broken?*

"The prophecy states that the shifter curse will be the

first to lift. Once it has been, the others will soon follow. For the wolf shifter curse to be broken, a shifter must find and mark their true mate. Once the bond is sealed, the curse will lift for all wolf shifters," Isolde says.

All eyes are on her, and no other voice speaks as everyone listens intently. I'm sure they've all heard this information before, but I wouldn't be able to tell.

Isolde turns to us. "Thank you all for agreeing to the offering. You hold the hope for us all."

I shiver at her words.

"We shall begin," Isolde says with a sly smile.

I don't trust her. I don't know if it's that she's a witch and my wolf instincts tell me not to trust her or if it's the woman herself I don't trust.

"Moonlight's offering," Isolde says.

"My name is Rowena." Rowena stands, ignoring Isolde's outstretched hand. Her long golden hair blows gently in the wind, and her body seems to glow brighter under the moonlight above. With her shoulders back and a focused look on her face, she walks forward with all the confidence in the world.

"Moonlight's offering is Rowena," Isolde announces to the crowd.

I hold my breath as the male alphas stand and form a circle on the opposite side of the stage. Rippling muscles, sharp cheekbones, and cutting gazes—every man is more attractive than the next, each shirtless with black pants.

Arousal and desire flick through me in spades, my body coming to life on its own accord. My mouth waters, my nipples harden, and wetness drips between my legs.

I want them. *All* of them. *Any* of them.

My female instincts have taken over any common sense. Any of these strong alphas could be my mate. I can smell each of their scents from here—musky, fresh, woody, citrusy, spicy. Somehow, each one seems like my own personal drug. I'm drawn to every smell for different reasons.

My eyes lock on Rowena as she enters the circle of alphas. The circle closes behind her as soon as she steps inside, the fifteen males caging her in.

I stare at the backs of the men closest to me. Their bodies are so large that I can barely see past them to the others. It takes everything inside me to stay seated instead of running into the circle and begging them all to kiss me, to lavish me, to choose me.

Somehow, I stay seated.

I hold my breath as I watch her through the gap between the backs of two of the men. I don't know what to expect. Through the heat pulsing through my body, I feel fear for her. She's the closest thing I have to a friend here, and she's moments from death if one of the alphas mistakenly chooses her.

Live—Rowena. Live.

Rowena smiles softly, basking in the attention. Her beauty shines even brighter as she grins. She's strong, standing with all the confidence in the world and showing no fear at all. She doesn't cower in front of any of the alphas. It's as if she was born to be an alpha's mate. It would shock me if one of these men wasn't her mate.

Rowena's hands grip her gown and bunch it up at her thighs before lifting it over her head.

I gasp at her nakedness so easily on display in front of the others. She doesn't flush or show any sign of embarrassment. *But why would she?* She's gorgeous—flawless skin and a perfect hourglass shape to her curves.

She nods to the first alpha. He walks forward, circling

her slowly as they both size each other up. Their eyes lock, and nostrils flare at each other. Growls leave each of their throats.

I flinch at the sound. From the way they are staring at each other, I can't tell if they are about to kiss or tear each other apart.

Suddenly, the male backs down and returns to his spot in the circle.

The dance repeats itself thirteen more times with each alpha. Despite the growls being distinct every time, each still sends shivers down my spine for different reasons.

Finally, the last one approaches her—Nyx.

My eyes widen at the sight of him. I don't know how I didn't recognize him earlier around the circle. Of course, he'd be here. He was the alpha of the Bloodmoon pack, and I'm his offering.

I grind my teeth together and fist my hands at my side. If anything happens to me tonight, it will be his fault.

He circles Rowena quickly, barely sniffing her before returning to his spot. His eyes hardly look at her. Instead, they look flat and bored with this entire event.

My own eyes scan his body like they have every alpha. He's as attractive as I remember, wearing the same dark pants as every man here. Without a shirt, I can see every line of muscle on his body. But unlike the others, I'm not turned on by looking at him. All I see when I look at him is anger. I want to make him pay for putting me in this situation.

As Nyx settles into his spot, I hold my breath again, not sure what's about to happen next.

A howl leaves Rowena—long and fierce. The other

alphas howl back. It's as if they're calling to each other, searching for the howl that matches their own—their mate.

And then, Rowena shifts.

My eyes widen at the beauty of watching her turn into her wolf form. A flash of gold surrounds her, and then a golden wolf with piercing yellow eyes stands where Rowena just was.

Her wolf form is as beautiful as her human one. Her fur is sleek, glowing with long, lean legs and a feminine fierceness in her eyes. She walks around the circle, sniffing each alpha.

None of the alphas shift.

None of them so much as move in her direction.

None of them are her mate.

None of them are choosing her, and she's not choosing any of them.

I may not know much about this ceremony, but I know that much.

Isolde sighs, standing just out of the circle.

"Blackwater is next," Isolde announces, defeat in her voice.

The alphas part, making way for Rowena to exit. She jumps off the back of the stage and disappears into the darkness of the forest beyond.

She lived.

I exhale.

She's alive.

I can live.

If none of them are my mate, I can live long enough to find the shifter who is my mate. That is, if they don't throw me out when they realize I can't shift.

I hope shifting isn't a requirement of the ceremony.

Hopefully, that was a choice Rowena made, and not all the women here can shift.

But as the offering from Blackwater walks forward and repeats the exact same steps as Rowena, shifting into her gray wolf form at the end before walking out into the forest in disappointment, I know my secret is going to be exposed.

Panic rises in my throat. I'm not sure what to do. All I can do is hope that someone finds their mate and breaks the curse before I'm called.

"Ironclaw," Isolde calls next.

A woman with waist-length, straight black hair walks into the circle. Adaluna is the name she gave Isolde. With striking features, she begins to repeat the same steps as the two before her, but as the fifth alpha—the one with red hair and a scar below his left black eye—approaches her, there's a shift in the air. We all can feel it.

Breathlessly, they both stare at each other with an intense focus. Their gazes seem to lock as if the rest of us no longer exist to them.

When the next alpha tries to approach Adaluna, the red-haired alpha bares his teeth in his direction, preventing him from getting close to her.

A gasp echoes, rippling up the hillside of the amphitheater.

Could this be it? Could they have actually found their mates? Could they be the key to breaking the curse?

"Baelor," the sixth alpha with the silver hair growls at him before he shifts into his wolf form on the spot. Baelor does the same—turning instantly into his wolf form and shoving Adaluna behind him.

She shifts instantly as the two alphas circle each

other, growling and baring their teeth as if preparing to fight.

Adaluna tries to intervene, but Baelor growls low in her direction, warning her to stay out of the impending fight.

All the other alphas shift in a burst of energy flowing from the stage.

I gasp at the sight of the alphas. My father is large in his wolf form, but these alphas put my father to shame. I've never seen such large beasts before. Baelor howls, battling the first silver wolf off with ease.

A brown alpha with yellow eyes attacks Baelor, going for the throat. But Baelor leaps in the air, avoiding getting his neck bit, and tackles the brown alpha, easily pinning him to the ground.

The brown alpha yelps and retreats as soon as he is let up.

The pattern repeats again and again, and I realize why the alphas are challenging him. Not because they think Adaluna is their own mate but to ensure that she is Baelor's.

Nyx puts up a strong fight. His midnight black fur wolf towers over Baelor. Nyx pins Baelor beneath him for a solid minute before he breaks free. Even though it's clear that Nyx would have won that fight, he doesn't challenge Baelor again, seemingly satisfied with the effort Baelor put in.

Finally, the largest wolf I've ever seen approaches Baelor, his howl louder than any I've ever heard. His fur is black with golden spots and streaks and glowing yellow eyes.

Ambrose—this must be Ambrose, the Moonlight's

alpha, and who Nyx was searching for when he carried me here.

He howls again. I instantly want to obey Ambrose's command, even though I don't know what he's saying.

Baelor cowers for a split second at Ambrose's howl, almost as if he wants to obey whatever command he's saying, but he fights it. Ambrose doesn't wait—he attacks. His teeth sink into Baelor's neck with ease, like a knife through butter.

I squeeze my eyes into slits and look away, afraid I'm about to see Baelor's death. There's a yelp and whimper from Baelor, and I force myself to turn back.

Baelor limps, holding one of his paws up, but he doesn't back down against Ambrose. Baelor continues to bare his teeth at Ambrose, as if he's willing to die fighting for Adaluna. It's clear that Baelor will die if Ambrose doesn't back down.

Ambrose howls one more time, enough that every hair on my arm stands up. His howl is a warning. Then Ambrose retreats, the other alphas already forming a circle and making room for him in it.

Baelor and Adaluna now face each other in the circle of alphas. The tension is thick in the air, and I find myself holding my breath.

Baelor howls and Adaluna matches with her own.

The sound is in perfect harmony as they circle each other and nuzzle their heads together. The embrace is as if they're finding the other piece of their soul.

A tear rolls down my cheek, and my lips curl up. This —this is how shifters were always meant to be. Finding their other halves. Living with love, not living broken.

The circle parts, and Isolde walks into the circle with

them. Her jaw is tense and her eyebrows are furrowed in determination.

There's a tingle in my chest, and my breath catches once again.

"Do you, Baelor, accept Adaluna as your mate?" Isolde asks.

Baelor nods and then barks his acceptance.

"And do you, Adaluna, accept Baelor as your mate?"

She howls.

Isolde nods. "Then, mark each other as such." Her hands outstretch as if magic is needed for the next part.

Silence stretches once again, and Baelor looks Adaluna in the eye.

I hold my breath, not sure what's about to happen. But I hope it changes everything. I hope the curse is about to be broken.

Suddenly, Baelor sinks his teeth into Adaluna's neck.

The howl that leaves her body is like none I've ever heard. It's the sound of agony spreading through her body, not joy at finding her other half.

"No," I whisper.

There are cries all around me. Howls, growls, and chaos as the pain reaches every one of us present, witnessing the scene unfold but unable to do anything to stop it.

Baelor's eyes widen, but it doesn't seem even he can stop. His teeth are sunk into her fur, unrelenting. Together, they sink to the ground until the life leaves Adaluna's eyes, and her body flops the remaining inches to the ground.

Baelor stands over her limp body. My hands fly to my mouth, holding back a cry. He howls—long and loud through the silence of the night. The howl is prolonged until his voice trembles.

The other alphas echo him before the entirety of the packs sitting on the hillside join in.

Baelor doesn't drop dead, and no one seems to expect him to. It must only be the females risking their lives in this ceremony.

Isolde waves her hand, and the howls instantly stop, even from the alphas circling her. Emeric and another man break through the circle and lift Adaluna's wolf body, carrying her to an altar near the woods.

I swallow hard when I notice two other altars, as if they are expecting more deaths tonight. "Alphas, return to your positions. Stormburst is next," Isolde orders with an unrelenting voice composed of zero compassion for the death that just happened.

My breath is hard and swift. Everything happened so fast. Isolde is trying to pretend like we didn't all witness a woman die right in front of our eyes simply because she thought an alpha was her mate.

But the alphas obey, shifting back into their human forms, now naked. Even Baelor returns to his place in the circle. His puffy eyes are the only sign of the pain he just endured.

I can't keep the tears from streaking my cheeks, mourning this young life, this woman. Even though I never knew her, the theft of the beautiful love she could have shared with the alpha is a crime.

I look up and see Rowena on the edge of the forest, staring at me with intensity in her wolf form. *All you have to do is say none of them are your mate; that's how you survive.* Her words from earlier repeat in my head before new words seem to be sent my way.

Survive, don't try to break the curse. Live.

I nod through my tears. When it's my turn, I will have no chance of breaking the curse. I can't even shift. I would never survive being marked like that. I just hope I'm not killed for being considered a traitor to our kind when they realize I'm from the Wintermoon pack. My pack is the reason the curse exists, the reason the offering is required, the reason Adaluna is dead.

CHAPTER 10
LUMI

"The Bloodmoon offering," Isolde says, staring at me like just saying the name of the pack is going to cause her to break out in hives.

There are murmurs and whispers all around the hillside amphitheater. I know the Bloodmoon wolves aren't popular, but I don't know why. It's clear they are at least tolerated, unlike my own pack. *Maybe everyone is intimidated by them?*

I stand up, my legs shaking as I feel the intense stare of the entire crowd on me. I'm the last to go, the last chance at this offering to break the curse. I can feel a swell of hope from everyone here all concentrated on me.

I'm not going to break the curse. It would be impossible, based on what I know of the ceremony. All I can do is survive.

I swallow down my fear, knowing it won't do me any good, and force my legs to move forward. When I reach Isolde, I say in a soft voice, "Lumi, my name is Lumi."

She nods and announces, "Lumi—the Bloodmoon offering."

More gasps echo through the hillside around me, but I don't dare look up. I'm too focused on what I have to do next and how to survive it.

The two alphas closest to me part, opening a space for me to enter the circle. Staring at my feet, I enter the circle, terrified I'll trip and embarrass myself further or blush at the sight of the naked men surrounding me.

Finally, hours into this ceremony, it's me standing in the center of this circle of alphas. My legs have stopped trembling, and I feel a warmth spread through my body.

Strange.

Is it a spell Isolde cast to keep me in place? Or is it being surrounded by the alphas that calms me?

When I look up, I don't feel afraid. I don't shake; my pulse has calmed, and my breathing has slowed.

"Remove your gown," Isolde's voice whispers into my ear as if she's standing right next to me. My head whips in her direction. If I don't do it on my own accord, she'll use a spell to force me.

Every man here is already naked. The women before me were as well. Nakedness isn't as sexual among wolf shifters as humans. It's a normal part of life seeing others naked. And I might as well be naked since this thin gown under the light of the moon is doing nothing to hide my body.

I pull the gown off my shoulders and then slowly lower it down my body, shimmying a little to get it over my hips until it's a puddle of cloth at my feet.

I don't allow myself to blush, but I feel the stares of the crowd and the nearby alphas on me. Slowly, I purse my lips and breathe out, remaining calm and confident. Looking at the man across from me with a steady gaze and a soft smile, I'm ready for whatever is about to happen.

Baelor is the alpha across from me, I realize. My smile drops, and my eyes well at the sight of him forced to continue after what happened to Adaluna. I don't know how any of them expect him to try to mate again after what happened.

To his credit, he doesn't hesitate. He's the first to approach me, probably to get this over with.

I stiffen as he gets close. In his state, he might do something reckless. He'll realize I'm a fraud as soon as he gets close enough to smell me. He'll notice I don't belong to the Bloodmoon pack.

He circles me once, barely breathing in my scent. I'm so frozen that I don't allow myself to sense anything from him. Baelor stops in front of me, his red hair blowing in the breeze and the scar around his eye looking more menacing than before.

"I'm sorry," I whisper.

I probably shouldn't speak, but I can't help but tell him how I feel.

His narrowed gaze and flared nostrils tell me he doesn't appreciate my sympathy. It would mean showing weakness to show that the loss of Adaluna affects him beyond what he's already shown.

I bite down to force myself from saying more but catch my cheek with my teeth and wince as a drop of my own blood spills onto my tongue.

Baelor returns to his place, huffing once in my direction like I disgust him.

I sigh.

I won't be making that mistake again.

The next alpha approaches, and I hold my head

steady and my emotions blank. I don't look at his naked body. I barely even notice which male is circling me.

But then he stops in front of me and breathes in heavily, his brown eyes locking with mine.

My pulse ticks up, and my skin grows warm and clammy under his gaze. I start to squirm as he continues to gaze at me while breathing in my scent.

The wind changes direction, and I get a whiff of him. He smells like the woods—of earth, dirt, and evergreens. I move, just a millimeter toward him, wanting to breathe in more of him.

For a second, he tries to move closer to me before stopping himself, too. But then he quickly retreats back to his spot in the circle.

Fisting my hands, I clear my emotions as the next alpha approaches. This man is taller than Baelor and at least a decade older, with a few gray strands in his jet-black hair.

He circles me in the same way the others did. I try to hold my breath, but his bold, peppery scent hits me hard. Warm desire floods my system, and my cheeks flush as he stops in front of me.

I swallow hard as he eventually retreats back to his spot.

I close my eyes briefly, trying to think of anything other than these alphas in front of me. I've only had three of fifteen approach me so far. *How am I going to survive twelve more?*

I'm attracted to them all. I want them all.

Closing my eyes was a mistake, as I can smell them more easily now. Hits of different fragrances overwhelm me—musky, fresh, citrusy, spicy, and woody from every direction.

An ache grows between my legs, and my nipples begin to harden under their gazes. My pulse drums in my chest, and every time the wind blows I'm afraid I'll moan from the brush against my sensitive body.

What is happening to me?

Is this how all the other women felt? This confusion and overwhelming desire toward all the alphas? Or is it just me?

I open my eyes, whirling around to look at all the alphas and Isolde, wanting to ask my questions out loud but stopping before I do. I pant, wanting the next alpha to come near, wanting so much more. I want to sink my teeth into any of them and...

This is because of the curse, I realize. I can't tell who my mate is between any of them. I want them all. I have no idea how they feel toward me, but I'll never be able to tell who my mate is. We are all doomed.

Another man approaches me, and I plant my feet firmly on the ground, holding my breath as best I can. But even holding my breath, I can smell his manly, fresh scent. It stirs dark lust in my belly.

The man smiles at me in a wicked way as if he feels it, too.

Fuck, my mind races, clearing of everything except how I can get with these men, how I can make them choose me.

"You better get ahold of yourself, or this is going to turn into an orgy."

My eyes fly open at his voice. I didn't even realize I had closed them as Nyx stands in front of me. His hair is perfectly tousled on top of his head, accentuating the sharpness of his jaw.

Suddenly, the heat leaves my body, and the ache vanishes. They're replaced by red-hot anger.

Nyx smirks as he shakes a dark lock out of his eyes. "Better, although I can still smell your arousal. No wonder all the males here are going mad."

"What do you mean?"

He raises an eyebrow up in the direction of the crowd. *Gods.*

Howls and panting meet my gaze. All the males seem to have gone mad, pacing and longingly gazing my way.

"You better hope you're mated tonight, or you're going to have to fight off a lot of guys if you want to keep your virginity."

I narrow my gaze at Nyx. "At least I know *you* aren't my mate."

His smile rises. "At least we know that." He finishes circling and stops in front of me as they all have.

"I don't know how, but I'm going to make you pay for this."

"You'll have to survive first," his coy voice teases.

I growl.

His dark chuckle echoes in my head before he returns to his spot.

The anger inside me remains as the next two males take their turns. All I can think about is Nyx, about the twisted fates that have led me here. *Why did Nyx choose me as his offering? Why not someone from his own pack?*

The world goes quiet as the largest alpha approaches, stopping right in front of me.

My breath is heavy in my chest as I let my gaze slowly sweep up his body. From his thick calves, getting a quick eyeful of his cock that has me blushing, over his rippling abs and strong chest, and then to his face.

His golden eyes glow in my direction, and his dark

black wavy hair with specks of gold rustles in the wind as is brushes over his shoulders. But it's his lips framed in dark shadow along his sharp jawline I can't tear my gaze from.

His lips are parted, and I have the strongest urge yet to kiss him. I need to kiss him. I have to; I'm not sure I'll be able to take another breath if I don't kiss him.

I blink, and he circles me slowly. I try to compose myself, to feel nothing, but hot, wicked desire burns through me. My skin crawls with need to touch this gorgeous man.

He's mine.

The words spread through my body like wildfire.

Mine, mine, mine.

Ambrose, I remember this man's name. Ambrose—*mine.*

He stops in front of me and takes a deep breath through his nostrils.

For once, I let myself breathe him in, and I shudder at his smell. He smells of the evergreens, of the earth, and of something far more ancient than this forest that I can't quite distinguish.

He smells like *mine.*

The howl that leaves his body rattles through me and makes my heart sing. I howl my own response, matching his tenor in perfect harmony.

In the blink of an eye, Ambrose shifts. Where the naked flesh once was is now large rippling muscles beneath black fur with specks of gold and glowing yellow eyes.

"I'm Ambrose, alpha of the Moonlight wolves," comes Ambrose's voice in my head.

I gasp at the easy intrusion of his voice in my head.

The mating bond—it allows shifters to communicate with each other in their heads.

"Lumi," I think back, unsure if he hears me or not, if I'm doing it right. I don't have a clue what I'm doing.

"Lumi, so beautiful. I've never seen such gorgeous moonlit hair as yours."

I blush. *"Thank you."*

His eyes bear into mine, and I swear he grins in his wolf form.

I smile back.

"Shift," he tells me.

My heart races at his command. *What do I do? I can't tell him that I can't shift. I can't say I'm from Wintermoon, and the magic that allows our pack to shift has long ago dwindled.*

"You can feel the bond between us. I know you can," Ambrose says.

Deny you feel anything. Stay alive, Rowena's words haunt me.

But I can't lie. I can't pretend that I don't feel the bond to him stronger than any male here, even if it means the death of me.

I nod.

"Ours is a true bond; it's not like what you witnessed between Adaluna and Baelor. Ours is real. I've never felt anything this strong in my life."

"Me neither," I admit.

"Then trust me. I won't let you die. Shift, so we can finish the ceremony. So we can mark each other."

"I can't."

"You can. I can tell how strong you are. That's why we're mates. You're worthy of an alpha, so strong. We have to accept the mating bond."

"*I can't,*" I say again.

"*You can. We are strong. Together, we can break the curse.*"

I shake my head. Fear ripples through me.

"*You can mark me first. That's how strongly I know that we are mates. If you mark me first, and I'm not your mate, then I'll be the one to die, not you. Trust me.*"

"*I do. I trust you with every part of me. I trust you completely.*"

"*Then shift. Accept the bond.*"

A tear rolls down my cheek. If there was ever a time to gain my wolf, now would be it. I look up at the moon. *Please,* I plead with it.

But nothing happens.

I look back to Ambrose.

"*I can't shift. I never gained my wolf.*"

His eyes widen. Even in his wolf form, I can tell the shock ripples through him.

"*No, then how can you be my mate? This can't be true. You seem so strong. How could I have been so fooled?*"

Suddenly, Ambrose's head snaps in Nyx's direction.

Nyx snickers, as if he knows exactly what's happening.

I wrap my arms around my naked body, unsure of what to do or how to save myself.

Ambrose shifts back into human form. "What did you do, Nyx? What half-breed did you offer?"

"Lumi is full wolf," he responds.

"A wolf who can't shift isn't a full-blooded wolf," Ambrose snarls at Nyx, moving to him in an instant and grabbing him by the throat. He could squeeze the life out of him with the closing of his hand.

"Who is she? She's not even Bloodmoon, is she?" he rages.

Nyx looks bored. No fear marks his eyes even though Ambrose is far larger than him and has his canines awfully close to his throat.

"No," Nyx says.

My pulse races. He's going to tell Ambrose the truth, that I'm from Wintermoon. I have no doubt the alphas will rip me apart in punishment for my pack causing the curse.

"I found her wandering in the woods. I scented her wolf, but she had no alpha to draw from to help her shift. I'm sure as soon as she's initiated into a pack, she'll be able to shift."

Nyx chuckles and continues his explanation.

"I sensed her power, just as you do, and I knew she had to be my offering. And I was right—she's your mate, Ambrose."

Ambrose growls.

Then all eyes snap to me. I don't know why Nyx lied. I don't know what he thinks he can gain by hiding my secret. I'm sure it's for nefarious reasons, and I don't trust him.

"Leave after the ceremony finishes if you want to live." Ambrose releases Nyx and then turns to me.

Ambrose's gaze on me has me hot and bothered and aching with lust-filled desire for him. Mate or not, wolf shifter or not, I need him to fuck me—now.

Ambrose's eyes widen in fear as he looks at me, and I'm not sure why.

"What's wrong?" I ask him through the bond.

"Run. Find Emeric. He'll take you somewhere safe."

"I don't want to leave you. What's happening?"

"The curse—every male here can smell you. You've become obsessively desirable to them. Since you're the unmarked mate of the strongest alpha who has ever lived, every male here wants a taste of you to try to change your mind before I make you mine. Run. Find Emeric. He'll hide you away while I deal with these beasts."

It's a command I feel through my entire body—an alpha command. His power must be immense if he can command those not in his pack.

I turn and run through the circle and into the forest, hoping Emeric will find me. I won't be able to outrun a wolf shifter who wants me, and Ambrose can't take down fourteen alphas and hundreds of others on his own.

So I run for my life.

CHAPTER II
LUMI

Run. Find Emeric.

The words blaze through me, forcing my legs to sprint through the woods and my eyes to brighten in the dark, darting around to look for Emeric through the trees and thick brush. My body obeys his command automatically—I don't have a choice.

But even if I did have a choice, I would choose running. I'm not sure I trust Emeric. Last time I trusted him he locked me in a cave, I ended up as an offering, and am now running for my life. A tiny part of me hopes I don't find Emeric.

I run as fast as my legs will take me despite branches carving into my bare skin with every step. Even running at full speed, having a head start, and Ambrose trying to hold them off, I hear male shifters behind me.

The curse—every male here can smell you. You've become obsessively desirable to them....

I glance up at the moon—fuck the full moon, not allowing me to shift.

The sound of crunching leaves under running paws

pounds in my ears. As they push their bodies to their limits, their deep panting grows louder, as do their howling and whining.

I don't dare glance behind me. If I do, the fear will overtake me. I can't think about what they will do if they catch me. Their own sexual desires combined with their wolf instincts to make me their mate will overpower any common sense.

I run faster, as if my human legs are capable of outrunning their wolf ones. But maybe Ambrose's alpha command was strong enough to make me run faster. He is the most powerful alpha—maybe he sent some of that power my way.

Closer and closer, I hear their heavy paws shrink the gap at my heels until I can feel the ground shaking under my own feet. A howl pierces through the cool air, and its nearness makes me jump.

I have seconds left before I'm caught.

Closing my eyes, I let myself succumb to my emotions as I catch my breath, leaning against a large tree trunk. The only chance I have to save myself now is to shift. My fear is at the front of my mind, but so is my shame, my sadness, my excitement, and my hot, wicked desire for an alpha I just met, my mate—Ambrose.

I let thoughts of him flood my mind—his thick black hair with glowing gold specks that I want to run my hands through, his lips that I have yet to kiss, his muscles that I need to feel contracting over me, and his cock that I refuse to die without feeling inside me.

My eyes pop open a second later. The emotions weren't enough. I can't shift, and I might never be able to. And if I can't shift, then I can't be marked as Ambrose's mate. I can't break the curse. But more importantly, I'll never be a bonded wolf. I'll continue to be an outcast or worse.

I've failed.

I fall to the ground as a wolf shifter lands on top of me—his weight crushing my frail, naked body. The ground, leaves, and twigs dig into the flesh of my stomach, breasts, and arms. But all I can think about is the fur pressing against me, the sharp teeth snapping at my back, and the wet nose nestling against my neck just under my ear.

He wants me. I can feel his desire, even without a bond or a word between us.

"No, please, no," I whisper, a tear rolling down my cheek. I don't know the rules of the mating bond. I don't know how to break the curse. But I do know that Ambrose was hesitant to accept me as his when he found out I couldn't shift. If another claimed me, my true mate might never accept me.

Sharp canines scrape over the skin of my shoulder.

"No, I'm not your mate!" I cry out. You can't change your mate. You can't change who you are destined to be with. No amount of lust, love, or desire can do that.

I won't survive if he sinks his teeth into my skin. Without the curse taking me, a wolf's bite can easily be lethal to humans when they go for the jugular. And he will—his instincts will take over. He's a predator; I'm prey.

I won't go without a fight. I try to wiggle out from underneath his heavy body, but I can't move. My heart races to uncontrollable speeds.

"No!" I yell again, like my own command must be obeyed as Ambrose's or any other alpha's.

I feel the tip of his canine press against my shoulder.

Then, a growl comes from the forest behind us, and suddenly, the weight is gone.

I crawl up, looking behind me to find two wolves fighting. One is dark brown, and the other a sandy blonde with golden yellow eyes tinged with blue.

Emeric saved me.

I'd know that sandy blonde coloring anywhere. Despite him obviously belonging to the Moonlight pack, giving him the golden glow, the tinge of blue in his eyes still remains.

He glances at me for only a split second, and I know what he's telling me.

Run.

The command Ambrose gave me weighs in my body. I'm supposed to run but also find Emeric, not run from Emeric.

I turn, fighting hard against Ambrose's command, willing the command to accept that I am following the command at the heart of it. I'm saving myself. I'm running.

Suddenly, my feet are flying again.

I hear the battle behind me. But I don't focus on the howls, the barking, the clashing of teeth and claws.

I sprint. I'm so focused on moving one foot in front of the other that I don't notice the hard body I slam into.

Hands grip my shoulders, easily keeping me from running away. But when I take a deep breath this man doesn't smell of the earth or the woods—he doesn't smell like a wolf shifter at all.

Could he be human?

Please, gods, let him be human.

A cold chill races through me as I stare at where he's

touching me on my shoulders. Slowly raising my head, I know what will be staring down at me.

Sharp teeth, pale, cool skin, and speed unmatched by any.

I take a deep breath as my eyes meet his—a vampire.

Vampires are our greatest enemies. They can kill humans with a single venomous bite. They're faster, more agile, and have more endurance than our own. They're immortal, and most concerning of all—they have mind control.

If he tastes a drop of my blood, he'll tap into my mind, and I'll be his willing slave. I'll do whatever he wishes, including digging a dagger into my own heart if he so desires.

"You have no reason to fear me, Lumi. It will barely hurt. I just need one drop."

Shivers race down my spine. I try to slow my heartbeat, hoping my blood won't be as enticing to him. And then I kick hard between his legs, hitting the steel rock of his body and almost breaking my foot as I do.

He chuckles, his grip tightening on my shoulder.

And then suddenly, he's on the ground.

"Rowena," the whispered cry comes out of me as she tackles him to the ground.

She goes for his throat in a vicious attack I didn't think her beautiful golden feminine body was capable of.

I hesitate for a split second, but there is nothing I can do for her. I can't help her. I can't even save myself.

All I can do is run and hope she's strong enough to outmatch a vampire.

Run, run, run.

I run as the moon dips lower, moonlight fading away and giving rise to the sun just over the horizon.

I'm exhausted from running all night. My legs haven't stopped for a moment since I saw the vampire. The sounds of my pursuers quieted hours ago, leaving only the soft breezes of the forest at night and now at dawn.

Still, I can't stop. I'm not safe. And Ambrose's command demands I keep going.

But I won't find Emeric in this direction. *Will he find me? Is he coming to get me?*

I have no clue; my brain is mush. I just keep going and going.

"I had so much faith in you," a woman's voice stops me cold.

I snap my head around. "Isolde."

She's leaning against a tree, still in her white cloak with thick, luscious blond curls hanging down to nearly her waist. She looks young, early twenties, and yet there is a wisdom in her eyes that tells me she's lived far beyond twenty years.

I don't know much about witches. I don't think they're immortal like vampires, but maybe they live extended lives like wolf shifters do. I don't know.

But I know I don't trust Isolde.

"I can't decide if I should kill you or pump you full of magic until you finally have the power to shift into a wolf."

My eyebrows jump up. "You have the power to help me shift?"

She nods as if it's obvious. She has the power to do pretty much whatever she fucking wants. "It would be painful—far more painful than if you figured it out for yourself. And you would lose control over your wolf—I would have that power." She pauses. "Forever."

My heart breaks. "No," I whisper.

Her eyes shift into dark orbs, and I feel her power flowing through her. "I don't have a choice. You are Ambrose's mate. You are the key to breaking the curse—for all of us. I have to kill you and hope the gods give Ambrose another mate—one who isn't as flawed as you. Or I force you to shift so Ambrose can mark you, break the curse, and then most likely kill you."

My gaze shoots daggers in her direction. "So either way, I die."

She shrugs. "Your sacrifice will save us all. I'm sure the gods will honor you in the afterlife."

I growl and feel a shift inside me—an awakening that wasn't there before.

Is she goading me into shifting? Or is her magic already working on me?

A howl pierces through the air, hitting me hard in the chest and forcing me to stop everything and wait.

Isolde, despite not being a shifter, stops and listens as well. A frown befalls her perfect face.

Ambrose and Emeric emerge from the forest in their wolf forms. A second later, both men are standing naked on two human legs. Emeric's eyes drag over me in concern, as if he's looking for any injuries. But Ambrose holds all his attention on Isolde and speaks to her.

"Leave. The sun has risen. We will have to wait until another full moon to complete the marking ceremony. You have no more use here, Isolde."

She smiles in a flirtatious way at my man. "Of course. I'll return on the next full moon."

With a flash, she vanishes.

My eyes bulge.

"How?" my mouth gapes.

Emeric chuckles at my response. "I take it this was your first encounter with a witch?"

I nod, my mouth still gaping.

Ambrose's head whips in my direction. His expression is emotionless as he drags his eyes over my naked body. Heat spreads through him, fueled by an unfulfilled desire for me.

My own desire mirrors his.

I want him, need him.

And yet, I can't help but see the disappointment in his eyes. I survived the night. I ran. I followed his command. The weak human without the ability to shift, who needed the help of Emeric, Rowena, and him in order to keep myself alive. I'm useless to him. He won't show me his feelings. He won't act on them, not until I prove myself worthy. He won't touch me until I shift and he sees the power within me.

"Come," Ambrose says. It's a command I can feel, even though he didn't need to give it for me to come with him. He did command me anyway, which means he doesn't trust me.

My mind doesn't trust him either, but my bones say he's my mate. I have no choice but to trust him completely and hope he's not the death of me.

CHAPTER 12
AMBROSE

"Is she really your mate?" Rowena asks as we all stare at Lumi, who has passed out in one of my guest bedrooms. I'm thankful to have a few minutes to gather my thoughts before I speak to her.

I don't answer as I stare at the woman who seems so small and fragile. I don't know how she's managed to even survive this long in the world without so much as a scar marking her flawless, pale skin. Her snow-colored locks are splayed out on the pillow, and her chest rises and falls heavily beneath the blankets. Her deep breathing is the only indication that she's unlikely to open her bright blue eyes anytime soon.

"Yes, she's his mate," Emeric says.

Rowena and I both turn to stare at him. Usually, I don't like Emeric answering for me, even though, as my beta, he knows everything about me. And because of the curse we both share—he feels everything I feel. But right now, I'm not sure how I feel about finding my mate or about the prophecy I was destined to fulfill finally coming true.

"Unbelievable," Rowena says, looking from me to Lumi in awe.

My jaw clenches as I stare at this woman lying on my guest bed. A woman I barely know. A woman who, by human standards, seems frail. A woman without a pack —an outcast, incapable of even shifting. The gods must be playing a cruel joke on me to give me her as a mate.

"I hate to say it, but you're sure Nyx isn't fucking with you?" Rowena can't process her disbelief, and I don't blame her. "You're sure he didn't convince a witch to put a spell on the two of you to make you think you are mates?"

My head snaps to Rowena. Most would cower when I look at them. They know the power inside me, but not Rowena. She's fearless and unrelenting in her ability to put me in my place.

"I'm sure. There isn't a witch powerful enough to put a spell like that on me," I say.

"Cocky, arrogant fool," Rowena says, rolling her eyes.

I growl, snapping in her direction. But she doesn't even flinch, completely unbothered by my outburst.

"I don't think it's a spell either, Rowena. I've never felt anything like this. If it's a witch doing this, then they'd be powerful enough to outright break the curse themselves," Emeric says.

I nod, turning my attention back to the meek woman still passed out. Warm anger spreads through my body because even though I know Nyx didn't do this, it does feel like a cruel joke. The gods above must have thought it'd be fascinating to pair me with the weakest woman they could find. *What am I supposed to do with her? How is she supposed to survive as my mate?*

"What pack is she from?" Emeric asks.

"I'm not sure. Somewhere north by the look of her hair. Silvercrest, maybe," I reply. We don't all carry physical markers of our pack, but I've only ever seen shifters with hair as white as snow come from packs that live in the far north.

He nods, sensing the anger in me. "She's stronger than she looks. She wouldn't be your mate if she wasn't. She wouldn't have survived tonight if she wasn't."

"Emeric's right. She's strong. I can feel it in her aura," Rowena says.

I narrow my eyes at Lumi as her chest rises and falls in slow, shallow breaths. Even how she breathes makes her appear weak.

There has to be more than meets the eye. A reason she was chosen by the gods as my mate. A reason I've yet to unveil, but I will. Time is running out.

I look up and meet Rowena's gaze. She knows how important it is for me to break the curse by the next full moon.

"Lumi's the one. I know it. Together, the two of you will break the curse," Emeric says, full of confidence as usual.

"I know," I say, walking out of the bedroom without another word.

I don't have to tell Emeric to guard Lumi with his life. He will. So will Rowena. They are the only people in the world I fully trust. The rest of the Moonlight wolves are good allies, but I would never trust them with Lumi.

I shift before letting out a commanding howl that I know every alpha within a hundred-mile radius can hear. The other alphas don't like to be ordered around, but when they are in my territory and I'm the only one powerful enough to break the curse, they have no choice but to listen.

Quickly, I jog to the outskirts of my territory, the usual meeting place where the alphas convene after every full moon. Usually, we meet to discuss what needs to be done at the next ceremony. If there is someone we are missing who needs to be presented in the offering. Trying to convince one of the witches with seer powers to tell us another part of the prophecy.

Not this time.

I'm the last to reach the clearing in the middle of the forest. The fourteen other alphas are all standing in a circle, refusing to turn their backs to any other alpha. They each dig their claws into the dirt below them and alternate growling and baring their teeth at one another.

I sigh as I shift into my human form. The others stay in their wolf form, like that would somehow offer them protection against me.

"Come on, guys. We need to talk," I say lightheartedly, trying to avoid giving another alpha command. But I'll do it if they don't shift willingly.

Nyx shifts into his cold, unsettling human form. "You want to talk about how I found your mate, and you weren't strong enough to convince her to complete the marking ceremony?"

I ignore him completely as I wait for the others to shift. But either smartly or stupidly they remain in their wolf forms, knowing that a fight is about to ensue. *Cowards.*

"And how do we know it wasn't your doing that prevented me from being able to mark her? You are the type who would find a way to break the curse and then spell her so you can control when the curse is broken," I say.

The others turn on Nyx, growling and snarling in his direction.

Cool calmness remains on Nyx's features as he holds me in his steady gaze. "And why would I do that when I am as desperate as anyone here to break the curse as soon as possible?"

I don't have an answer for him, but Nyx is up to something.

"I told you to leave if you wanted to live. The fact that you're still alive is proof of my benevolence for finding my mate. Take your pack and leave before my kindness runs out."

"So, she is your mate?" Baelor says as he shifts into his human form.

"Yes, Lumi is my mate. And at the next full moon, I will mark her and break the curse."

"Not without a challenge to prove that she's your mate. That's how it works, right? The challenge is supposed to ensure that the feelings you feel are correct, right?" Baelor says, his voice dripping in sarcasm.

"Baelor, I'm sorry—"

"You're not fucking sorry! You didn't lose your mate!"

"Adaluna wasn't your mate!"

His eyes narrow at me, and I can see the shift in the tension of his body. I shouldn't have said what I said, even if it's the truth. But he has to face reality. We all need to stay focused if we are to break the curse.

Baelor's pupils dilate, and his canines begin to sharpen. "I think you're a coward."

A hush spreads through the other alphas. Zephran, with his need for peace, tries to approach Baelor to calm him down, but I shake my head slightly. This is between me and Baelor.

"Don't do this, Baelor. It's not going to end well for you."

He chuckles manically as fur begins to form down his spine, as he slowly continues his shift into wolf form.

"My life is already over. I can at least ensure that the others see how much of a coward you are. You aren't the strongest among us, as you claim. When it comes down to it, you won't sacrifice your mate for the marking. And even if you are strong enough to keep her alive through the marking, you won't allow her to mark you in return and risk your own life. You're nothing but a two-faced coward," he says.

I wait until he fully shifts before I move. I give him every advantage I can, knowing it still won't be enough. I wish it didn't have to be this way. But as the alpha among alphas, I have no choice. I have to accept Baelor's challenge. And I have to win, no matter the cost.

CHAPTER 13

LUMI

Light splinters through the window shades, flooding my room. My eyes squint open, and my body barely moves, begging me to go back to sleep. If the sun is any indication, I've slept most of the day, and there's too much that needs to be done. There are too many unanswered questions. A curse needs lifting, and I need to talk to Ambrose—now.

I sit up quickly but immediately regret my actions as my head pounds. The sheets fall down my body, and I realize I'm still naked. The details of last night are foggy. I remember following Ambrose and Emeric back to the campgrounds. I remember Emeric showing me to the bedroom, and then I must've passed out.

My eyes cut around the room, looking for clothes, but I find none.

Damn wolf shifters and their inability to realize that most people don't like to strut around naked.

I rip the sheets off the bed and wrap them haphazardly around my body until I am at least covered. I run my hand through my long hair, wishing

I had a hairbrush or, better yet, a bath. Grit and grime coat my strands, while sweat and oil coat my pores. Hopefully, I'll be granted a bath and a brush soon enough.

I cautiously open the door, expecting Emeric or someone else to be guarding it, but I find no one. *Huh? Strange.*

I walk down a long, empty hallway, listening for signs of Ambrose, but there are none. The house is huge—a maze of hallways and doors. I'm shocked to find that no one was guarding my door. *Did Ambrose trust me enough not to flee? Did he trust that the other males would leave me alone?*

Finally, I hear a pan clanking, and I turn a corner to find Emeric standing over a pot on the stove with a cup of coffee in his hand.

Emeric beams at me like I am the sun itself.

"Good morning, beautiful," Emerics says, his voice is sweet and kind. He looks at me like Kael used to look at me—in a loving, sister sort of way.

"Morning. Where is Ambrose?"

"He's out doing alpha stuff."

"What does that mean, 'Alpha stuff'?" I lean against the counter opposite Emeric.

"Not that it's any of your business, but he is saying goodbye to the other alphas and their packs before arranging the marking ceremony next month."

Next month—that's my deadline. I have one month to learn to shift. One month for Ambrose to fall in love with me and me with him. One month to ensure that he is indeed my mate. One month to break the curse.

"And why aren't you out there with him? You are his beta, right?"

"Because I have far better things to do than say goodbye to a bunch of arrogant, hot-blooded alphas."

"Like what?"

He hands me a cup of coffee. "Like ensuring you don't run away."

"I'm not going anywhere. I want to meet with Ambrose. I want to break the curse."

Emeric's eyes shoot through me sadly for a split second. He turns back around to stir the eggs in the pot, and then he flips the bacon in the other pan.

"You weren't doing a very good job of guarding me all the way on the other side of the house."

Emeric chuckles. "I can guard any human like you from a far greater distance. My hearing and smelling abilities far outweigh your own. I knew the second you woke up, and I heard every footstep you made down the hallway. I smelled you the second you entered the room. You weren't getting away without my knowledge. And as I am ten times faster than you, you wouldn't have made it farther than a step outside before I caught you."

I glare at him. "I'm not a human."

"You could've fooled me."

I snarl and growl.

Emeric just laughs again. "You're going to have to work on that menacing growl. It's adorable."

"And what would stop someone else from breaking in and taking me? Another wolf shifter—an alpha, perhaps —could have kidnapped me before you had a chance to stop them."

Emeric's eyes fall and darken. "No one is a threat to you in this house."

"What is that supposed to mean?"

"You're in Ambrose's house. The alpha of the Moonlight wolves. He is the alpha that trumps all others. No one would dare break into his house. No one would dare harm you, not here. You're safe here."

The seriousness in Emeric's voice hits me. It's the truth, but I can't help but think he's not telling me something.

"Does this house happen to have any clothes that would fit me?"

Emeric seems to finally realize I'm wrapped in bedsheets. He's standing in nothing but loose athletic shorts and no shirt, perfectly at ease with his semi-nakedness. He's a superbly sculpted man with sun-kissed skin, blonde hair, and bright blue eyes. He's so lovable and good-looking at the same time. But I'm still pissed at him for leading me to that cave, for tricking me. And I'm pissed off at him now for not telling me the whole truth.

"I'm sure I can find you something to wear. But do you want to get dressed or eat first?"

My stomach growls, and my mouth salivates at the smell of the eggs and bacon he's making.

He grins knowingly. "Eat first. Maybe there is a wolf inside you after all if you pick eating over clothing yourself."

He dishes up a plate of eggs and bacon, and I snatch it from his hands, not bothering to make it to the table before digging in. Emeric and I eat in silence, too hungry for words. After eating, he finds me jean shorts and a tank top for me to wear.

I need to talk to Ambrose. I need to figure out where we stand and how he's going to help me learn to shift. I need to learn everything there is about the curse because, obviously, I don't know the whole truth if the witches and vampires are also affected by it. And I need to figure out what Nyx did to Kael without revealing that Kael and I belong to the Wintermoon wolves. I don't believe that Nyx sent him deep into the forest until he could control his shifting, not after Nyx sacrificed me in the offering. Not after I saw the way everyone stared at Nyx in complete terror. He and Emeric are enemies as well. I'm terrified to learn what Nyx might have done to Kael.

"I need to get showered and dressed," I say.

"Take your time. You can use the bathroom next to your bedroom."

"I'll be right back," I say, hoping that Emeric's hearing isn't as good as he claims. I need to get out of here.

———

THIRTY SECONDS IS ALL the time I allow myself in the shower before I'm out and pulling clothes onto my still-damp body. I quickly run my hand through my long, wintry mane to brush out the tangles, not bothering to dry it as it drips water onto my shirt. Leaving the shower running so Emeric thinks I'm still showering, I sneak out the front door.

As the house door falls shut behind me, I take a deep breath, taking in the warm sun on my cheeks before facing the challenge ahead of me. An unsettling feeling hits me hard in the chest. Slowly, I glance around and find I'm surrounded by six shifter men.

Waiting—they were all waiting. I gulp down a swallow. For me—they've been waiting for me. Apparently, there *was* a reason Emeric didn't want me to leave the house.

I should go back inside. It's only a couple of steps behind me. Emeric said the house was protected, and that no shifter would attack me inside. But I'm not inside, and by the way they are all looking at me, I'm fair game out here.

I'm not even sure I could make it to the door before one of them could grab me. They are all so freaking fast, and I have nothing but my human speed. It doesn't matter that I've barely taken a step outside the door. They can close the gap in the amount of time it takes me to blink.

"Easy guys, you know Ambrose will kill you if you touch me."

"Not if we mark you as our mate. He won't have a choice but to accept the marking," a blonde man says.

"I can't complete the marking with anyone, not right now. It's not the full moon. And Ambrose will kill you long before there is another full moon." At least, I think Ambrose would kill them. I honestly know very little about the man.

Mine—that word sounds into my head again. *Ambrose is mine.* It's such a strange feeling to have such strong feelings for a man I don't even know. I've only spent a few minutes with him, but I can feel it with every part of my body, with every one of my senses. The connection to him is a living, breathing thing. It's as part of me as my heart or lungs. I need it to survive. Even without the curse, if something were to happen to Ambrose, I'm pretty sure I would die, too.

The men don't back down. Their nostrils flare as they breathe in my scent. Their eyes dilate into slits. And I smell their male scents—pheromones trying to draw me to them. They're all fools. Even if I wanted to choose one of them, I couldn't.

I run my eyes through the six males. At the last one,

my heart beats so hard in my chest that I think it's going to break my ribs.

"Kael!" I shout in shock.

Tears fill my eyes, and my heart warms. "I never thought I would see you again."

I truly thought Nyx killed Kael. I thought I had lost him forever. He was the only one left of home, the only thing keeping me going when everyone else I love is most likely dead.

Kael doesn't look at me like he's glad to have finally found me, though. He doesn't look at me with that brotherly love I'm used to seeing from him. Lust—pure, unadulterated lust is all I see in his hazel eyes marked with silver strands.

"Kael, it's me—Lumi. Your best friend that you think of like a sister. Remember?"

Kael looks at me as if in a daze, as if under some spell himself.

"Kael," I plead, my body trembling.

He stalks toward me, and the other males move in as well. I inch backward, knowing that if I run, it will just make their predatory instincts kick in, and they'll lunge for me. Inch by inch, I gain a quarter of a foot, but it's not close enough. I'm not safe until I'm back in the house.

"Kael, remember who you are. This isn't you. You're better than this. You're my friend. You don't want me. This is some curse, some spell you're under. This isn't the real you." Another inch back, another inch closer to the door. I'm so close now that I can feel my hair brush against the wood I just have to find the handle.

I keep my eyes locked on Kael, ignoring the other males. My only chance of survival is Kael. If I can break through whatever spell he's under, then maybe the two of us can find a way to escape.

Kael moves closer—he's the closest of all of them to me.

Please, I say, but the word never leaves my lips. Kael grabs me before I have a chance to move another inch. His lips slam against mine in a devouring kiss. My hands go up to his chest, trying to push him away, but he's a wall of muscle. There is no moving him.

I'm not strong enough.

I don't know how to fight back.

I'm weak, and I hate it.

I hate how uneven a match we are.

And I hate that most of all, when Kael wakes up from whatever spell he's under and realizes the mistake he made, he'll hate himself. This isn't him. Ambrose will kill him before he has a chance at redemption.

Please, I think again. *Please, please, please.*

The other males franticly close in further. Hands reach out, stroking my back, threatening to pull me out of Kael's arms. I don't know which is worse—my friend claiming me against my will or strangers touching me.

Tears stain my eyes, and my heart beats quickly in my chest, like a prey seconds before it's slaughtered. I push against Kael with everything I have, as I try to bite down on his tongue he's shoved into my mouth.

But he barely flinches—I don't even think the pain registers in his head. That's how consumed he is by his lust for me. I don't understand it. Days ago, he was so clear that we weren't mates, that we are nothing but friends, nothing but brother and sister to each other. And now he has his tongue shoved down my throat, threatening to fuck me right here in front of all these males.

A menacing growl vibrates through the air, warning us on a deep, primal level that we have to obey. Our movements halt immediately. Our lungs don't even expand to take another breath.

Another low growl, snapping of teeth, and the sound of claws scraping over skin break through the silence. Paws pound against the ground as some try to flee. But the snapping of sharp teeth keeps them from escaping.

I take the moment to shove Kael as hard as I can, finally breaking his hold.

He shakes his head, his eyes clearing a little.

"Lumi?"

I nearly sob. "Yes, it's me. Your Lumi."

He exhales in relief. But I see the large black wolf with golden flecks in his fur, and I know what's about to happen. "Run, Kael. Run," my voice breaks.

"No, I'm not leaving you. Not again."

Ambrose releases the last of the five men he held in his jaws. The man slips to the floor lifelessly. Ambrose turns his eyes towards Kael. His eyes lock on him, and he crouches down as if he's about to pounce. He's going to kill him. I can't tell how many of the other five are dead or just in so much pain that they can't get up.

But I can't let Ambrose hurt Kael.

Ambrose lunges for Kael. Time slows as I throw myself between them at the last second. Ambrose halts, his nose brushing against mine as he huffs out a hard breath.

"Please, no. He's my friend. He won't hurt me, not again. He was just under some spell, but he's not now," I plead.

Ambrose bares his teeth in Kael's direction and rolls his shoulders, his fur moving in the wind as a shift changes in the air. We're eye to eye, even though he's in his wolf form and I'm a human—that's how big and terrifying he is.

And yet, when he looks at me, I know he'll do what I ask. He feels the same way about me that I do to him.

I don't take my eyes off Ambrose as I speak to Kael. "Kael, find Rowena. She'll help you. I'll come find you soon." I don't know if she will, but she's the only person I trust not to kill him at the moment.

"But—"

"Trust me. I'm safe with Ambrose."

"He looks like he's about to bite your head off. I'm not leaving you," Kael says.

"He's my mate," I say matter-of-factly, saying it as much for Kael's sake as Ambrose's. They both need to hear it. Ambrose is stuck with me. Together, we can figure out how I can shift.

Kael's eyes widen in disbelief.

"Go," I order Kael.

Ambrose and I continue to stare into each other's eyes, both tense. Neither of us backs down, but Kael finally leaves.

Finally, I can breathe again. As I exhale, Ambrose shifts back into his human form. He stands naked before me, his pale skin in stark contrast to his dark hair that hangs in loose curls down his neck.

That's when I notice the fresh scars, the thin lines of blood rolling down his muscled skin. My heart beats slow and steady as I take him in. I realize the cost to him. I realize how he spent his night and this morning. Fighting off men. Fighting for me. He wasn't hiding from me. He was fighting for me. Fighting to keep me. Fighting to keep me safe.

And this is how I repaid him? By disobeying his orders and doing something so foolish. And he had to fight even more shifters because of me.

"*Get inside,*" he snaps in my head. It's an alpha command, but he didn't need to use his power to get me to listen to him this time.

"*I'm sorry,*" I think back to him.

He hangs his head in exhaustion but doesn't say anything back. I can feel the disappointment rolling off of him as I obey his command and walk back into the house.

CHAPTER 14
LUMI

"I'm sorry," I say again as I close the door behind me.

Ambrose is pouring himself a cup of coffee in the kitchen, not bothering to put any clothes on first. Emeric is nowhere in sight.

Instead of responding to my words, he turns and faces me.

It takes everything inside me not to gasp at the sight of him. I knew blood coated his body before, but I didn't have time to study the volume of blood on him. An overwhelming metallic scent fills my nostrils, and fear curls in my stomach as I scan every inch of his skin, not even blushing when my gaze flicks over his long, thick cock. I desperately search for the wound that must be gushing blood as he sips coffee.

"Where...? How bad are you...?" My voice slips with each word, unable to ask if he's injured. I just met this man. I barely know him, but my heart would shatter if he were to die.

He smirks, dark and devious. "The blood isn't mine.

I'm not wounded, but my ego may be if you think I'd get hurt that easily."

"I didn't mean…" I snap my mouth shut as he grins at me.

He has a sense of humor.

"Whose blood is it, then?"

"Do you really want to know?"

"Yes. If you're expecting me to be the obedient type who doesn't want to know any details or the dangers we face, then you need to find yourself a new mate," I scold.

He cocks his head to the side, his face void of any emotion, and takes another sip of his coffee. He's as calm as a Sunday morning, not like he's not standing here naked, coated in someone else's blood, while I drill him on what he was doing last night.

"Baelor's."

I suck in a breath. He fought the alpha with the red hair, who thought he'd found his mate, but when he went to mark her, she died.

"Baelor? Why?"

"He challenged me. He didn't believe we're mates."

I frown. "How bad?"

He furrows his brow. "You really don't know? You can't smell what happened on me?"

I shift uncomfortably on my feet but shake my head. All I smell is that cool metallic smell of blood. But it doesn't give me any clue as to what happened.

"How long have you known you were a wolf shifter?"

"My entire life." I could lie, but I decide I only want to lie about the things I have to lie about. Keeping as close to the truth as I can without telling him I'm from the Wintermoon, the better.

"And yet, you didn't grow up in a pack?"

I shake my head. "It was just my father, Kael, and me. My father could shift." I blow out a slow breath, knowing the words I'm about to speak are the truth, and I'm not sure I can say it out loud. "He died..." the words catch in my throat. "He died about a month ago. After that, Kael and I came in search of other wolf shifters. Nyx found us and brought us here."

"I'm sorry for your loss. I know what it's like to lose your family." His words are a gentle caress, and I feel empathy ripple off him.

Our eyes meet in joined grief, strengthening our connection even deeper.

"What pack did you belong to before your numbers were decimated?"

I shake my head. "I don't know. My father never talked about the pack before. It was too painful for him. My mother died in childbirth."

He nods. "You smell like Silvercrest. Their numbers have been dwindling, and we haven't had any members of their pack at the offering in over a decade. That would be my guess."

"Silvercrest," I whisper, pretending it's the missing piece of my family puzzle. But I hate myself for lying to my mate, a man I'll spend the rest of my life with. But I don't have a choice—at least, not yet. I need to know how he would act if he found out the truth. He needs time to get to know me before he judges me for my pack.

I don't know why he can't smell the truth on me like Nyx did, but I'm not going to argue with him.

"I want to be initiated into the Moonlight pack. And then you can help me get my wolf."

He chuckles. "You are a bossy thing, aren't you?"

"I am." I fold my arms and smirk at him.

He sets his coffee down on the counter and walks toward me, stepping into my space.

Now I can really smell him—the evergreen, earthy, ancient scent that smells like coming home. The metallic smell falls into the background of my mind.

Kiss me, I think. *Dammit, kiss me.* I need to know what it's like to kiss him. Just one kiss.

His eyes darken, and his tongue runs over his bottom lip. He's going to kiss me, my heart sings.

Finally.

He takes another step closer, until our bodies are brushing together, but it's still not close enough for me. I hold my breath, waiting for him to make the first move. It seems like the right thing to do since he's the alpha, and I wouldn't want to break his fragile ego by kissing him first.

"You aren't ready to be initiated into the Moonlight pack."

I frown, but my eyes are too locked on his lips to fully register his words.

"And I won't be the one helping you to get your wolf."

My heart immediately shifts from a rampant thunder in my chest to a grinding halt.

"What? Why?"

"I'd probably kill you long before you got your wolf."

I narrow my eyes at him as I glare. "I'm not afraid of you."

"You should be. I'm the most powerful alpha alive. I could snap your neck in a second if I desired it. No one would question my decision to end your life. I would suffer no punishment for it."

"You won't. I'm your mate."

"And you're weak. You haven't been trained even to fight as a human, let alone as a wolf. You can't even smell what happened on me. You don't have any of the basic wolf instincts. You can't shift. You're useless to me."

"I'm not weak!"

He growls, trying to get me to back down, to bow to him. I stand taller, growling back.

"I'm. Not. Weak."

His jaw twitches, and his eyes glow that bright yellow color of the moonlight.

"That is yet to be determined."

I huff.

"But whether you are weak or strong, you should still be terrified of me. If I don't find you worthy of being my mate, I'll kill you. It's the only way to ensure the universe brings me a new mate, one I actually find up to the task."

"I'm not the only one who needs to be found worthy. You need to prove your worth, too, if you expect me to accept the mating bond between us."

He grins approvingly. But right now, I couldn't care less about what he thinks. This is a two-way street. I don't care if he's the most powerful alpha. I know my own worth, and I won't be bossed around by anyone, especially an egotistical male on a power trip.

"Emeric will train you. He's the only male you can trust. Do not venture out of this house without him by your side."

"What about you?"

"You can't trust me, and you're not safe with me. I think I've made that perfectly clear."

"Maybe I can't trust you, but I'm not afraid of you."

"How bad, you asked? How badly did I hurt Baelor?"

He pauses, and my heart skips a beat.

"I killed him."

I don't react. I know he's looking for a reaction from me, but he'll find none. I lock my emotions up tight.

"Learn to shift. Become worthy of being part of the Moonlight wolves. And stay away from me until then."

I grind my teeth together.

"Otherwise, you'll end up dead."

CHAPTER 15
LUMI

My jaw slackens as I process his words. Ambrose killed Baelor—just like that.

Suddenly, it hits me—I know very little about Ambrose, my mate. He's the man I'll spend the rest of my life with if I learn how to shift and complete the marking, but I don't know him. I'm not in love with him, and he sure as hell isn't in love with me.

Everything we feel toward each other is because of a supernatural bond, part of how our species is fighting for survival. It's beyond either of us. This bond is predestined, something we have no control over.

The mating bond doesn't guarantee love. It doesn't guarantee that we will even like each other. All it does is guarantee a physical match—one that will produce strong offspring.

I thought when I found my mate, he would be easy to love; maybe it would even be love at first sight. Instead, Ambrose is a killer. He killed another alpha, and from the look of Ambrose, it took very little effort. He killed Baelor rather than risk him threatening us. I don't know if that's supposed to be romantic or terrifying.

And he'll kill me, too, if he finds out the truth. He's already doubting me. He thinks I'm not worthy of being his mate if I can't even shift. I'm a weakling, clearly not strong enough to be an alpha's mate. The alpha's mate is supposed to be his equal in every way and strong enough to carry his heirs.

If he finds out I'm from the Wintermoon pack, I'll be dead. He won't have a choice but to kill me. I may not know Ambrose very well, but he won't accept mating with someone he views as a traitor. And my pack is just that to the rest of the packs.

I need to talk to Kael. We need a plan to keep our pack identity a secret.

And...*fuck*...I need to talk to Nyx. He knows the truth. He could destroy me. *Why hasn't he already outed me?*

Anxiety pumps through my body, filling every inch of me as I look up to find Ambrose gone. I need to talk to him. I don't know what I'm going to say or what I'm going to do, but I have to do something. I didn't come all this way just to die. I'm stronger than Ambrose, or anyone else, thinks I am.

Instinctually, I head down the hallway and stop outside a closed door that I know Ambrose entered, most likely his bedroom. My wolf instincts may be pathetic compared to his, but at least I can sense where my mate has gone.

I stare at the door, unsure of how to handle this. I need to talk to him. We weren't finished with our conversation, and I need to arrange a time to speak with Kael at the very least. Maybe he can help with my Nyx problem.

I reach for the door handle without fear but find it locked.

"Ambrose, we aren't done talking."

I wait a few seconds, hoping that he'll respond or, better yet, open the door and finish the conversation we barely started. But he doesn't. I press my ear against the door and hear the faint sound of the shower running.

He's not responding because he can't hear me.

No, that's a lie. He has supernatural wolf hearing. He can hear me. He could respond if he wanted to, but he's not.

I start to talk to him in my head, but nothing comes out. I can't speak through the bond we formed. I realize it's the first time I've tried when we weren't in the same room. *Does it work through doors, through walls? How far away can I speak to him in my head?*

I close my eyes, concentrating on Ambrose. He's in the shower. *Water rolls down his ripped muscles and turns red as it washes away Baelor's blood. Drips fall down his body over his long, thick cock that swells larger...*

I shake my head, opening my eyes, realizing that I can't focus enough to send him a message that way. I have no choice but to sit outside his bedroom until he opens the door.

"You're going to be waiting a long time," Emeric says.

I fold my arms as I sit cross-legged outside his door.

"I don't care. I need to talk to him."

Emeric leans against the wall with a glowing smile on his face and a sparkle in his eyes. "You're both stubborn. I can see why you're mates."

"Well, Ambrose doesn't. He thinks I'm a weak, pathetic girl who can't even shift. He thinks he might as well kill me in hopes of finding a new, better mate."

Emeric chuckles.

"I don't find anything I said funny."

"No, but I do. Trust me—the last thing Ambrose thinks of you is that you're weak."

"He told me I'm weak to my face."

Emeric shrugs like he's been told the same thing by Ambrose a time or two. "What are you going to do about it?"

I look down at where I'm sitting. "I thought it was obvious. I'm sitting here until Ambrose opens the door and talks to me."

"And when he does, what are you going to tell him? That you aren't weak?"

I frown.

"Sorry to tell you, but yes, I heard every word of your conversation. Wolf hearing and all that. The only reason those outside of the house can't hear is because Ambrose has had this house's walls reinforced to the point that no shifter could invade his privacy."

"No one but you."

Emeric's smile broadens. It's an infectious smile—genuine, warm, and kind.

"What did you do to become his beta?"

Emeric chuckles. "You haven't earned that story yet."

I turn my head toward the door.

"Come on, why don't we spend an hour or two training while Ambrose sulks in his bedroom? That way, when he decides he's ready to talk to you, you'll have a few new muscles growing on you and skills to back up that mouth of yours."

I narrow my eyes at Emeric. "I still don't trust you."

He shrugs. "Maybe I don't care if you trust me or not."

"But you do—because if this works, one day I'm going

to be your alpha's mate. And I would have the power to get rid of you as beta. You'll only stay if I trust you."

He smirks. "Good thing that you trust me then."

"I don't trust you."

"Except you do. You pretend you don't because I tricked you into that cave at the offering. When really, you were planning on entering the offering all along. No one had to force you."

He's right. I do trust him. Probably more than I should. But he did save my life. And I was planning on finding my mate. Even once the risks of the offering were explained to me, I still would have chosen to go through with it.

"I'm not the only one who saw your truth. Ambrose sensed how brave you truly were. And when he told you that he killed Baelor, he could hear your heart beating the same as I could."

I swallow hard. "He heard it sputter in fear?"

Emeric's eyes darken as he speaks in a serious tone. "No, he heard it continue to beat slow and steady, just like I did. He may have said you are weak physically, and that's true. But you aren't weak where it matters most. I can whip you into physical shape in no time, but teaching you how to be stubborn, brave, and fearless—I don't have to teach you that."

I smile. "Are you always this charming?"

He flashes me a smile back. "Always."

I stand up. "Fine, then whip me into shape."

He nods.

I stare at the door for another second, trying to will a message to Ambrose. But it's like I've forgotten how to speak. Nothing works.

I frown. "Does the mental bond we share only work

when we are in the same room? Or is that something I have to practice and get better at the same as physical training?"

Emeric stares at the door and then at me. "It's been a long time since anyone had a connection that allowed them to speak mind to mind. I don't know exactly what it means to be mates or even how it truly works. But I remember stories from my parents having mental conversations with each other from miles away."

My frown deepens as I try once again.

"But I'd guess if you can't get through to Ambrose, it's because he doesn't want you to. His powers are immense as an alpha. He could easily be shielding you from talking to him."

"Gods, he isn't going to make it easy for me to love him, is he?"

Emeric chuckles. "No, but would you ever love a man who made it too easy for you?"

I don't answer him as I pull my long silvery-white hair into a ponytail on top of my head and follow Emeric out the back door to train.

CHAPTER 16
LUMI

"You have no endurance or muscles. Your form is crap. Speed isn't going to do anything compared to a shifter or vampire. You can't shift, not even a tingling of anything. No claws are randomly forming, or canines sharpening, or anything. Honestly, I don't know how you're even alive," Emeric says, chuckling to himself, his blue eyes shimmering in the fading sunlight.

"Please, tell me what you really think," I say between heavy pants as I roll my eyes at him. We've been training all day, taking breaks only to refuel, and then we've been back at it. Running, strength training, practicing hand-to-hand combat. But even if I was the fastest, strongest human alive, it wouldn't be enough to defend myself against a shifter, vampire, or witch. Not that I'm even close to being a strong physical human.

After tossing me a towel and a water bottle to where I've collapsed on the grass, Emeric still stands shirtless above me. There's not even a drop of sweat or at least a sign he exerted any of his rippling muscles today. I wipe the sweat from my brow as I down the water in long gulps.

When I look up again, Emeric is sitting next to me on the grass as a strand of his sandy blonde hair falls over one of blue eyes. I reach up and sweep the hair out of his eyes without thinking.

I pull my hand back abruptly, like I just touched a hot fire.

Emeric grins cockily as he studies me. "Don't do that."

"Do what?" I sit on my hands, so I don't do anything else stupid.

"We've just spent the entire day together. I pushed you to the limit of what your fragile human body can handle."

"Can we please stop pointing out that I have a fragile human body? I'm well aware that I can't shift."

"I'm sorry." He sighs, leaning back on his elbows. We both stare up at the fading sun dipping below the trees just beyond the stone walls that surround the massive backyard we've been training in all day. This place is a fortress of thick stone walls, but I don't know if they are just meant to provide privacy or actually keep anyone out. A shifter in his wolf form could easily jump it, so could a vampire, and a witch could blast through the wall.

I look back at the mansion of glass walls that face out into this backyard. I keep expecting to see Ambrose's golden eyes staring out the window each time I do. But if he's watching us, he disappears before I spot him.

"What is going to happen to Ambrose? Are the others going to try to kill him for killing Baelor?"

A dark chuckle leaves Emeric's throat. "No, Ambrose is the most powerful alpha that exists. No one would be foolish enough to try to take him on. They'd end up dead just like Baelor." He pauses. "Well, Nyx might be the only other alpha stupid enough to challenge Ambrose, but he'd lose. The others respect the hell out of Ambrose and know he's the only real hope we all have of breaking the curse."

Nyx—my heart jumps into my throat before I remember that Emeric can hear every beat of my heart and change of my respirations.

"But you don't have to worry about any confrontation happening anyway. The other alphas all went back to their respective territories until the next full moon."

"How will the next alpha of Baelor's pack be chosen?"

"There will be a challenge the day before the next full moon. Their beta will be in charge of the pack until then. And usually the beta becomes the next alpha, but not always. Whoever wins the challenge will become alpha at the full moon ceremony."

"Is that how Ambrose became alpha? He challenged someone?"

Emeric bites his bottom lip. "It's really not my story to tell."

I frown, staring at Emeric intently. Warmth spreads through me as I stare into his crystal blue eyes. A lump forms in my throat as I let my gaze dip down across his bare chest. I swallow it down quickly, but I can't hide how my cheeks pinken, or my heartbeat quickens.

Emeric frowns as he stares at me, and I know he notices my body's reaction.

I open my mouth to ask what's happening to me. Why I'm so attracted to him, but he speaks first.

"It's the curse."

I take a slow deep breath, hoping it will ease the hot, tingling ache starting in my core and working itself wild through my body. But all it does is give me an inhale of his crisp, clean scent. The tingle turns into an unquenchable ache.

"The longer you go without completing the marking ceremony, the worse these symptoms will get. The other males will go wild, trying to make you their mates, and you will become intensely attracted to every male around you. It's meant to confuse you, to prevent you from finding your true mate, and keep the curse alive."

I bite my lip and clench my fists to keep from jumping Emeric's bones. "How do I know that Ambrose is my true mate?"

"I can't answer that. Only the two of you can."

"Well, that's not helpful."

Emeric chuckles and every muscle in my body trembles trying to keep from touching him, kissing him, choosing him.

"Don't do that," I grit out, closing my eyes and trying to block the feelings out.

"Sorry. It's why it's so important that you are ready to complete the marking ceremony by the next full moon."

I grind my teeth together as the agony overtakes me. Sweat drips down my brow and off the back of my neck, and my hands become clammy.

"Why is it affecting me so much right now? And why don't you seem to be affected?"

"Because we spent so much time together today. Any male you spend this much time with is sure to cause this reaction in you. But soon, it won't take this long for you to have these feelings. Soon, it will be only a matter of minutes with another male before your lust overwhelms you."

Fuck, I'm not going to make it a month. And I have no idea how I'm going to learn to shift. We spent a whole day training, and I'm no closer to figuring it out than I was when we started.

"And you?" I spit out, cracking my eyes to look at Emeric, concerned that he might be affected now. That he might have just as strong an urge to kiss me as I do him.

Emeric smiles brightly with his kind eyes as he tucks a loose strand of my hair behind my ear.

I shiver at his touch, but he doesn't take things further. He doesn't lean in to kiss me. He doesn't draw our bodies closer together.

"You never have to worry about me being affected by the curse."

I frown. "Why?"

He shakes his head, staring off with a faraway look on his face. "It doesn't matter. What matters is teaching you how to shift."

I roll my shoulders back, trying to control my feelings as well as Emeric can. But I can't help but wonder why he isn't affected by the curse.

"Why are the vampires and witches cursed? I always thought it was just the wolf shifters after the Winter-moon pack member rejected their mating bond," I ask, trying to change the subject.

He raises an eyebrow at me. "No one knows for sure the details of the other species' curses. The wolf shifters were the first to deal with the wrath of the gods. But shortly after, the witches and vampires angered them enough to have their own curses inflicted upon them."

"What are their curses?"

He shrugs. "Everyone is secretive about the details. No one wants to give another species the advantage of knowing their weakness."

The sun dips below the horizon, and the sky quickly begins to fade into darkness.

"You told me that your eyesight at night is the only heightened sense you have, correct?"

I nod.

"Good. Then we will start practicing at night, see how good your eyesight really is. If it's not as good as a wolf shifter, then we'll see if we can improve it with practice, see how much you can control it. From there, we can see if we can get any other senses or flickers of you being more than just a human girl." Emeric stands up.

"I am more than just a human girl," I snarl, joining him at his side. The attraction immediately vanishes as soon as he calls me a human girl.

His eyebrows shoot up in my direction, and he bites back a smile. He did it on purpose to get rid of my lust, so I can't stay mad at him for long.

Suddenly, his head snaps up. His body becomes still as a statue, and I know he's listening to something.

"Get inside the house and lock the door. Now!" Emeric barks his order at me.

Before I even take my next breath, a sandy-colored wolf with crystal blue eyes and a golden hue is running toward the outer wall. My eyesight sharpens as I look toward the wall, but I don't see anyone other than Emeric. But I know we are under attack. It's most likely another male that scents me and thinks I'm his mate.

Fuck, I need to get inside.

I start running toward the house, following Emeric's order. I search the windows, looking to see if Ambrose is going to come bursting through one to help Emeric with whoever is attacking. I know Emeric is a beta, and that means he's plenty strong, but that doesn't mean he's capable of fighting off another alpha or multiple pack members at once if they decide to attack.

The windows are empty as they've been all day. I'm three feet from the door when I dare to turn to see who is attacking and if Emeric can take them or if I need to find Ambrose.

My feet stop when I see them—white fangs, black clothing, and speed that is unmatched as they surround Emeric.

Vampires.

"Ambrose, Emeric is being attacked by three, maybe more vampires in the backyard. He needs your help. Now." I try to tell Ambrose with my mind, but the emptiness that returns tells me he either didn't get my message or is too far away to help.

I take three more steps and reach for the door handle.

I should go inside.

I should lock the door.

I should keep trying to reach Ambrose or anyone else who can help Emeric.

"Ambrose?" I try one more time, pleading with everything I can in my mind.

Nothing.

Fangs dip into Emeric's fur at his neck, and he's tossed hard against the brick wall. A high-pitched yelp whirls through the air, as a mass of blood pours out a gash at Emeric's neck.

I don't know how to help him, but I can't leave him. I can't leave him to die. I'm not strong. I can't shift. I don't even feel a tingling. And even if I could, I wouldn't be skilled enough to take on three vampires alone. Emeric isn't even able to. I do the only thing I can think of, and I'm not even sure it's going to do a damn thing to stop them from draining every drop of Emeric's blood.

"Stop. I'm Lumi—Ambrose's mate. And if you let Emeric live, you can have me."

CHAPTER 17
LUMI

The world freezes at my words.

All movement ceases, and the creatures in front of me go still as a statue. I count them: two males and one female.

With a flash, two witches appear out of thin air.

I blink as if I'm imagining them. But I know the two female witches that appeared are as real as the three vampires. I've always known of their existence, but it's still hard for me to get used to the idea of them actually existing.

The vampire sinking his teeth into Emeric releases him, spitting out a wad of fur as blood oozes down Emeric's sandy hue.

"Stay wolf," the vampire snaps at him, and I realize he tasted some of Emeric's blood, which means he has the ability to control Emeric.

"Leave him alone!" I shout, terrified they'll kill him.

Emeric stops moving, but he's still breathing. Even I can see that from here, as my eyesight sharpens in the night.

"And why would you offer yourself up?" the blonde-haired vampire with a charming grin to rival Emeric's asks.

I frown. "He's my friend, and he doesn't deserve to die. Let him go, and you can have me." I don't know what possesses me to say the words that leave my mouth. They could move on me in less than a second. Their fangs, speed, and magic would defeat me before I even had a chance to turn toward the door.

"Does it matter why she wants to trade, Draven? Make the trade, and let's go," the shorter, bulkier one says with jet-black hair.

"Silence, Nikolai," Draven says, appearing to act as their leader.

Nikolai rolls his eyes, seemingly unfazed by Draven's tone.

The female vampire scoffs.

"You can't agree with him, Vespera," Nikolai says.

"Patience," Vespera says, watching me closely.

All of their blood-red eyes are watching me without blinking. They are waiting for something. *But what?*

For Ambrose to come to rescue me?

If he hasn't already come to my rescue, I fear he won't make it in time.

"Hmmm," Vespera says, turning toward Draven.

"What do you want?" I ask. My eyes cut to Emeric, looking for any clue as to what they are doing here and what they could possibly want.

Emeric barely shakes his head. I know he's telling me to run, to get into the house like he told me to earlier.

I grind my teeth together. "*Not happening*," I shoot back mentally to him, even though I know he won't get my message.

One of the witches steps forward, until she's standing next to Draven. She's in long, white, willowy robes that her long white hair blends into. I can't imagine the witches spend all their time in these robes, but so far, it's the only thing I've seen them wear.

"You were right, Serenity," Draven says.

"You're a brave, foolish girl," Serenity says, studying me a minute longer. They all study me, still waiting.

"Let Emeric go and take me in his place," I say again, knowing I'm exactly as Serenity called me—brave and foolish. If they do take me, I'll be dead by the end of the night.

Time goes still once again. All eyes lock in on me—waiting. Then I realize what they're waiting for, a second before they say it.

"You really can't shift?" Vespera says, whipping her long, thick brown curls over her shoulder in annoyance.

"I—" I start.

"She can shift," Ambrose's deep voice booms through the courtyard as his breath heats the skin of my neck. My entire body burns and aches to lean back into his chest, for his arms to wrap around me in a comforting embrace.

But I don't dare move, and he doesn't move to touch me either.

"But why waste her time doing so on the likes of any of you? You can hear her heart, how steady it is. She's not afraid of any of you. But you should now all be afraid of me. Leave before I rip out your throats," Ambrose growls.

I finally get the touch I've been seeking, but it doesn't offer me any comfort. Ambrose grabs my bicep and practically throws me through the backdoor of his house.

"Will Emeric—?" I start, but Ambrose cuts me off.

"He's fine," he snaps.

"But—"

Ambrose moves so fast, stopping only millimeters in front of my face. I've never seen anyone move that fast, not even the attacking vampires I just witnessed.

My heart is pounding fast in my chest. It seems it only responds like that to Ambrose.

He growls. It's an authoritative growl that rings through every bone in my body. A growl meant to serve as an alpha command.

He turns, and I feel the pull to follow him. I don't speak, just follow. Step by step, my heartbeat quickens with each step.

I want to look back to see if Emeric is safe inside the house or if the others left so easily. *Could Emeric really take on three vampires and two witches alone while under the mind control of a vampire?* I don't think so. But Ambrose is confident he'll be fine.

I don't look back. My eyes are laser-locked on Ambrose's bare, muscled back, contracting with each step he takes. And then up to his hair that he's pulled half up in a loose bun.

He opens a door I haven't been through and starts walking down the steep staircase, not bothering to flick on the lights. *But then, why would he when his vision is perfect in the dark?*

Thankfully, mine is as well, or I'd be falling down the steep staircase.

Every instinct I have tells me not to follow Ambrose down the stairs. And yet, there's a tiny part of me that tells me I must follow. That's the part I have hope in. The part of me that is still a wolf. The part of me that is capable of shifting.

We reach the bottom of the stairs before Ambrose whips around.

"You disobeyed me," Ambrose growls.

"Yes," I nod.

"I can't trust you."

"I can't trust you, either."

He shakes his head. "Then you leave me no choice."

Before I can open my mouth to ask what he's talking about, I'm moved. My feet are lifted off the ground, and I'm set roughly down a few feet away. Then I hear the quick clanking of metal doors.

"Do not leave this cell," Ambrose roars, the alpha command washing over me in an unbreakable order.

Ambrose locked me in a cell in his basement and used an alpha command on me to ensure I stayed put, all for trying to save his friend's life. Ambrose can't be my mate. We are never going to recover from this.

And yet, even as I think the words, they aren't true. I know with every part of my being that Ambrose is my mate. Only the two of us can break the curse. But first, I want to break a few of Ambrose's bones for locking me in this cage. Then I'll figure out how to fall in love with the bastard.

CHAPTER 18

AMBROSE

I fling my back door open and grin—the vampires and witches haven't left yet. I roll my shoulders back, a thrill zipping through me at the impending fight. I need this so I can stop thinking about what I just did.

Without a word of warning, I leap off my deck, shifting mid-jump. The second my paws hit the ground, I'm flying through the air again at Draven.

He squats down and hisses in my direction as he prepares to launch his own attack, ignoring my warning to leave.

As I'm about to land on him, he launches his body up, and we collide in the air.

My claws dig into his back while his teeth scrape against my neck. It's the only time I'll let him get this close to my blood.

The impact of the ground forces us to release each other as we land. Back on our respective feet, we circle each other and prepare for our next moves. Draven smirks at me as he licks the single drop of my blood off his lip. He thinks he's already won. Most shifters fall completely under a vampire's control as soon as they get a taste of our blood, but I'm not most shifters.

"Tell me the truth about your *mate*. She can't shift, can she?" Draven commands.

I don't have to answer. I'm not under his control, but I can feel the eyes of the others on me. And I know if I don't handle this perfectly the rumors are going to spread throughout the communities and they'll keep attacking until they get her to shift or kill her. I shift back into my human form.

"For the last time, my mate can shift. But if you don't leave my territory until the next full moon, I'll make sure you shift into a million little pieces."

"He fought your mind control, Draven," Vespera says.

Draven's face turns whiter than it already is, and now it's my turn to smirk. I see the third vampire standing next to Emeric, but I know that he doesn't have control over him either. Still, he's going to need to see a healer to address the wound the vampires caused.

"If your mate could shift, then why didn't she? Why didn't you mark her? Why isn't the shifter curse already broken?" Vespera asks.

I snap my head in her direction. "Nyx—he fucked with her before he brought her to the offering. But she's mine now, and she'll be ready by the next full moon."

"She better be," Draven says.

"She will, not that you'll be alive to witness it." I attack without another word. My muscles contract and release at the thrill of a fight as I set my wolf free on these bastards.

But of course, they are cowards and flee the second

they see that I'm a worthy opponent. The vampires and two of the witches I don't recognize vanish instantly.

But Serenity lingers behind, her blue eyes locked open as if she's watching a movie that none of the rest of us can see. I look to Emeric, who shifts into his human form as we wait for Serenity to return to us.

When she finally blinks, I ask, "What did you see?"

Most seer witches don't like sharing their visions or prophecies. But I hope she will if she thinks it will help me break the curse.

"Tell me," I snap at her.

She doesn't jump at my outburst. She calmly turns her head, her long white hair blowing gently in the breeze.

She's not going to tell me. I'm going to have to attack her, bring her near death, and then…

"Lumi's the one—she'll break the curse," Serenity says.

I freeze, knowing there's more. There is always more to these prophecies. The prophecies aren't set in stone. Just because she sees something doesn't mean it will actually happen—just that on the current course that everyone is on, it will.

Her blue eyes look deep into mine as she speaks the next part, "But the heartbreak…" She doesn't finish her sentence before she vanishes.

"Fuck," I say.

Emeric looks at me. "Fucking witches and their inability to tell you anything useful."

I stare at the space where Serenity just was. As much as Emeric thinks what she said wasn't useful, it was. I know so much more than him. And the burden I carry is unlike anything he'll ever experience. I know what heart-break she's talking about.

I look back at the house, and the fear grips hold of every nerve in my body as I think about Lumi locked in my basement.

Emeric studies me closely as his blood drips down his neck. "Where's Lumi?"

I don't answer him.

"Where's Lumi, Ambrose?"

"Leave it alone."

He frowns as we both walk back into the house. The second he's inside, I know he knows exactly what happened. He can hear her. He knows exactly where she is.

"She'll never forgive you."

"Good," I snap.

Emeric doesn't flinch at my word, but I know he can feel the turmoil swirling through me—the pain and fear and loss of control.

"You won't hurt her," Emeric says softly.

I close my eyes as the pain overwhelms me. Flashes of thick dark curls, golden eyes, and red lips splatter across my mind's eye.

I shut the visions out as quickly as they came. I don't want Emeric to be any more privy to how I'm feeling. But when I look at him, I can see the softness in his eyes. He knows exactly how I feel, but he'll never truly understand because he doesn't know the truth of what happened.

"She's your mate. It's real this time. Together, you'll break the curse. But locking her up isn't the answer."

It's the only way to keep her safe, I think, but don't speak aloud. "Go see Serenai. You're going to need help healing from that wound," I command as my heart thumps wildly in my chest, and I know that there is no way to keep her safe.

Lumi's the one—she'll break the curse. But the heartbreak...

The brown curls and her infectious laugh through her red lips flash in my mind again before I switch my thoughts to the silver-haired beauty locked in my basement.

Lumi thinks I'm a monster, but she has no idea. It's going to happen again—the heartbreak—and I have no idea how to stop it.

CHAPTER 19
LUMI

Anger ripples through me until my muscles begin to spasm uncontrollably. My nerves ignite, begging for an outlet before they combust.

But I sit.

And I wait.

And I wait.

I will wait until Ambrose returns. Then, I will make my move.

The basement is veiled in complete darkness. Thankfully, my eyesight is the one thing that proves that I carry the wolf shifter blood in my veins despite not being able to shift. I can see the entire room perfectly. Three cells and I am in the center one. And from the marks on the walls and in the ground, it looks like the cells are frequently used.

Even at the sight of evidence of torture, my anger doesn't turn to fear. I'm not afraid of Ambrose. I don't care that he's the strongest alpha that ever lived. He shouldn't have locked me in a cell. Shouldn't have used an alpha command on me.

I don't care how little he knows me. I don't care how angry he was with me for disobeying his orders. I don't care how if he's not used to other people disobeying him. He should've talked to me. I shouldn't be here.

I don't know how long I wait—somewhere between minutes and hours—but it's not as long as I expected. Maybe he was just dealing with his own temper and needed me somewhere safe where he wouldn't hurt me. But no excuse will dampen my disgust with him.

I hear heavy footsteps descending the stairs. I don't have to look up to know it's Ambrose. The way my body reacts instantaneously is enough for me to be sure. Heat floods my body, and a beginning to be familiar ache forms between my thighs. I grit my teeth together, angry at myself for feeling any attraction for a male who could get so furious with me that he locks me up like a prisoner. *Damn the bond between us.*

"How is Emeric?" I ask, staring straight ahead at the wall, ignoring him and my body's reaction.

"He lives, for now. However, I haven't decided if I'm going to kill him for putting you in danger."

His words cause me to look up and into his golden-flaked eyes. He's standing on the opposite side of the metal bars; there's a deep but unclear emotion on his face. I don't know him well enough yet to be able to discern what's going on inside his head.

"Don't be mad at Emeric. You're not the one who gets to be mad," I growl.

He raises his eyebrows. "And you are?"

"Yes, I get to be angry." I stand, stomping across the cell until we are face to face. I have to crane my neck to look up at him, though, which ruins the effect. "I get to be incredibly angry with you."

"For keeping you safe? That's what you're angry about?"

"For locking me in this cell like I'm your enemy!"

His nostrils flare, but mine flare right back. I won't back down, not this time. If I do, I know what my future will look like. I'll be following one step behind this man for the rest of my life. I'll be blindly expected to follow orders. I'll live in this house, but it might as well be this cell for all the freedom I'll have.

"You're not my mate. You can't be," I shake my head, glaring at him, my anger overpowering the sexual tension I felt earlier. My rage masks every warm feeling I have toward him. If we are really mates, then I shouldn't be able to squash those feelings so easily.

For a second, neither of us says anything. I don't know how he's going to react to my fuming.

A slow grin works its way up his face, and then he cocks his head to the side.

My heart flutters in my chest. *Down heart, don't fall so easily. This man is nothing more than a controlling alpha asshole. He's not my mate. He can't be.*

"You don't think we are mates?" he asks, with a sly grin and quickly darkening eyes.

I shake my head. "I think we were fooled, like so many before us."

"Hmmm." He moves to the cell door and pushes it open. I'm not even sure if he bothered to undo the lock or not.

My legs instinctually try to take a step backward, but I force myself to hold my ground and not show any fear.

"You're too cruel to be my mate."

"I am cruel." He takes a step toward me, invading

every bit of space between us until I can't breathe without inhaling his scent.

Still, I refuse to retreat. I won't allow him to intimidate me.

"I'm an alpha; I don't have a choice but to be cruel and ruthless. If I'm not, my pack and all the shifters would be vulnerable. The witches and vampires would be constantly attacking us. I have to exude power at all times. Otherwise, we're all dead."

I frown. "You locked me up to control me. To try to make me yield to your power. If I'm your mate, then you don't get to manhandle me. I'm your equal. And I can't be equal to a cruel monster like you."

The second my words leave my mouth, my back hits the wall behind me with a gentle thud. Ambrose pushed us back so quickly that I didn't even realize we were moving. His body stands in front of me, boxing me in with his large, powerful arms on either side of me. His hips lightly push against mine.

"You don't think I'm your mate?" he says again, his breath hot against mine.

"I don't think you're my mate," I say for what feels like the millionth time. Each time I say it, it feels more and more true.

His golden eyes drag down my body, assessing me for himself. I try not to flinch under his stare, but my body can't help but twitch. My breath comes hard and fast as my heartbeat leaps out of my chest.

I swear I see his lips curl up at my reaction to his perusal of my body. It just pisses me off more.

"You're right; you're not my mate," he says. His words are a dagger in my back—hard, cruel, menacing. He says it so casually, like he's deciding on his next meal, and I don't make the cut. I shouldn't be angry at him for repeating my own words back to me, but I am.

"My mate wouldn't have silver, snowy white hair. She'd have golden yellow hair." His fingers run through my long silver locks, and I tense at his touch.

"She wouldn't have bones more pronounced than muscles." He runs his hand down my neck, over my clavicle, and then over my ribcage.

"She'd have wide hips for bearing my future heir and the rest of my offspring." He slides his hand around my ass and tugs me tightly against him.

My hatred of him burns and burns inside me at every insult. Unfortunately, it's not the only thing burning.

I grind my teeth together and grip my hands into fists, trying to keep from letting my body heat with desire for this man.

"Then let me go. You're wasting your time with me," I whisper.

His nose nuzzles against my neck as silent shivers race down my spine. I refuse to move. I refuse to give in to this desire.

"My mate would also react to every single word I speak. She'd shiver at my breath on her skin. Her heartbeat would race at my touch. And a kiss...a kiss would have her soaked, ready for me to fuck her."

I lick my lips, and he smirks at me in a knowing way. "Should we test it out? See if you are truly my mate or not?"

I shake my head quickly, refusing to let him win no matter how much I want the bastard to kiss me.

"I'm sure my body would react to any number of men kissing me. My reaction to you would prove nothing."

He shakes his head. "Your body would only truly react

to your mate. Only your mate would be able to satisfy the urges you feel. Only your mate would make you think of them and only them. Only your mate would be enough for you."

"I know about what the curse does. I know it tries to survive by making me desirable to every male and every male desirable to me. How do I know that's not what's happening between the two of us?"

"Have you kissed a man before?"

I nod slowly.

"And what did you feel?"

I think of my kiss with Kael. "Nothing."

"I'll parade every man in the pack in here to kiss you until you realize the truth."

"I'm not your mate."

He chuckles. "You really don't get it, do you? It took me a while, too, to realize how perfect we are for each other."

"I hate you. We aren't mates."

He runs his thumb up and down my hip, driving me slightly mad.

"Being mates isn't about being in love. It's not about liking or not liking each other. It's about being each other's match. Their equal."

"I'm not a savage beast like you," I say.

"No, you're not. But that's only a tiny part of who I am. I'm strong, ruthless, determined, and a leader, and I will do anything to stop this curse. You're the same."

"You said I was weak! You don't think I'm any of those things."

"You are weak—physically. You don't have the muscles or endurance you need to match me or any other supernatural creature. You're weak because you haven't gotten your wolf yet. Which, of course, wouldn't appear when you are packless and don't have an alpha to guide you."

My nostrils flare with rage.

"But you don't let that physical weakness stop you. You're foolish enough to think you could still stop vampires and witches alone. You're the bravest, stubbornest, most determined female I've ever met. That makes you strong. You aren't afraid of me when everyone else is, including Emeric. You're my mate, and you know it. Denying it won't change anything."

"I'm—" I start but cut myself off. He's probably right, but I still hate it.

"It doesn't change anything," I finally say. "It doesn't change that I hate you. That you want to control me. That I still refuse to be yours and follow your every command the rest of my life."

His eyes narrow, and he takes a deep breath, his gaze softening. *"I was afraid."*

My heart stops as I hear him through our bond. His words going straight to my mind feels so intimate, like he's pouring his soul into me.

"I was terrified that I was about to lose you out there."

"But you didn't. You're the strongest alpha the world has ever seen. You didn't even have to fight to get me to safety."

He shakes his head as a strand of his hair falls in his face out of the half up bun on top of his head. And then I see the change, the moisture gathered in his eyes. The air changes between us. "Nyx sent them—the vampires and witches."

"Nyx?"

He nods. "He's the only alpha who can rival me. All he

wants to do is defeat me and take over as head of all the packs. If he does, he'll unleash hell on all the packs for exiling his Bloodmoon pack for all these years. He'll let the vampires and witches wreak havoc until we are all destroyed."

I study him closely and see that he's truly afraid of Nyx. Of what could happen. But right now, I don't care about Nyx. Or the vampires. Or the witches.

"Do you know what the mating bond does to a male? Especially an alpha?"

I shake my head slowly, trembling slightly as he moves his hands up my body.

"Let me show you. And then you can tell me if you think we are mates or not."

CHAPTER 20

LUMI

Every time he speaks to me in my mind, it overwhelms me. It feels like an invasion, a caress, and an intense look into his mind. But then I remember he has the same access to my mind, and I freak out. I still don't know how it all works. What he can hear or feel, or how he blocks me out when he wants to—I don't understand any of it. I don't understand how the mating bond works, or the curse, for that matter. Not really.

But I do know that it's real.

"Why block me before?" I finally speak back into his mind, opening myself up to him again, feeling incredibly vulnerable.

"Because you shouldn't grow close to me. It's not safe. Not until you can shift and have your full strength. I don't trust myself around you."

"And now?" I raise my eyebrows.

He stills. *"I still don't trust myself around you. I'm not sure I ever will. But I don't have a choice; letting you in seems the only way you'll listen to me so I can keep you safe."*

155

I growl at that, but before I can respond, fear over-whelms my mind. A bitter taste engulfs my tastebuds as my skin grows clammy, and my breath becomes shallow. My eyes are blinded by darkness despite my sharp eyesight.

"What's happening?" I ask as dread turns my skin ice cold.

Before Ambrose can answer, my sight has returned, but instead of seeing Ambrose standing in front of me in the cell in the basement, I'm looking out a glass window at the back garden, looking at my side profile. I'm looking through Ambrose's eyes and feeling everything he's feel-ing. White-cold terror freezes me to the spot for a split second.

Less than a second—that's how long it would take one of those vampires to sink their teeth into her neck. A witch could kill her even faster with the flick of their magic, breaking her neck. I have to move, I think. But should I jump out the window? Or do I have time to move to the door? How do I save her?

Suddenly, we're walking inside the house. My body has turned from ice cold to flaming hot fire. The fear quickly turns to rage and an intense desire to keep her safe. My mind is a whirl, trying to figure out the best place to keep her safe. I consider sending her away, just locking her in my room, but it's not enough to keep her safe. Not from me.

I only have one option. One that will keep me from claiming her in every way possible. One that will keep me from forcing her to shift, to become a member of my pack, of completing the marking ceremony, of fucking me over and over until she's mine, completely mine.

Next, I'm locking the door to her cell, and shame

floods my mind. *It's the only way.* The only way to keep her safe from the alpha male that is overwhelming me, shouting at me that *she's mine, mine, mine. That I can't let her go.*

I snap back to reality as intense desire replaces every drop of fear. I'm no longer looking at the past through Ambrose's eyes. I'm in the present in the cell with Ambrose staring at me, waiting for me to respond.

"How'd you do that?" I ask, my stomach curling and my head spinning like I just went on a wicked roller coaster ride. I search Ambrose's eyes for the truth.

"The mating bond. It allows me to show you my deepest thoughts and memories. It allows us to connect on a level so deep that we are practically one soul. So when I say I care about you, that I find you as my equal, I mean it. I wouldn't bond with just anyone, even if I felt the pull of the bond."

"I haven't done anything to be called your equal or you mine. Not yet."

"Maybe." His lips curl. "But the bond is still here between us. What are we going to do about it?"

I still. I'm not sure. I felt his intense fear. I understand why he did what he did, but...

Before I can answer him, his breath is hot on my neck for a second before his lips brush ever so slightly against my flesh.

I hold my breath, trying to keep my breathing steady and my heart from racing. I'm still determined that we must have gotten it wrong, that we can't truly be mates. This alpha, this ruthless predator, this hot-as-sin man can't be my equal.

His eyes meet mine in challenge, as if he knows exactly what I'm doing. He moves his head to the other side of my neck and breathes slowly while hovering his lips against the shell of my ear.

My toes curl in my shoes, but I keep my heartbeat steady.

That is until he moves his hands, starting at my shoulders and gliding down my body. He finds the outer curve of my breasts before gliding them across the curve of my ass.

I hold my breath as if waiting for something. He's going to kiss me, and I'm not sure I'll stop him. I stare at his lips, waiting for them to close the distance between us. They get closer and closer but stop an inch away. He's close enough to feel the tingle of his breath against my lips but not close enough to actually be kissing.

He closes the distance between our hips, and I jolt at the hardness I feel pressed against my lower stomach. Liquid desire pools between my legs at the thought of his hard cock filling me.

"So you want me. It means nothing. It doesn't mean we are mates. It just means there's an attraction between us," I find my words, even though every word is thick with desire.

"You're right; the attraction between us doesn't mean we are mates."

My breath heaves heavily in my chest, and my nipples brush against his bare chest, causing them to pebble in my tank top. He says the words so casually, like he doesn't care if we are mates or not. But the way he's looking at me like I'm the only person who exists in the world tells me otherwise.

"Deny our attraction. Deny that we are mates. Save yourself, Lumi. Save yourself from me," his voice drops low.

I close my eyes, trying to do what he says. To forget how attracted I am to him. I was attracted to Emeric earlier, too. It means nothing that I'm attracted to Ambrose. He's a killing machine. He's nothing like me. He can't be my mate. We must have gotten it all wrong. Mates wouldn't treat each other like this.

Warmth swirls in my belly, slowly growing all the way to my fingertips. My heartbeat is erratic. Butterflies flutter in my chest. And there is an ache between my legs I've never felt when thinking of a man before.

I've only ever kissed Kael. I've never had the chance to experiment with teenage boys or young men. Never made out on a basement couch or in the backseat of a car. Never made it to second base. Never felt anything like this.

How do I know this is normal desire or something more? There is only one way to find out.

"Kiss me. Please, fucking kiss me. I'll die if you don't." I didn't realize I sent the words through the link we share until I feel his lips against mine.

A spark races through my body the second our lips touch. My eyes fly open, and I find Ambrose's eyes glowing back in my direction as if shocked by the spark, too. But then his tongue licks at the seam of my lips, and I open to allow him into my mouth.

My eyelids fall closed as I lose myself to his kiss. His hand curves behind my neck as he angles my head to deepen the kiss.

I wrap my arms around his neck, pulling him closer to me as my fingers tangle in his waves of long hair. I forget the pain he caused me by locking me in this basement. I forget that a monster dwells in the man I'm kissing. I'm overcome with the intense sensation that this is the thing I've been searching for all my life. *This feeling. This man.*

And I know, despite my limited experience with kissing other men, that this isn't what kissing other men is like. That can only mean one thing.

Before I can speak my thoughts out loud or even loud enough in my mind for Ambrose to hear, an intoxicatingly sweet, musky smell invades my nostrils. I open my eyes in confusion at the strong, overwhelming smell. Ambrose's eyes are still closed as he continues to kiss me.

The smell races through my nostrils like a zap of electricity.

Am I...am I getting more of my wolf instincts?

I don't know if I send the thought to Ambrose or not, but a low groan trembles through his body and across my lips. And all my thoughts dissipate.

I'm hungry, so hungry for more. But Ambrose is slowing his kisses and barely touching me instead of increasing the intensity of our pleasure.

I need more, so much more from him. I know I'll spend every second of every day aching for him now that I've kissed him until he's fully claimed me in every way possible and I him.

"Touch me," I purr in his mind in my most forceful demand.

His eyes flash open at my command, and the gold glow is swirling, mixing with the dark of his pupils as he stares back at me.

Fear should be my response. I know that, but my belly coils as heat spreads through my body as his dark stare.

He grabs my hand, plunging our joined hands between the band of my shorts and panties until I can feel how drenched they are.

"How wet are you?"

"Soaked."

He growls his approval.

"You should see for yourself," I say seductively, needing his touch more than I need air.

He stiffens and looks at me with such longing that I know we are going to tackle all of my firsts in one night, but I don't care. I need this man. I don't care about his past. I don't care who he's killed. I don't care that he locked me up or why. I need him. The rest we can figure out later.

I reach out to pull him back into an aggressive kiss, but before I can brush my fingers against his locks of hair, he's gone. Vanished, as if he wasn't even here in the first place. In his place, his two lingering words echo in my head.

"I can't."

CHAPTER 21
AMBROSE

Lumi's going to die, and it's going to be my fault. I know her fate—I know both of our fates—the second I kiss her. And I'm desperate to change our destiny.

There is so much she doesn't know, so much that I can't explain to her yet. The only thing I know for sure is that if I don't get ahold of myself and fast, she'll die.

I stand on my back deck, sucking in lungfuls of air as I try to cool off after that kiss. I thought kissing her was for the best. I thought she needed to see how our physical connection was different than anything either of us had ever felt before.

Instead, I almost killed her.

Flames dance through my body, and my wolf is burning to be let free. To run. To kill.

I force more air down my throat—more, more, more. And I try to think of anything else, anyone but her. Because if I think about how her soft lips felt pressed to mine, or how she fit perfectly in my hands, or the soft whimpers she made when I touched her, then I won't be able to stop myself. And she'll end up dead.

I grip the railing on the deck until my knuckles turn white, and my muscles tremble as I force myself to stay frozen where I stand instead of returning to her. But even with the door shut and Lumi in the basement, I can still hear her. Her shallow breaths and erratic heartbeat are like a siren's call, begging me to return to her.

I can't.

I fucking can't.

We aren't going to survive until the next full moon. I'm not sure I can survive another minute without returning to her. Without tasting her again. Without claiming her and exploring every seductive part of her.

"Ambrose," his wicked voice slithers into my head. It's not like my connection with Lumi that feels warm, like sliding into a second home when I talk to her through our bond. A very seductive, desirable home that I want to fuck until we've both lost all control. Nor does it feel like talking to Emeric, which is less talking and more intuitively reading each other's mind, as we've been friends for so long that it's impossible not to know what the other is thinking.

No, Nyx's voice in my head is like an invasion that I immediately want to block. It's only possible because of how strong we both are as alphas, but we can only communicate the most basic of thoughts.

I grip the railing harder. He didn't leave. He's still here. It's the only way he'd be able to communicate with me.

"Where?" I send the word flying back like a bullet intent on killing him.

"Here," Nyx says, and images of evergreens fill my

head. Despite the vagueness the images would invoke in most people, I know exactly where he is. I know every tree and every landscape of my territory.

I don't try to speak to him again, and I don't question whether his summons is a trap or not. The energy flowing through me at the moment makes me stronger than he could ever imagine. Even if he's set a trap, I have the physical advantage at the moment. I'm going to end this once and for all.

Kill, kill, kill.

The words fly through my head as I leap from my deck, shift in midair, and sprint to him. I'm finally going to kill him. I'm not giving him another chance.

I should thank him, really, because killing him might be the only thing that saves me from killing Lumi.

Blood stops me in my tracks as I run through the village my pack has created. The scent floods my nostrils until it's all I can inhale.

I slow when I spot the first body—Calix. He's one of my best fighters, and yet he's bleeding out on the ground with two puncture marks on his neck. I run to his body, shifting back into my human body.

"Calix! What happened?" I scoop his head, cradling it in my lap.

He starts to open his mouth, but I realize I already know what happened. I don't need his explanation. I just need him to live.

"You're going to be okay. I won't let you die," I say with the command of an alpha behind the words, ensuring that he doesn't die while I heal him.

"Go, I'll heal him and the rest," Serenai says as she kneels beside Calix.

The rest...I look up and see body after body lining the

street. At least a third of my pack lays lifeless, bleeding from vampire wounds. But I can hear their heartbeats. They're alive.

Whether the vampires didn't have time to kill them or tried and failed to control them once they took their blood, I don't know, nor does it really matter.

"Go! I won't let any of them die," Serenai says, starting to tend to Calix's wounds. She's the best at what she does, so they'll all be okay. But it still feels wrong to leave my pack when I can help.

Serenai lays her hands on Calix's wound, while looking up at me. "Make him pay for what he did."

"I will. I promise."

And then I shift, my dark fur and muscles forming in less than a second.

Nyx dies for this.

He deserved to die for what he did before, but this... this is the final straw. I won't let this action go unpunished.

"Nyx!" I scream through the woods as I approach the spot where he told me he was. I don't bother to shift back into my human form. I know he can hear me, and I'm not here for a conversation. I'm here to kill him.

Nyx barely moves, but I see him there in the shadows —always in the fucking shadows. Standing in his human form, he doesn't speak. He knows what I've discovered. He knows I know what he's done. And there will be no more talking.

A deep, guttural growl works its way through my body. Every shifter, vampire, or witch in my territory can hear it.

"I told you to leave or die."

Nyx doesn't flinch. His blackened eyes lock on me in

an unblinking focus. There is no emotion in his features. He's lost whatever emotions he used to have years ago.

"You can't kill me, Ambrose." His voice is bored and unbothered.

"Watch me." I squat, ready to leap and slash his throat in one jump when I see her—the reason he's so sure I won't kill him.

I freeze.

Nyx smirks; his vile, evil grin covering his entire face. "Now that I see I have your attention, let's talk."

I shift as my heart sinks. "What do you want?"

"I want collateral. I want insurance that the curse will be broken on the next full moon."

"It will be."

Nyx cocks his head, looking at me in his deranged way. "I know it will."

CHAPTER 22

LUMI

My hand keeps reaching out into the empty space in front of me. I keep thinking if I reach out far enough, I'll feel Ambrose's hard body again. But no matter how long I keep reaching, my hand comes up empty.

Slowly, I pull it back to my chest, feeling my heart rapidly beating and the warm flush that still floats through my body. I'm barely able to process what the hell just happened or what my feelings toward Ambrose are now.

The room is still cascaded in dark shadows, but my eyes cut through the darkness and clearly see the cage door shut. *Shut, but is it locked? And did he lift his alpha command?*

I suck in a deep breath, and I swear I can still smell every musky, evergreen, and lusty scent of Ambrose. Layers of different smells continue to invade my nostrils even though he's gone. But I know he's gone, not just from this room, but from the house because his scent is muted. My sense of smell has been enhanced—wolf scenting. Another tiny part of my wolf unlocked. I'm one step closer to my full wolf unleashing, and it's because of Ambrose.

I stare at the caged door once again. *Is it locked?* That's the question. The question that will tell me how I feel about Ambrose. *Is he continuing to keep me locked in this cage, or is he letting me be free?*

I tremble slightly, but I don't move toward the door. I'm not sure I'm ready to find out the answer.

"Lumi, you down there?" a high-pitched voice echoes down the stairs.

"Yes," I squeak out.

Before I can even register what is happening, Rowena is standing in front of me.

"Thank gods, you're okay," she says, breathing hard. She looks like hell. Her golden eyes are bloodshot, and she has bags under them like she hasn't slept in days. Her long hair is pulled up in a tangled knot on top of her head, making her appearance even more disheveled.

"What happened?"

She swings the door open. "Come on, I'll explain as we go. There's no time."

She starts heading for the stairs, but I can't keep my mouth from gaping at the door she just swung open. It wasn't locked. Ambrose set me free.

"Lumi!" Rowena gets my attention again.

"Sorry, coming." I race after her, struggling to keep up as we climb the stairs. I have no idea what's going on, but in the limited time I've spent with Rowena, I know I can trust her.

"Where's Ambrose?" Rowena asks me.

"I don't know."

Rowena furrows her brow. "I can smell him all over

you. It's fresh, like he was just here. He didn't tell you where he was going?"

I blush, like I should be able to answer the question. "Ambrose doesn't tell me anything."

She sighs. "He should. He can't keep things from you. You're going to be an alpha, equal to him in every way if you're mates."

I swallow at that thought. Becoming Ambrose's mate is more than just becoming his. It means becoming an alpha. I'm not sure I have what it takes. When I look at Rowena, I see an alpha. She's confident, strong, and experienced. She'd be the perfect woman for the job.

"Are you sure *you* aren't his mate?" I ask.

She breaks out laughing. "Yes, I'm very sure."

"Did Ambrose do something to you?" Worry etches my eyes. I know what he's capable of. But...

"No." Rowena narrows her eyes at me as if just registering that she found me in the basement in a cage. But then that cage door was unlocked, so she shakes off any thoughts of concern for me. "Emeric isn't here either."

I frown at that. "Really? You're sure?"

She listens carefully and then sniffs. "He's not here."

I sniff, mimicking her movements, not finding any of Emeric's scent either. But I can't believe that Ambrose would have left me here unprotected.

"You're safe in this house. Ambrose would never leave you unprotected. It's spelled by a powerful witch to keep others out."

"It didn't keep you out."

"Because I'm not a threat." She smiles genuinely.

"Tell me what's going on."

Her smile drops. "There was an attack. The vampires and witches, along with the Bloodmoon wolves..." She pauses as if she can't speak the rest of it but then forces the words out. "They attacked. I'm not sure how many were hurt. I'm sure that's where Ambrose and Emeric are right now, helping the injured. But..." she trails off again.

My heart sinks even though I have no idea what she's going to say. "Spit it out!"

"Kael is gone. The last I saw him, he was being dragged off by a vampire."

I gasp, my hands shooting to my mouth to cover my shock. Water fills my eyes at the thought that Kael is most likely dead. That everyone I ever loved or cared about is probably dead. My father, my pack, and now Kael.

"I don't understand. I thought they just came here to see if I could shift and break the curse. They attacked after they came after me?"

"They came after you?"

I nod.

"Yes, they attacked the rest of the pack about an hour ago. I'm not sure why. These things happen from time to time about territory or revenge or threats. I would guess it would be a warning to Ambrose that if he doesn't break the curse on the next full moon, they will attack again and destroy us."

I frown. "I have to find Kael."

Rowena nods, like she knew I would say that. "Come on, I'll help you."

She starts jogging out of the house, and I follow as quickly as I can, pushing any sense of dread down, knowing it won't help me find Kael. The second we step onto the main dirt road that leads through the village, I gasp again. I don't know what I expected to see, but it wasn't this. Smoke billows out of several rooftops. Wails and cries echo through the woods, and blood—so much blood marks the grass and dirt, even where bodies aren't lying in agony.

This is my fault. This happened because of me. Because I was distracting Ambrose. Because I can't shift.

Moans and groans fill the air, and the overwhelming metallic scent infiltrates my nostrils. Ambrose's house sits on top of a hill overlooking the rest of the pack's homes. The number of people tending to half-broken human and shifter bodies seems like the entire pack was affected in one way or another. And Kael could be among them. I have to find him.

I know that wolf shifters can heal from remarkable injuries, but I don't have enough experience with vampires to know what wounds can be healed and what can't be. For a moment, I'm torn between staying and trying to help save the pack members that I can and finding Kael.

"Last time I saw Kael, he was being dragged this way," Rowena says, heading into the forest at our right.

I hesitate for another moment, but ultimately, I know my limits and who I have the chance to save. "Let's go." I start running full out, but the second Rowena starts jogging, I know I won't be able to keep up with her. And she'll waste valuable time staying with me.

"Go ahead, I'll catch up."

"I can't leave you unprotected."

I frown. "Please."

She shakes her head.

I sigh but don't try to ask her to go on ahead again as we trudge through the forest, following the scent of blood. But I haven't picked up on anything specific of Kael's. I don't know if that makes it better or worse. *Does that mean he was dragged in this direction, or is he back with the pack healing his injuries?*

A howl of agony rings through the forest.

"Kael," I gasp, knowing that howl anywhere. I look at Rowena, knowing the howl is too far away. Whoever is threatening him, we won't get there in time.

"Please, he's all I have," I whisper through my tears.

Rowena hesitates for just a second, looking in the direction of the howl and then back at me.

"Tell Ambrose where you are, and then don't move until he gets here. I'll go after Kael." Gold fur splits through the air where Rowena's soft pink flesh was before. She doesn't look back at me as she runs full speed through the forest.

"Thank you," I whisper after her, wishing I could shift and join her. But I trust her to do everything she can to save Kael. She's as strong as any wolf I've seen, maybe even as strong as an alpha.

I start to search for that connection to Ambrose in my mind to tell him where I am and to come find me. But I stop before I speak to him. He's back with the pack. They need him. I can't be the reason that he's not there for them again.

I listen carefully, but I hear nothing out of the ordinary. I don't smell anyone or see anyone. I'm safe here. I want to run after Rowena, but my conscious stops me. My relationship with Ambrose is fragile, and I know he won't forgive me for putting myself in danger.

The urge to flee after her is impossible to resist, though, especially when a deep voice surprises me from behind.

"Looking for someone?"

CHAPTER 23

LUMI

I didn't hear so much as a twig move before his deep voice trembled through me. For a moment, I don't move as I process my next move. I should tell Ambrose I'm in danger. But if Nyx wants me dead, I'll be dead long before Ambrose could get here and save me. Rowena is miles away. I'm all alone with Nyx.

Chills race up my arms, but I calm my breathing as I turn and face him.

"Where is he?" my voice holds demands an answer, refusing to let a drop of fear tremble in my voice.

Nyx leans against a tree casually, like he just went out for a stroll and came across me. He sweeps a strand of his black hair out of his eyes.

"Kael is safe with the Bloodmoon wolves."

I glare at him with a deep intensity, trying to figure out if he's lying or telling the truth. I've only ever spent a couple of hours with the man. I know he's the only other alpha that Ambrose is afraid of, the only one that rivals his powers. I know there is more between Ambrose and Nyx, more than just two competitive alphas.

"Why did you take him?" *Keep him talking.* I decide that is the best way to stay alive. Keep him talking; let the rage flow through my veins. And hope my wolf finally decides to make an appearance today.

Nyx stares at me, seemingly confused as to how I don't already know the answer to that question. But when I don't balk, he finally says, "Someone needed to make sure there were no distractions for you before the next full moon."

"Kael isn't a distraction."

Nyx narrows his eyes playfully. "Isn't he? He's the male you care most about. He's the male you shared your first kiss with. He's the male that you dream about at night. The one you want to fu—"

"Stop," I growl. "Just stop. Kael is just a friend. He's not my lover. And he's not my mate; Ambrose is."

Nyx stares at me, unblinking. A cold breeze wafts toward me, making me shiver.

"If you say so. But personally, I'm not taking any chances. I want the curse ended as soon as possible."

"Then return Kael, or I'll refuse to mate with Ambrose." I grind my teeth as I speak. I'm not even sure if I know if I'm bluffing or not.

"Shift, and I will," he replies.

My eyes widen. *That simple, huh? Just shift. He knows full well I can't shift.*

I huff angrily, letting my anger at this man fill me. This man who could kill Kael with a snap of his fingers. A man who could take the last remaining person of my past.

I take a deep breath, then another, and another, letting the burning feeling flow through me.

He chuckles. "That isn't going to work."

I glare at him. "Take me instead."

"I can't do that. I need you to break the curse. Although, at the rate you're trying to shift, Kael has a much better chance at breaking the curse than you do."

"Then. Let. Him. Go."

"And what motivation would you have to learn to shift if I did that?"

"I don't need any motivation. And I'm not going to complete the marking ceremony if it means freeing you from the curse. You deserve every ounce of pain you and your pack feel. You're working with vampires and witches. You sent them to kill the entire Moonlight pack. You kidnapped my best friend. I'm not going to do anything for you."

Nyx just stares at me, unmoving. I'm not sure if he processed any of my words or not. I'm not sure if he's going to call my bluff or not.

I can't not complete the marking ceremony. I have to break the curse for everyone, even if it means freeing Nyx as well. But Nyx doesn't know that. Threatening to not break the curse to get Kael back is the only option I have. I can't fight Nyx. I can't shift.

"I could tell Ambrose your little secret. Tell him that you aren't packless. That you belong to the Wintermoon wolves. That you are the reason for the curse."

I swallow hard, unsure of how to respond. He's got me. I'm powerless. There is nothing I can do to get Kael back, short of fighting him. Ambrose can't know my secret. He'll kill me in hopes of finding a better mate.

"If you did that, then the marking ceremony wouldn't happen. Ambrose wouldn't choose me as his mate. He'd kill me. And you'd still be cursed."

"Won't matter since you can't shift anyway. And I'm not sure you're worthy of being an alpha's mate."

I growl, hoping something kicks in. Claws, sharp teeth, speed—anything to help me attack this man.

Nothing appears. No new traits or senses. But I'm not going to let Nyx get away with everything he's done.

I run at him with everything I have, throwing my arm back like I'm going to punch him and then sweeping my leg into a kick just like Emeric taught me.

Nyx simply takes a step to the side as I fly through the air, landing hard on the cold ground.

"You're fearless; I'll give you that. You and Ambrose have that in common. Along with that annoying, determined attitude that causes you to never give up. But let me stop you before you hurt yourself." Nyx pushes a foot into my back, applying enough pressure that it makes it hard for me to breathe. I have no idea how to get out of this position.

He wins.

But if I can shift. If I complete the marking ceremony. If I become an alpha alongside Ambrose, then maybe together we can defeat him and his pack once and for all.

"Keep my secret, and I'll end the curse. Hurt Kael and I'll kill you. And I won't end the curse. If Kael dies, I won't have a reason for ending the curse."

"Kael is completely safe as long as you complete the marking ceremony on the next full moon. If you fail, I have limited reason for keeping him alive."

I wince as his foot digs deeper into my back. "I won't fail."

"I know; you'll do anything for your friend. So I'll keep your secret. But you'll owe me a favor. You'll learn I don't do anything for free, little snow wolf. Especially not any favors for Ambrose or his mate."

I growl, knowing I need to talk to Ambrose. I need to

let him know where I am. And I need to know what happened between him and Nyx. I need the whole story. And I need a better plan to get Kael back before the full moon. Despite how badly I want this, I'm not sure if I'm going to be able to shift in time.

"Oh, and one more thing before I let you go. Ambrose was the one who gave me Kael. He traded his life to me like it meant nothing to him. So if you want someone to blame for my capture of Kael, blame Ambrose."

CHAPTER 24
LUMI

"*I need to talk to you. Now,*" I growl at Ambrose through our mental connection. It doesn't matter how far away he is or if he's trying to block me out. Nothing is going to stop me from getting the message to him.

"*I'm a little busy at the moment,*" Ambrose snaps back out of breath.

"*I don't care. Where are you?*" I'm already sprinting back to the Moonlight wolve's home, assuming he's still helping them recover instead of out looking for Kael.

"*Fighting a couple of vampires. Get back to the house. I'll be there as soon as I'm finished with them.*"

I roar at his alpha command. I'm done taking orders from him. The hold his command has on me withers away with each step I take, until it feels like tiny little bubbles floating around me. *He's not my alpha; he doesn't get to command me.*

I run faster than I've ever run before. I'm not sure if it's new wolf abilities developing, or I'm just so angry with him that my legs carry me faster than ever before.

"Why did you give Kael to Nyx?" I send the words before I think better of it. If I truly care about Ambrose, I shouldn't distract him while he's fighting. But then again, I'm so furious with him right now that I might just kill him myself.

There's a long pause. If the bastard doesn't answer me, then I'm done giving him more chances; I don't care if he is my mate, I'll—

"I'm on the west end of town. You're close. I'll finish these three off and then answer any question you have for me." There's a sadness and fear that he pushes through with his words.

I snap my mind shut, blocking him out in an instant. I'm not even sure how I block him or if I'll be able to repeat it, but I'm not going to let him pour emotion into me that will confuse how I feel. There is no excuse for what he did to Kael. And if Ambrose still expects me to play his mate, he has a lot of explaining and graveling to do.

Ambrose is right, though; I am close. I hear the cheers of the crowd that has gathered to watch Ambrose fight. Before I make it out of the forest, Rowena collides with me.

"Are you okay?" She looks me head to toe before her eyes widen. "You know—you know what happened to Kael."

I nod.

She sucks in a deep breath as a loud cheer has us both turning our heads toward the sound.

I don't know how she knows what happened to Kael. But the sincerity in her eyes tells me she just found out as well. I'm glad she wasn't hiding it from me.

She grips my shoulders firmly. "Give him hell. I'll have

your back, and you'll always have a place to sleep if you decide he isn't the one for you."

I nod slowly, unable to speak for fear of taking any of my wrath out on her.

She seems to understand as she grips my hand, and together, we walk out of the forest and into the crowd. The crowd is cheering as if they are watching a boxing match instead of a real life or death fight.

Rowena and I both shove through the crowd, pushing people aside as they grunt at us, that is until they see my face. I don't know how many of the shifters recognize me, or they just see my look of pure resolution. Either way, they begin to part for me instead of needing to be shoved out of my way.

At the edge of the crowd, I stop as I see Ambrose's large wolf form tear into the neck of a vampire. His teeth sink hard into his cool flesh, and then, with a flash, he's human. Emeric tosses him a dagger, and he shoves it through the vampire's heart.

The crowd roars with applause as Ambrose drops the vampire's body to the ground before immediately shifting back into his wolf form. I scan the ground and find another vampire already dead with a stake in his heart. Only one female remains.

I look the three vampires over quickly, but none of them are the same ones who attacked Emeric and I earlier.

The female bares her teeth at Ambrose. But he doesn't so much as break a sweat as he stands to his full height and lets out a warning growl—one that says you're next.

They both stare at each other for a second longer, and then the female runs. She's fast, so fast that my eyes can barely track her as she moves.

The crowd parts, no one brave enough or stupid enough to try and stop her.

I turn back to Ambrose, curious to see what he'll do.

"She doesn't get to escape. Not after what she did," he growls in my head.

I don't know how he plans on catching her. Vampires are faster than wolf shifters, and she already has a head start.

But he breaks out into a run, darting through the crowd where she just zipped through. I hold my breath even though I expect it could take hours or even days for Ambrose to track her down. And I don't have that long.

I'm about to send a message telling him that in my head when a high-pitched scream echoes above all the other noise. The voice falls silent quickly, and so does the crowd. All eyes are locked in on a break in the crowd.

Ambrose drags the limp body of the female vampire with his teeth to the edge of the crowd and then drops it unceremoniously onto the ground before shifting back into his human form.

The crowd cheers once again. But Ambrose's eyes lock in on me in a serious manner. He may have just defeated three vampires, but he hasn't dealt with my wrath yet. And I may very well kill him for what he did to Kael.

Rowena places her hand on my shoulder and gives me a gentle squeeze, reminding me that she has my back. But I don't need her help to deal with Ambrose. I don't need anyone's help. I don't even need my wolf's help, if she even exists at all. I've got this.

I take a step forward, out of the crowd, and into the center of the circle that Ambrose just fought the vampires in. The crowd is still reeling from Ambrose slaughtering the three dead vampires. Those who notice me don't notice the expression I bear. I'm not about to congratulate my alpha mate on a job well done.

Ambrose is frozen as he watches me approach. Sweat-soaked hair frames his face in dark waves. His face is a stale, somber white, and his eyes never leave mine, not even to blink.

I'm burning with my rage as I stride across the grass. I don't hesitate a single step. I don't think about how strong he is and how weak I am. I don't think about his threats to kill me so that he'll get a new mate if he doesn't find me worthy.

"You traded Kael to that monster. You traded his life like it meant nothing to you. You gave our enemy the only friend I have in this world." I narrow my eyes, my teeth grinding together so hard that I feel the enamel turning to powder in my mouth. "You, Ambrose, are not my mate."

A gasp ripples through the crowd as one by one they hear my words. I was their hope, their chance at breaking the curse. And here I am publicly admitting that I was wrong. We both were. There is no way this man is my mate.

Ambrose doesn't so much as twitch a muscle at my outburst. He still hasn't blinked as he stares at me. He's processing, deciding what to do next. That's his move, I realize. He guards his emotions and thoughts until the last moment. It's probably served him well hundreds of times before. But now, it just gives me more time for my rage to swell inside me.

"Fight me. Kill me. Get a new mate. Because I won't help anyone who trades away innocent lives like that."

"I'm not going to fight you," Ambrose says like a caress in my head.

"Coward," I fire back.

"I'm not a coward. I don't want to hurt you."

"You already did."

He swallows hard, his throat bobbing. It's the first outward sign that anything is bothering him. And then he makes a move toward me—an outstretched hand most likely to grab me and drag me back into that cell in his basement to keep me locked up until he's seduced me into submission again.

I won't let him lock me up. And I won't let him get away with being the proud alpha defending his pack when he can't even protect and defend his mate and her friend.

I duck as he reaches for me and then swing as hard as I can at his stomach. It's like hitting a brick wall. But my hand doesn't feel the pain, just the hardness of his body as I hit him. I know once the adrenaline wears off I'll feel that. I most likely broke a bone.

A sharp inhale is the only reaction I get from Ambrose that he was affected by my punch.

"Fight me, you monster," I yell, letting the entire pack hear me.

I can feel the shocked faces on me, and hear the muttering and gasps ringing all around me. I'm sure no one speaks to their alpha this way. I come from a small pack that was more family than anything, but even in that small pack, my father's word was law. No one dared to disobey or defy him. And that's exactly what I'm doing to Ambrose.

Low growls pierce the air, spreading through the crowd in a warning to me.

Ambrose holds up a hand, though, and the growls cease. He has absolute control over his pack. He just doesn't have control over me.

I blink, and Ambrose is gone from the spot where I last saw him. I try to spin, sensing exactly where he went, but I'm no match for his speed. His arm wraps around my neck, yanking me to him in a hard embrace.

"I'm sorry," he breathes against my neck.

"Sorry isn't going to bring Kael back." I elbow Ambrose as hard as I can, but once again, he doesn't move. In fact, I think he tightens his grip on me.

I writhe harder in his arms, doing everything I possibly can to break free. But I could barely have a chance at fighting a human male, let alone an alpha wolf shifter. His strength is unmatchable by anyone here. He just fought off three vampires on his own. He's probably fought countless males to keep his job as alpha.

I should stop trying to fight him. I should give up. I should surrender.

"Promise me we'll get Kael back. Promise me you'll do whatever it takes."

He stills, and I swear I hear his heart stop beating. "I can't."

That's all I need to hear. I whirl, breaking his hold on me. My hands fly up, intending to smack him across his face, to break any hold he thinks he has on me, both physically and emotionally. I'm not his fucking mate. I'm not his anything.

Snarls and growls and gasps ring out at once. Suddenly, there's blood leaking down Ambrose's face. He breathes deeply, settling himself as I watch more blood pour—blood I caused.

I narrow my eyes, not understanding how I caused such a deep gash on his cheek from my nails alone. Until I look down at my hand and nearly fall on my ass at the sight.

Claws.

I have long, sharp claws where my fingernails used to be.

I stare at them and then up at Ambrose.

His lips curl up just the tiniest bit in satisfaction. I'm one step closer to becoming a wolf shifter. One step closer to being able to complete the marking ceremony with him.

Ambrose opens his mouth to speak, and as soon as he does, the crowd grows quiet. "You, Lumi, are my mate. You are my hope. You are our hope. But you are so much more than that. You are worthy of being an alpha. You have that strength, that fire in you. Your pack at the moment may be small—only you and Kael, but you already have the instincts of an alpha to defend your pack at all costs. You are my equal."

I shake my head slowly, not believing a single word he says. "I can't trust you."

"I know. And I'm sorry for that." And then the voice changes from out loud to crystal clear in my head. *"I'll spend the rest of my life earning your trust. As soon as you are part of the pack and my mate, I'll tell you everything I can't tell you now. I'll spend my life being worthy of you. But for now, have faith in me and in us. We are mates. You know it. It's why you are closer than ever to getting your wolf."*

"Promise me you'll help me get Kael back. And that as soon as you can, you'll tell me everything and never keep secrets or make decisions without me again."

"I promise. I couldn't promise before in front of the pack to save a nonpack member. But I promise you, my mate, that I'll help you get your friend back."

There's a twinkle of hope in his eyes.

Warmth spreads through me, and my newly formed

claws begin to retract until I'm once again looking at the pinks of my fingernails.

"To your soon-to-be new alpha female. She'll do anything to protect you, as I always have and will continue to do by her side." Ambrose kneels, and I find that as I spin around, the entire crowd does the same.

I'm their hope; that's why they accept me so easily. They've been cursed for twenty-one years, and I'm beginning to think that I only know the most basic parts of the curse. As I look into the eyes of those around me, I see their suffering in their puffy eyes.

This is bigger than me and Ambrose. Or Kael. Or the promise I made to Nyx. This is about saving them all.

Suddenly, a man with straight long black hair comes running up the dirt path. He's completely out of breath, but everyone stands silently at the sight of him. He stops just in front of Ambrose, who is the only one still kneeling in front of me.

The man drops to his knees in front of Ambrose.

"Is Freya...?" Ambrose asks, croaking out her name as if it hurts him to even speak it.

A slow, deep smile spreads across the man's lips. "She lives. Serenai says she'll make a full recovery. Because of you. You saved my daughter when you made the trade."

I process the words as Ambrose's eyes fly to me.

"How old is she?" I ask Ambrose through our bond.

"Seven."

"How?"

"She's human, not wolf shifter. Adopted her when her human parents died."

"And you traded Kael to save her?"

"Yes, Kael wanted to trade. He was the only one I could

offer. It goes against my oath as an alpha to trade any of my own pack members. I'm sorry."

There's a softness in Ambrose's eyes as he looks at me.

"You weren't going to tell me that you saved a girl? That Kael wanted to be traded?"

"I knew you needed to get your anger out. Nothing I said would ease your pain. I'll always let you take your anger out on me. I'll always be the man you need, even if I'm not always the man you want."

Mate—that word echoes in my head again. And despite everything, I know the word is true. I know Ambrose is my mate. *Fuck, he's my mate.*

CHAPTER 25

LUMI

Rowena approaches me and we don't have to be able to speak mind to mind for me to know what she's asking me. *Do I need her help when it comes to Ambrose?*

Yes and no.

He's such a contradiction that I have no idea what to think or feel about him. The connection I share with him...there's just something there that I can't explain other than saying we are mates. I don't need her saving me. I have to learn to deal with Ambrose on my own.

With determined eyes, I smile gently at her.

She smiles back, looping her arm in mine as she whips her long golden hair over her shoulder. "I'll walk with you back to Ambrose's place; then you can tell me what the plan is to save Kael."

I nod, still feeling the stares of the entire Moonlight wolves on me. The looks I get from them are varied—from admiration to fear to anger. I haven't won them all over as much as Ambrose tried to convince me that I did.

Emeric joins Ambrose, and then wordlessly, they take

off through the village. I have no doubt they won't rest until they've ensured every pack member is accounted for and on their way to healing. Ambrose doesn't look back, but Emeric keeps glancing over his shoulder at me with concern in his eyes as I lean against Rowena's shoulder until they finally disappear from view.

"Thank you for helping me. Kael has been my only friend for so long. It's nice to have another friend."

She squeezes me harder against her. "We are going to get Kael back."

My lips curl up as she says the word 'we' like we are a team, like she's invested in this too.

"How are you feeling about Ambrose being your mate?"

She says it like it's a fact, like it's already been determined.

"I haven't fully accepted that I have a mate, let alone that it's Ambrose."

She opens her mouth like she wants to say more but then thinks better of it. Finally, she says, "Ask him. Ask him all the questions you have. Ask him everything."

She stops walking, and I realize we've made it to the door of Ambrose's house.

"I will," I say, even though I have no idea if Ambrose will answer any of my questions.

Rowena hugs me and then slides a phone into my pocket. "My number is already programmed in. Call me if you need anything. I'll see you tomorrow."

"You don't need to worry about me. I can handle Ambrose."

She smirks. "I know—we all saw that tonight. If anyone still doubts that you are his mate, his equal, they won't after tonight."

I shake my head. "I still can't shift. How can I be his equal when I can't even shift?"

"You will, you're so close. You just have to tap into that last little bit of yourself that you have yet to fully discover."

"How?"

"It's different for everyone. For me, it was about accepting my beauty instead of fighting it. I used to hate that people only saw the beautiful golden-haired woman when they looked at me. They didn't see more—that I was intelligent and brave and strong. Once I accepted my beauty as a positive thing and not a negative, once I fully accepted myself, I was able to shift."

I frown, unsure what parts of myself I have and haven't accepted yet.

She squeezes my hand. "They're inside."

I raise my eyebrow, not expecting them to have beat us to the house. I thought I would have a few minutes on my own to collect myself.

Rowena studies me for a minute as if she's able to read my guilt. "It's not your fault that we were attacked. The Moonlight wolves are stronger than Nyx or the vampires. No pack member died. Ambrose being our alpha makes us all stronger than the other packs."

I don't respond because there is nothing I can say that would stop the guilt I feel for distracting Ambrose. If it wasn't for me, Nyx and the vampires wouldn't have attacked. Ambrose would have stopped the attack before anyone was hurt.

Rowena doesn't say anything else as she starts walking down the path from the front door down to the street, while I open the front door to face Ambrose.

Emeric spots me first.

"He send you to lock me up again?" I fold my arms across my chest, while staring him down with a look that dares him to try it and see what happens.

Emeric's face drops. "No. I was going to stand guard outside and give you two some privacy, unless you don't feel safe with him."

I scoff. "I feel perfectly safe with him. But I'm not sure how safe he is with me."

Emeric rubs the back of his neck as if unsure how to respond to my comment.

"I'm fine; go outside."

He nods and is gone before my eyes can even track his movements.

"I'm glad you aren't afraid of me," Ambrose says, appearing in front of me as if out of thin air.

I blink, annoyed that my vision isn't as good as I thought it was. And I do everything I can not to shiver at his unexpected presence in front of me. Despite my visceral reaction to him, I'm not full of bravado. I'm truly not afraid of him.

"We need to talk. And we're not going to stop talking until you answer every question I have."

He stares back at me with his piercing gold eyes before gesturing for me to follow him into the living room. As he walks, my eyes lock in on his broad back, rippling with every step. I want to run my tongue all over him and...

"You could put a shirt on," I mumble under my breath.

"Why? I know you like ogling my body."

"I can't focus when you're shirtless."

He smirks, and his eyes twinkle as he lowers himself onto the couch. "I like seeing your attraction for me. I need that reminder when you're angry with me."

I sit on the other end of the couch and whip my tank off, until I'm sitting in my bra and jean shorts. I watch his reaction, and I swear I see his golden eyes swirling as he takes in my body. For a second, I consider taking more clothes off, but his reaction would distract me more than him. And as much bravado as I appear to have, I'm not as comfortable in my bare skin as he is.

"Tell me what happened between you and Nyx."

"Nyx killed someone I loved. Someone so powerful that I didn't think they could be killed. And it changed the trajectory of my life forever. I became alpha and, ever since, have had the weight of keeping my pack safe and trying to find a way to break the curse on my back. I never wanted this responsibility, especially at twenty-two, but I knew that I was the only one strong enough to defend against Nyx and eventually kill him."

His father—he's talking about his father. I have the urge to move across the couch and hold him as I see the tear drop down his cheek, but I force myself to stay, at least until he's answered all my questions.

"I should have never let Kael go with him, even to save Freya."

I frown, my heart torn in two. "You saved that little girl's life; no one can fault you for what you did."

"You do."

I bite my lower lip, "I don't. Not anymore. Not now that I know the truth."

"Do you love him?"

I blink, my mouth drying. I wasn't expecting that question. "Yes, I love Kael, but as my best friend. He's the only family and friend I have."

He's silent for a moment. "Rowena seems to be growing close to you. I hope soon that you don't think of Kael as your only friend."

"What happened between you and Rowena?"

He stills to the point of not blinking, not breathing.

I hold my breath as well, preparing for his answer.

"Everyone thought we were mates. They were wrong."

He says the words so nonchalantly that I know it wasn't that simple, but I don't prod. I wait, hoping the silence will drive him to speak more.

"Rowena is the strongest female in the Moonlight pack, so it was natural that everyone thought she was my mate. But we knew even without exploring it that we weren't mates."

"Did you date?"

"We did go on a couple of dates to appease the pack. They needed to see us trying after everything they've been through. And I was willing to do almost anything to try and save them. But I wasn't willing to kill Rowena just to prove that she wasn't my mate."

He runs his hand through his hair. "But some in the pack didn't want to let it go. They still don't."

I frown.

"It's why Rowena entered the offering this year. She needed to prove to everyone that she wasn't my mate."

My heart jumps in my throat. *I can understand why the pack would think that Rowena is his mate. She's a better choice than me.*

"She's not a better choice. She's not as fearless, deviant, or demanding as you are. She doesn't have the natural leadership and protectiveness of the rest of the pack like you do. She wasn't born to be an alpha, and you were," he says as if he can read my thoughts. I'm sure I didn't send them into his head.

"I wasn't born to be an alpha," I say. It doesn't matter that my father was an alpha. Alphas don't always follow family lines.

"You broke free of my alpha command."

"That's because I'm not part of your pack—"

"No, it's because you became the alpha of a new pack that you and Kael created when you were on your own. I'm strong enough to command every wolf shifter, even those not in my pack. I can even command alphas, but only alphas are strong enough to break free of my commands. You're an alpha."

I suck in a breath, and his eyes roll down my body, taking in every inch of my flesh.

"She's not as beautiful. My body doesn't ache for her with raw, uncontrollable desire like it does you. I don't crave her like I crave my next meal. And she sure as hell isn't as brave as you, my queen."

"I'm not brave, and I'm not your queen."

"You're brave. You've stood up against me multiple times now, and you most definitely are my queen, my mate, my equal, my future everything."

I shrug. "Well, maybe you aren't as much of a big bad alpha as you let on."

His eyes alight at my words. And suddenly, he's sitting right next to me on the couch with that predatory stare that says I should be very afraid of him.

When I don't react in fear, his eyes fill with lust as if my lack of fear turns him on.

I run my tongue over my lips in anticipation. Ambrose watches every second of my movements with a stillness that I didn't think was possible.

"I want to kiss you. I want to shred every drop of clothes from your body and fuck you against every surface of my house."

Yes, I think, but I'm not sure if I actually send the word to him or not.

His eyes peruse up and down my body as he inhales me. I know he can smell how wet I am, how badly I want him, too.

"I need to tell Emeric to come back into the house first so he can ensure I won't hurt you."

I frown. "You won't hurt me."

He shakes his head. "You're my unmarked mate. I'm struggling more and more not to lose myself around you, and I've barely touched you. If I do more than kiss you, I'm not sure I'm strong enough..." he trails off.

I raise my hand to his warm cheek, which feels like I've touched fire. He's burning up.

My eyes widen as I slip my hand around his neck, pulling him toward me. But he's still strong enough to resist my tug and stops an inch from my face.

"I already sent a team to ensure nothing happens to Kael. I don't want you worrying about him. Or hating me..."

My heart sputters. *Oh, this man. How could I have ever doubted his feelings for me? How could I have ever doubted that he's my mate?*

"Thank you. When I talked to Nyx—"

I fly across the room until my back is pinned against the large window, and Ambrose's entire body is flush against mine, holding me in place.

"*When and why did you talk to Nyx?*" his anger is palpable as he speaks into my mind.

I glare at him defiantly. "I talked to him when I went to find Kael."

"You have no idea who Nyx is or how terrified of him you should be. But you're about to learn how much of a big, bad alpha I can be, my brave, foolish queen."

CHAPTER 26

LUMI

I raise my eyes at him as he growls low and deep, the sound vibrating through my body, sending equal parts fear and electricity zipping through me.

"You going to lock me up again? I'd like to see you try. I don't care if you are my mate; I'll never complete the marking ceremony if you lock me up again."

His eyes widen in amusement. "Have I told you that I love how brave and sassy you are? But no, I've learned my lesson about locking you up. I won't resort to that again unless you leave me no choice. Which, based on how you're acting, might be what we are left with." He leans in closer until his breath is hot on my neck. "But don't act like you can resist becoming my mate. You can't resist me any more than you can resist breathing."

I narrow my eyes. "You underestimate how stubborn I am if you think I'll ever choose a mate who treats me poorly."

"Oh, I know. But you won't get to choose who you mate with if you end up dead. Do you know how dangerous Nyx is? Do you know he aligned his pack with vampires? Do you know he's willing to do anything to defeat us as soon as the curse lifts?"

I swallow. "I know he's dangerous, but I couldn't leave Kael to die either. He's my best friend."

"There is so much danger for you. It's everywhere. Nyx, the vampires, the witches, the other shifters...me."

I snap my teeth at him, catching some of the flesh of his earlobe between my teeth and biting until I draw blood before he pulls his head away. "I thought I was your strong queen."

"You are. And you have so much untapped power that I have no doubt you will soon be powerful enough to take on anyone. You're not there yet, but I can't wait until you have that strength."

"Why? So you can mate with me? Mark me as yours?"

He smirks, his eyes glistening with dark, lust-filled thoughts. "Maybe, but also so that I don't have to worry about you dying anymore. I'll know you can protect yourself. And when we are together, I'll be able to fully unleash myself on you."

"No one's stopping you," I taunt him.

The guttural groan that emanates from his throat has my core heating and dampness dripping in my panties.

We stare at each other for a moment, locked in a battle of wills, waiting to see who will break first. We both want the same thing. Simultaneously, we move— our lips colliding in an aggressive kiss.

My arms are still pinned to the glass window behind me, so the only thing I can control is the kiss. I kiss him brutally, bruising and nipping and tasting every inch of his flesh that I can reach. Blood drips from the nicks on his lips, and his tongue battles mine.

His bare chest pushes against my skin, but it's not enough. I want more, more, more.

I hate the bra I'm wearing.

I hate the shorts blocking us from truly joining together.

I want to know once and for all if Ambrose is my mate. Once he's buried inside me, I'll know without a shadow of a doubt that he's mine. That we were made for each other. That the universe fated it from the very beginning.

I don't know Ambrose well enough, and he doesn't know me. Not in all the ways we should before we are to be mated, but time isn't on our side. We'll be constantly attacked if we don't complete the ceremony on the next full moon. The entire pack is in danger until we do. And I won't let that continue to happen if I can do something about it.

His tongue pushes deeper into my mouth in a claiming, possessive kiss that has me writhing. But it's not enough. I want my hands free. I want to grab onto the length of his hair. I want to rip the rest of the clothes from his body. I want him thrusting inside me.

He chuckles against my lips. "Your thoughts are very loud when I kiss you."

My cheeks burn red.

"Don't be embarrassed by your need for me. *Never.*" And then his lips move from my mouth to my jawline and then down to my neck.

I shiver, arching my back, pushing our bodies further together as his lips kiss so tenderly against the skin on my neck. My body heats to the brink of explosion. Electric energy flows through me faster than lightning as my eyes roll back in my head. I'm going to come from his kisses alone.

I can't think. I can barely speak but manage to say, "More."

A rumble of a growl vibrates through the room, shaking the decor on the walls.

"Only if you promise to never put yourself in danger again. To never leave this house without an escort of either me, Emeric, or Rowena."

My heart stutters in my chest. "That sounds an awful lot like a prison to me."

He shakes his head as he nuzzles against my neck. "It's the only way I can give you freedom while keeping you safe. Just until the marking ceremony."

I frown, but then he kisses me on the neck again. And I want him so badly that I could very easily agree to any terms. Even keeping me locked up and only letting me free for sex and food.

"Fuck me, and we have a deal." My eyes glisten with dirty thoughts. It's only a couple of weeks until the full moon. I can make this promise to him easily enough.

His teeth rake over my neck like it's as much of a struggle for him to accept my terms as it was for me to accept his. "It's all I want to do—fuck you, explore every part of your body, claim you, but..." he chokes on his next words as I thrust my hips forward until I can feel his hard length against my lower stomach. "I don't trust myself with you, not to hurt you. I need you to be at your full strength first."

"You won't hurt me."

"And when I fuck you, it can't be a part of some deal. It needs to be because we both want it."

"We both want it," I counter.

His eyes darken as he stares at me. "Nyx made a deal with the vampires. I don't know what the exact deal is, but he's powerful and dangerous, more than either of us even realize. He's taken so much from me." He shakes his head. "Never again."

"Never again," I agree.

"You don't understand everything—you don't know the implications if we don't break the curse this time. And it's more than being attacked by others trying to get us to break the curse faster. It's so much more." He places his forehead against mine in a desperate attempt for me to understand. "It's so much more, and I want to tell you. I want to tell you fucking everything. But I don't want to put that burden on you."

I suck in a breath.

"I wish everything was different. That I could court you properly, that we could take our time, fall in love first. We don't have that time."

I capture his mouth with mine and then speak in his mind. *"I promise."*

Everything changes after I speak those words. There's a trust and hunger that wasn't there before, for both of us.

He releases my wrists, and both of our hands grab onto each other at the same time. My hands grab onto his neck and tangle in his thick hair, holding him to me as if my life depends on it, while his hands grip my ass, holding me so tightly against his body that it's hard for either of us to breathe.

"I need you," he says, his face buried in my neck.

"Then have me."

His eyes blaze with a golden light, shining brighter than I've ever seen his eyes before. Nothing else changes about him. No claws form. No sharpened teeth. No fur. No shifting, but I know his animal instincts have kicked in as much as his human desires have. And I know what he means about not being able to stop himself. This is my last chance to stop him.

I don't want to stop him. Instead, I let out a soft whimper filled with need.

His hands clasp the front of my bra, shredding it open as easily as if it were paper. He doesn't hesitate as his mouth captures one of my nipples, encasing it fully as his tongue licks around the sensitive bud.

I hold on harder to his head, barely keeping myself upright, knowing I'd topple over if the glass window wasn't still behind me. He quickly moves to my other nipple as his hand cups my breast, and his thumb flicks its peak.

Heat courses through me in a way that it never has before. I'm flooded with blood and heat and emotion.

I must fuck him. I must have him. He's mine.

The thoughts flicker through my head, coming so hard and fast that I can't process anything but my need for him.

He slides down my body, and my shorts go with him as he kneels in front of me, staring hopelessly at the spot between my legs, dripping with warm desire.

He takes a deep breath, taking in my scent, and shudders as his eyes roll back in his head. "You smell better than anything I could ever imagine."

"Taste me." Before the words have even fully left my throat, his tongue is licking up my slit and locking on my clit.

The heat spreads faster through my body at every sweep of his tongue. Heat like I've never felt before. Heat that spreads like a wildfire through my body, flooding me to the point that I might pass out.

Ambrose must notice my reaction because he lifts me

up, sweeping my legs over each of his shoulders while never once letting up his devouring of my clit.

In a second flat, I'm tossed onto my back on his bed, and his pants are gone as he stares at me bare-naked and spread out on his bed. I stare right back, taking in every muscle rippling down his chest all the way down to his large cock straining in my direction. It's all I can really focus on, even as I notice a glow of something on his skin that's supernatural and not something I've ever seen before, even on wolf shifters.

I lick my lips, and then he's on top of me. His lips on my lips. His cock is hard between the moisture soaking between my legs.

"Hot," is the only word I can get out as my body blazes and sweat soaks my body. I've never been so overtaken by anything in my life.

Ambrose growls, his lips kissing me hard and punishing. His cock is so fucking close to sliding home, to completing our own private ceremony declaring each other as mates.

Something shifts in the air, in us. I don't know what exactly, but suddenly Ambrose is moving faster, too fast. My mind whirls. Claws shoot out of my fingers and dig hard into his back. His teeth sink into my neck, and he starts shifting—fur, ears, teeth, and claws all begin to form where he was before.

I gasp as the hunger remains in his eyes as he's half wolf, half human on top of me. The heat propels through my body, and I realize this is it. This might be the moment I finally shift. For a single second, I feel joy, but the shift doesn't happen.

I'm burning up. And Ambrose is lost to his wolf and desires as he sweeps down my body, biting down on my clit so hard I scream my orgasm out both in agony and sweet release of pleasure.

My heart flutters hard and fast. I have to stop him, but I can't. I don't know what's happening—to either of us. All I see is his predatory stare as his features remain half wolf, half human. If we are truly mates, it's not going to be enough to save me from him.

The burning in my body says I'm not strong enough to survive even if I stop him. That I need him as badly as I need this to stop. The fire will never burn out of my body. I'll never shift until I have Ambrose, until I'm sure he's the one.

Before I can process what to do or how to save myself, Ambrose is thrown from my body, pinned against the wall by a fully shifted Emeric.

"Wait, I need Ambrose," I cry out as Rowena scoops me from the bed. I'm too weak to even fight back or lift my own body.

"We need you alive," she says simply. And then I'm carried so quickly from Ambrose that I can't even begin to understand what happened to him or me.

I'm alive, but I've never felt more dead as the heat continues to burn me alive from the inside out. Until finally, I succumb to the feeling, and blackness takes over me.

CHAPTER 27

LUMI

A chill races through my body, jolting me awake. Wet, cold towels cover my entire body as I lie naked on a bed. Judging by the pink satin comforter, I know this isn't Ambrose's bed.

"Thank heavens," Rowena says, and I turn my head to my right to see her fussing over me.

My head aches like I've just been run over by a truck. "What happened?"

"Drink." She shoves a straw to my lips, and I take a long sip of ice-cold water, knowing I'm not going to get any answers until she's satisfied that I've drunk enough, which turns out to be the entire thirty-two-ounce water bottle.

"What happened?" I ask again after draining it.

Rowena adjusts some towels on my body and looks me over, avoiding my gaze.

I grab her wrist, stopping her from adjusting another cool towel on my body. "What. Happened?"

She sighs. "You don't remember?"

I start to shake my head no but then stop. "I

remember being with Ambrose. I remember feeling really hot, like unnaturally hot. And then I remember you and Emeric…"

She nods. "You were trying to shift but couldn't."

I frown. "That's what it feels like to shift? Like your body is being burned alive from the inside out?"

Her face pales. "It can be. It's different for everyone."

"Why did you stop me, then? Why didn't you let me shift?"

She sits down on the edge of the bed I'm lying on. "Ambrose sent out an alpha call. He wasn't in control anymore. And you—you weren't going to survive much longer in your state. You were burning up but not actually shifting. Your human body wouldn't have survived, and even if you did, Ambrose would have torn you to pieces. He was too out of control."

"But he was in control enough to tell you that he needed help?"

"He didn't consciously do it. It's a pack thing. If the alpha is in trouble, the rest of us can sense it."

"Why couldn't I shift?"

Rowena strokes my hair. "I don't know."

I stare up at the ceiling, frustrated that, once again, I failed. "Does this mean I'm closer to being able to shift?"

"I don't know."

"What do you know?"

"I know that you are incredibly strong and caring and that you and Ambrose are perfect for each other. And you still have a couple of weeks before the next full moon. You'll figure it out by then."

"Why does it have to be the next full moon? Why the pressure to do it this time?"

"I don't know. I can just sense it—time is running out. It has to be this full moon."

I narrow my eyes at her, trying to sense if she's lying or at least not revealing the entire truth to me.

"You really don't know more?"

"I don't. Ambrose keeps his secrets close to him. He doesn't burden anyone he doesn't have to burden. He carries the entire weight of the Moonlight wolves on his shoulders alone." She pauses. "Until you."

I scoff. "He hasn't told me anything."

"Maybe not yet, but he wants to."

I open my mouth and then hesitate because I know she's right. I know he wants to tell me. He wants to share everything with me. I just have to prove to him that he can trust me. That he can share his burden with me.

"I need to train. I need to learn to shift. I won't let anyone else get injured or die because I can't break the curse."

Rowena nods. "I'll get you some spare clothes."

———

I'm a pile of sweat in Rowena's backyard. We've been at this for hours, but I haven't even made my claws reappear. And despite how hot and sweaty I am, nothing came close to how I felt last night with Ambrose. No earthy moving change in my body that rattles me to my core. Not even a flicker of anything supernatural happening in my body. If I didn't know better, then I would think that wolf shifter DNA doesn't run in my blood.

I heave a deep breath. "What now?"

Rowena runs her hand through her golden hair, her

face unreadable. "Maybe if you watch me shift a few times, you'll get some inspiration?"

I nod, sinking into one of her back patio chairs. I suspect she's doing this to give me a break. But I'll try anything at this point. I've tried concentrating, exercising hard, and letting my emotions overtake me—but nothing has worked.

Rowena takes a step off the deck, tossing her robe off, and shifts as easily as if she were breathing. One second she's a human, the next a beautiful golden furred wolf with a feminine fierceness in her yellow-eyed stare. She winks at me and then she's back in her human form and completely naked in front of me.

I gape at her, remembering how beautiful her body is and how perfect she would make as a mate for Ambrose. She should be his match. She should be alpha female. She's strong enough, beautiful enough, and she can shift.

Rowena picks up the robe and puts it on, eyeing me suspiciously. "What are you thinking about?"

"How beautiful you are and how effortlessly you shift."

"Ambrose told you?" She sits down in the chair across from me.

"Yes."

She nods. "Good, I wanted to tell you but thought he deserved to get to tell you first."

"Are you sure you two aren't mates?"

She chuckles and stands. "We're going to need some wine for this." She returns a few minutes later with two glasses and a bottle of red wine. She pours us both a glass and hands one to me.

"No, thanks."

"Alcohol can help you get out of your head. It can sometimes make it easier to shift."

I sigh. "Give me."

She smiles, and we both take a long drink. "Ambrose and I make perfect sense on paper. We are both the strongest in our pack. Both determined and fearless. Both care deeply about the pack and breaking the curse. We are both beautiful people. I will admit there was an attraction between us that we explored."

I hold my breath. She got to explore him—fully. It's clear in her eyes. She's not holding back when she speaks. She got to have him in every way before she made her decision, while I had to be rescued from him because I'm too weak.

"The attraction between us was strong. Strong enough that we didn't leave the bedroom for weeks. But that lust quickly faded. That wouldn't have happened if we were mates. There was nothing like love between us. And we both knew, deep down, that we weren't compatible. Not really. He was focused on being alpha. On taking care of the pack. And I've never wanted anything more than my independence. I was never born to be an alpha."

She looks at me over her wine glass. "You are."

I frown. "Why does everyone keep telling me that?"

"Because it's a wolf thing. We can sense when someone is born to be an alpha. There is a different scent and aura to them," Emeric says as he walks through the back patio door.

"How is he?" I ask, knowing that Emeric will know exactly who I'm talking about. Ambrose could tell me himself, but he hasn't reached out through our mental bond, and neither have I.

Emeric sinks into a chair next to Rowena, wincing in

pain as he does. "He's angry with himself for putting you at risk."

I frown. "And otherwise?"

"Perfectly fine."

"What about you?"

"What about me?" Emeric says with a wide grin, trying to hide whatever pain he's in.

"Don't think I didn't notice that little wince. Did Ambrose hurt you?"

Emeric shakes his head. "No, nothing like that." He pauses and then snatches the bottle of wine from the table and takes a drink straight from the bottle. "How much do you know about the curse?"

"Not enough," I say, downing the rest of my wine.

Emeric and Rowena share a knowing glance, and then Emeric says, "The curse affects each of us differently. Some it weakens their powers, others it shortens their lifespans, and others suffer in pain."

"How does it affect you?" I stare intently at Emeric.

He sighs. "As Ambrose's second, I'm in pain when he's in pain. I take on all of his hardships through physical pain. All of his worry and fears become pain for me."

I look him over, confused as to why he's always smiling and happy if he's always suffering. Because from what little I know about Ambrose, he's constantly worrying.

"That's not fair."

"The curse isn't fair," Emeric shrugs and then smiles.

Rowena places her hand gently on his shoulder as if she's trying to comfort him.

"What about you?" I ask Rowena.

She sighs. "Mine is far less annoying than Emeric's. I

can't be intimate with a man without intense pain afterward."

I frown, especially after the story she just told me about being with Ambrose.

With a twinkle in her eye, she says, "Don't worry, I can still enjoy intimacy with women."

We share a smile, but it's forced. I know it's not Emeric's constant pain, but it still affects her. I know her beauty causes every male from every pack to lust after her. Her curse affects her as strongly as Emeric's affects him.

My guess is that the curse plays to each person's unique personality. It seems to find a way to hurt that person in the cruelest way possible.

It hits me like a freight train, and I sink back in my chair.

"Lumi, what is it?" Rowena asks with fear in her voice.

"What if my curse is that I'll find my mate but never be able to complete the marking ceremony by not allowing me to ever shift."

Silence stretches between Rowena and Emeric. Their mouths gape open as they process my words. It could be true.

The gods who cast the curse care about one thing and one thing only—ensuring that it continues forever.

This would ensure that.

"I don't accept that, and neither do you, Lumi. Even if that is your curse, we will find a way to break it together," Ambrose says from the doorway.

CHAPTER 28

LUMI

"How? We've tried everything. It should have happened by now," I say, tired and defeated.

Ambrose's jaw tightens. "We haven't tried—together."

I raise my eyebrows at that. "You're really going to help me?"

"Yes, I'm sorry I didn't do it sooner. I thought you were better off training with Emeric and Rowena. But I think we've been going at this all wrong. You've come the closest to shifting when you're with me. We will figure this out together."

I eye him up and down, taking all of him in. I walk over to him and then glance back at Rowena and Emeric. "I'm fine, guys. He's not going to lose control again. You can leave us alone—"

"No, they can't," he says.

I frown. "I'm safe—"

"You're not. You're not safe with me. Not like you should be. And I'm sorry, so fucking sorry, for what happened."

"Don't—don't take back what happened between us. I'm not sorry about any of it."

Ambrose's eyes glisten, but he doesn't say anything in response. Instead, he sweeps me toward him and crashes his lips down on mine in a hungry kiss. At the touch of his lips against mine, I realize why he didn't want Rowena or Emeric to leave. I realize how he plans on evoking me to shift.

Amusement dances in my eyes at the idea of claiming him here in Rowena's backyard while both Rowena and Emeric watch. But then I think better of it.

I pull away, sucking his bottom lip into my mouth as my body resists what my mind is saying before finally releasing him.

"We can't," I whisper, even though I know no matter how quiet I am, every wolf shifter within a couple-mile radius can hear our conversation.

Ambrose rests his forehead against mine. "Why not? You've come the closest to shifting when we're together."

"I know, but..." my eyes cut to where Rowena and Emeric are sitting, still drinking the wine and trying to act like they aren't listening to every word of our conversation.

He strokes my face before running his hand through my hair. I want nothing more than to kiss him, fuck him, and let my emotions run wild, but I don't think it would help me shift. My emotions are too intense when we are together.

"Show me how you shift."

"You've seen me shift before," he says.

"I know, but show me again. Walk me through it step by step. Tell me how it happened the first time."

He grips the back of his neck and rubs gently, his bicep flexing and drawing me back to my lust-filled daze.

"I honestly don't remember my first time; I was so young. I think five or six. But shifting now is the same as breathing. It's instinctual. It happens when I need it to. It's as fluid as walking or running."

One second he's standing in nothing but his jeans in front of me, the next he's the impressively large wolf that still shocks me every time I see him. The gold flecks flickering bright against his dark fur, and his golden eyes beaming with hope that I can join him in my own form.

"I want to see what your wolf looks like. I want to know her as I know you," his words are a seductive caress in my head.

I bite my lower lip. *"Me too."*

I close my eyes, imagining what my wolf might look like. I imagine my silvery-white hair with dark undertones and my piercing blue eyes. Or maybe being Ambrose's mate would give me some flecks of his signature gold color that he and the rest of the Moonlight wolves seem to share.

I let those warm thoughts fill me and try to invoke that hot fire that had burned before, but this time I try to channel the energy into shifting.

I stay like that for several long minutes, but nothing happens. The warmth never turns to the hot I felt before. Nothing changes, not even my nails sharpening into claws.

I open my eyes and sigh as I look at Ambrose, knowing the disappointment that is going to be heavy on his face.

He shifts back, and I can barely look him in the eye as my shame fills me.

"Hey, we will figure this out together. There is nothing to be ashamed of. It's the curse doing this, not you." His fingers lift my chin up to meet his gaze.

Heat fills my body as it does every time he looks at me. Desire pools between my legs as my ache for him grows.

"*Use it,*" he says.

I let the fire build in me. I let the heat spread as I peruse Ambrose's body with my eyes. I run my fingers gently over the tuft of hair on the center of his chest as I bite my lower lip.

Shift.

Nothing happens.

Ambrose doesn't grow impatient with me, though.

"Can you try to explain it to me again?" I ask.

He frowns and runs his hand through his hair. "It's hard to explain. It would be like explaining to someone how to make their heart beat. It's a natural process that just happens."

"But you can control when you shift, so there has to be some practice to it."

"Yes and no. Once it happens, all you have to do is think about shifting, and your instincts take over."

"So I just have to figure out how to trigger it the first time?"

He nods.

"Isolde said she could use her magic to help me shift—"

"No!" His voice is loud, commanding. "No, that isn't even an option. It would give Isolde untold power over you."

"I thought you trusted Isolde."

"Not with you." His golden eyes soften.

I just have to trigger my shift one time, and then it will be as easy as breathing.

But it doesn't happen. No matter how hard I try. No matter how many times Ambrose shows me how to shift. How patient he is. How he tries to get me to tap into my emotions. How he goes through the mechanics of it, nothing helps.

"Maybe we should try the marking ceremony anyway. Even if I can't shift, if we are truly mates, it would still work, right?" I say suddenly as I sit next to Ambrose on Rowena's couch in her living room, with my head resting on his shoulder.

Rowena and Emeric are making food in the kitchen, but the gentle clang of moving pots and pans around stops the second I say the words.

Ambrose shakes his head. "It would kill you."

"Will it break the curse, though?"

Silence is my answer. I don't know if it's because Ambrose is trying to think it through or if he's trying to find a way to talk me out of doing it. Finally, he says with a low growl. "It doesn't matter because I'm not risking your life to break the curse."

"Why? The curse has to be broken. I know you haven't told me everything. And I don't know how it affects you personally, but I know that it does. I know that time is running out. I'm willing to do it, no matter the conse-quences."

He shakes his head. "I'm not."

"Why?"

"Because we are mates!" Ambrose jumps up and throws his hands up like he thinks I'm crazy.

"So? You'll get a new mate if I die; that's what everyone keeps telling me."

Ambrose turns to me. "I won't. Once the marking ceremony is completed, it will only be you."

"Then you'll find someone to love. They may not be your mate, but you could love again. Choose your own partner and forget about all this predestined bullshit."

"You're not listening to me. I don't want anyone else. I want you. I won't accept you dying as a way to break the curse."

"But we don't even love each other. We're just compatible. We're just—"

Ambrose cuts me off with another growl. "Stop acting like you aren't worthy—of being my mate, of me falling in love with you. Just because it hasn't happened yet doesn't mean it won't. We will find another way, but you aren't sacrificing yourself to break the curse."

I frown.

Rowena is suddenly in the living room. "I have an idea."

We both snap our heads in her direction.

"Ambrose should initiate Lumi into the Moonlight pack. It might be just what she needs to feel like she belongs. Maybe she needs to feel part of the pack in order to be able to shift."

My eyes brighten at her idea, but then I see Ambrose's expression. He's as upset as when I suggested completing the marking ceremony as a human. I realize I have no idea what it takes to be initiated into the Moonlight wolves, but whatever it is, I have to do it.

CHAPTER 29
LUMI

"What would I have to do to be initiated into the Moonlight pack?"

Ambrose isn't looking at me; he's looking at Rowena like he might kill her for bringing up the idea in front of me. It makes me feel like it isn't the first time that she's brought this up to him.

"Lumi is going to have to do it sooner or later," Rowena says.

"Later then," Ambrose growls.

I fold my arms as I watch them argue in front of me like I'm not even here. But it gives me time to study both of them and their relationship together. If they once had feelings for each other, they're not there anymore.

"It's not really your decision," Rowena says with a smirk.

Ambrose steps in front of me like I need protection from Rowena. "I'm not putting her through that."

"You can't stop her if she wants to initiate."

"I'm the alpha. I can deny her."

"And how would that look to the rest of the pack? You

want them to accept her. You want them to believe she's your match and to respect her as your mate. If you didn't let her initiate, they would think it's because you don't think she's worthy enough."

"Lumi is more than worthy," his growl vibrates through me and warms my heart even though he's denying me a chance to join the pack.

"I agree, and she's capable of making her own decisions," Rowena's eyes twinkle as she looks at me.

I smile at her, appreciating her help, but I'm capable of fighting my own battles when it comes to Ambrose.

I step out from behind Ambrose. "Maybe you two should talk to me and let me have a say instead of arguing like I'm not right here."

"Initiation isn't an easy way to solve our problems. It might not even help you shift. And then you would have gone through everything for nothing," Ambrose says, finally looking at me.

"But I would be part of the Moonlight wolves. Even if it doesn't help me gain my wolf, I would belong somewhere."

Ambrose's eyes soften as I speak, but I immediately regret my words. I've always belonged to a pack. I've never felt like I didn't.

"You can join after you gain your wolf. It will make it easier to endure."

"But it would make her stronger now. And as much as she has the internal strength, she needs the full support of the pack with all the attacks currently happening," Rowena pushes.

Ambrose continues to stare at me, and I can see his resolve ending.

"Lumi can know the truth," Rowena hits him with the final nail.

He sucks in a breath, like being able to tell me everything would ease some suffering that he's been battling all this time.

"Initiation won't be easy. It will be the hardest thing you've ever been through. I can't tell you more than that. But I have no doubt that you'll be able to get through it and become part of the Moonlight wolves, whether you do it later or now."

I smile, but my heart suddenly starts racing. If I'm part of the Moonlight pack, then I'm no longer part of the Wintermoon pack. I'm leaving my past behind.

What if they find out I already belong to a pack? Can I still initiate into the Moonlight pack if I'm still technically in the Wintermoon pack?

My heart sinks when I realize that isn't going to be a problem. My father is dead. The pack is gone. I'm truly packless right now.

Ambrose turns to me with a lightness in his eyes. "I could tell you everything. No more secrets between us."

I force my smile to widen as he does, even though I feel anything but happiness because there will always be secrets between us. Maybe not his anymore, but mine. I can never tell him what pack I came from or who I truly am. But maybe it doesn't matter if I can find a way to break the curse.

"It's your choice," he says.

"I want to initiate into the Moonlight wolves."

He pulls me in tight in a hug, his arms wrapping around me like he's never letting me go. And for once, I feel like I'm home.

"Tomorrow night—I'll arrange everything for

tomorrow night," he says, releasing me before jogging off to talk to Emeric and arrange the initiation, leaving Rowena and me in her living room.

"Everything okay?" she asks, and I know she can see through my fake smile.

I let it drop, knowing there is no point pretending. I trust her, but I can't trust her with my secret.

"It will be after initiation."

CHAPTER 30

LUMI

"We should leave soon, you don't want to be late," Rowena says as I brush my long white locks into a high ponytail, and she watches me from doorway of my bathroom.

I swallow down my nerves as I turn and face her. "Where is Ambrose?"

"He and Emeric left while you were showering."

I frown. "Ambrose didn't want to wish me luck or tell me goodbye before he left?"

"Maybe he would have if you didn't take an hour-long shower," Rowena chuckles.

I shoot her a dirty look. "Well, maybe I wouldn't have taken that long if I knew what I was getting myself into. You guys have told me practically nothing about what initiation entails."

Rowena sighs. "I would tell you if I could."

"But you can't." I take a couple of steps toward her, not even bothering to look at myself one last time in the mirror. I'm wearing black leather pants with a grey T-shirt and a black leather jacket. Black combat boots are waiting for me to put on to complete my ensemble. Rowena picked out my entire outfit, which is my only clue as to what I might be facing tonight.

She straightens my jacket and takes a deep breath herself, like she's holding something back.

"I don't want you to tell me. I know it goes against pack rules to tell an outsider anything about your initiation process. I don't want the pack to exile you."

"You don't have to worry about that. I couldn't even if I wanted to—alpha command and all that."

"Ambrose was the one who came up with the rule about initiation?" I raise my eyebrows.

"It's for the best, trust me. Even if I could tell you, I'm not sure you should know ahead of time."

"It's that bad, huh?" I chuckle, trying to lighten the mood as I push past her.

She grabs my arm, turning me back toward her.

"It is—it might be the hardest thing you have ever gone through."

I think about losing my father. About never knowing my mother. About Kael being taken by Nyx. About being Ambrose's mate and not being able to shift.

She sees the pain I've experienced racing through the blue in my eyes. "But then again, you're not an ordinary shifter. You're stronger than all of us." She smiles softly. "I think you'll initiate into the Moonlight pack just fine."

I clench my jaw and nod at her. "I will."

We both head to the living room and slip on our shoes. As I'm lacing my boots up, Rowena speaks up.

"I can say this. Initiation is nothing about being able to shift or not. It has very little to do with being a wolf shifter and more to do with having the spirit of the Moon-light wolves. We're known for our bravery, our cunning-ness, our strength. We're known as leaders among the packs. We're the guiding light. The pack just wants to make sure you fit those qualities before you join."

"Thank you," I say, even though I'm not sure if anything she said was helpful or not. "I am surprised initiation doesn't have to happen on the full moon, though."

"For most packs, that's the case, but as long as there is moonlight out, then it's enough for our pack. We're that powerful." She winks at me.

I laugh and roll my eyes at her. My face immediately drops when I see the sun setting out the window. Initia-tion is about to start as soon as the sun fully dips below the horizon.

"I wish I could go with you," Rowena starts.

"It's okay. I need to do this on my own." I lick my lips, and my eyes narrow in determination.

And then Rowena runs up behind me and hugs me tightly. "The next time I see you, you'll be a full member of the Moonlight wolves. Then you can know everything. There will be no secrets. You'll get your wolf soon after, I'm sure of it. And then I'll be bowing down to you as my alpha queen."

I roll my eyes but hug her back, already feeling like she's a sister to me.

Finally, she releases me after the hug goes on a little too long, and I start to feel some of her anxiety for me that she's been trying to hide.

"You've got this," she says, but I can hear the fear in her voice for me. It only drives me.

I don't look back as I walk out the door and follow the directions into the woods behind Ambrose's house. I don't think about what awaits me. I'm confident that I'm as prepared as I can be to face it.

I shiver as the sun begins to fully set and the last streams of sunlight turn to shadows. The air quickly turns cool, but it will still be a few hours until the moon fully rises in the sky.

I was given very few directions of where to go once I got into the woods. I'm shocked that Ambrose didn't give me more instructions after the attack by the vampires and Nyx, but then again, I get this sense that every step I take is being watched. I know I'm not alone. I'm safe—well, as safe as I can be considering the hell the pack is about to put me through.

A glow at the base of a tree draws my attention, and I walk closer. I stumble as I see more of the yellow glowing marks.

Magic.

Runes.

Something I've never seen before but only heard about in fairytales marks the base of the tree.

My heart races, unsure of how magic plays into this. A sense of dread overwhelms me as I stare at them.

I can feel him close—Ambrose. I scan the bushes and trees, but I don't see him.

"Look up," a tiny voice says, but it doesn't belong to Ambrose.

When I do, I gasp.

Ambrose is bound high in the tree. Blood drips from a gash on his neck. And two vampires guard either side of him.

It's clear to me what happened. They got news that I was to be initiated tonight. They knew everyone was focused on that instead of watching for an attack, and they took advantage. And now Ambrose is going to pay the price.

CHAPTER 31

LUMI

"*What do I do?*" I ask Ambrose through our bond.

Silence greets me.

Ambrose's eyes don't change, nor do they acknowledge that I spoke to him. And I don't feel any of the fire in my belly that I often feel when I'm connected to him.

I stare at the glowing marks at the base of the tree he's in. Runes by witches. My eyes scan over them quickly. I don't know much about witches, but I do know the runes are impacting Ambrose and my ability to speak to each other.

"*Ambrose, talk to me. Tell me what to do,*" I try again, hoping against all odds that I'm wrong.

Ambrose stiffens as if he realizes what I'm doing, but I don't think the message went through.

Fuck, what do I do?

I don't recognize the vampires holding onto Ambrose. I don't know why they have him, but I suspect they want what all of us magical creatures want—to break the curse.

"Don't hurt him. He's your best chance at breaking the curse. He's my mate. And I came here tonight to initiate into the Moonlight pack so I can complete the marking ceremony at the next full moon and break the curse."

The vampires just stare at me with their blood-red eyes. One raises his upper lip so I get a clear view of his lethal fangs. But neither of them speaks or moves an inch as if they are frozen in stone.

I frown as I scan the woods for the rest of the Moonlight wolves. They have to be here if they were expecting me to initiate tonight. *Did other vampires and witches grab them? Or are they safe?*

I don't sense anyone else near. At the moment, at least, I'm on my own.

Fear rolls through me. I don't stand a chance on my own against vampires. I don't know how to reason with them, and I don't know how to free Ambrose from the runes that seem to be silencing our connection and keeping him bound high up in a tree.

What are they waiting for?

"What do you want?"

The vampires barely even glance in my direction when I speak, but I swear I see Ambrose's jaw tick. And then he mouths a single word that slams into me as hard as the fear—*run.*

I glance behind me just in time to see the glow of yellow eyes in the darkness behind me. I don't hesitate. I run.

I hate running, and I vow whenever I do get my wolf, I'm never running from a fight again. But it's all I can do. Run and find help because I'm useless on my own.

But I don't know where to find help. I don't know where the pack is. And I'm running in the wrong direction from town.

I whip my head quickly behind me to try to get a sense of how many are following me. The yellow glowing eyes are there in the dozens.

Wait. I holt to a stop when I realize who has glowing yellow eyes—the Moonlight wolves.

It's a huge gamble. I could be wrong. But I won't get much further running.

I turn at the same time I stop. My breath is heavy, and my heart is sprinting at full speed, ready for me to run again as I stare down those glowing yellow eyes that number in the dozens.

The eyes stop growing closer, but they seem to grow in number. A chill races up my spine, and I glance over my shoulder to see that some of the eyes have moved behind me, until I'm completely surrounded by those Moonlight wolves.

I scan them, looking for someone I recognize. It's then that I realize I haven't spent enough time with the pack. But then again, that's not my fault, as Ambrose hasn't let me out of his sight.

Several of the faces are familiar, but I can't come up with any of their names.

"I think Nyx has Ambrose," I say calmly, trying to take deep, relaxing breaths. *This is the Moonlight pack. They aren't going to hurt me.*

No one speaks.

The moon begins to rise high in the sky, and my eyes begin to adjust to the darkness enough that I can make out that some of them are in their wolf forms and some in their human. The ones that are human are completely naked, as if they were in their wolf form but recently shifted back.

I keep my eyes on their faces, waiting for someone to speak to me. To tell me what they know or don't know about who and why they have Ambrose.

Shivers overtake me again, though, when I realize something odd about the faces—they're all male. Only the male members of the pack are here. I don't see any females. I don't see Rowena.

"Emeric?" I say suddenly when I see his blonde hair and a hint of a smile.

"Oh, thank gods. Ambrose is being held by a witch's spell and two vampires, maybe more, in a tree..." I trail off as Emeric doesn't respond to the words I'm saying. He shouldn't be smirking at me like that, not when Ambrose is being held hostage.

"Emeric?" my voice says hesitantly.

He runs his tongue across his lips in a seductive manner. He sees me as his next meal.

I swallow down a lump in my throat. I made a mistake. Whether the witches cast a spell on them or this is the curse driving the males of the pack into a frenzy, there is no reasoning with them. And now I'm trapped by all the male members of the Moonlight wolves, while my mate is held hostage. I made a grave mistake that there is no saving myself from, unless I can shift.

CHAPTER 32

LUMI

*S*hift.

I command my body to shift like I force air down with my next breath. But unlike my lungs, the rest of my body doesn't listen. I can't even conjure up the claws I was able to form earlier. The only thing that tells me I have any wolf blood in me at all is my eyesight—crisp as it's even been. But my eyesight won't save me.

And even if I were able to shift, I'm not sure that would save me. I'm far outnumbered.

They all take a step closer, many of them now less than five feet away from me. One easy leap for a wolf, and I'd be in any of their clutches. One snap of their jaw and they could inflict a wound that would have me bleeding out in seconds.

I don't know what's causing this behavior. And that's my first step. I can't break through whatever this is if I don't know if it's a spell, the curse, or something else.

"Emeric, what are you doing? What's happening?" I start, trying to keep my voice calm and my heartbeat regular. Any fear could cause them to react even faster.

Emeric cocks his head, studying me like he didn't know I was capable of speaking.

I suck in a breath. Maybe my words can get through whatever spell he's under. If it's the curse, I know he isn't as affected by it as the rest of them. He's so connected to Ambrose. If Ambrose is being tortured, Emeric will feel it. That's his curse. And it's my saving grace that if Emeric is still standing and not hunched over in pain, then Ambrose must be alright, at least for the moment.

They all take a step closer to me in unison. *Spell or curse?*

"Emeric, who have you talked to tonight? Did you talk with anyone before you came here?"

Emeric takes a step toward me, while the others remain frozen. All of them look at me without blinking, with an intensity that makes my skin crawl.

"Such a silly, naive wolf to think you get to ask us questions. Or that we would answer them," Emeric says, his voice deeper than I've ever heard it, almost like he's the new alpha.

I shutter. *No, Ambrose isn't dead. Emeric is just the beta. Of course, he commands the attention of the others when Ambrose isn't here.*

"What do you want?" I ask, even though I'm terrified that I already know the answer.

Emeric's lips thin in a wicked smile as he glances over his shoulder at the other males. I can see it happening even before he gives them the cue, but there is nothing I can do to stop them.

"You," he says simply, like that explains everything.

In a split second, my arms are yanked in two different directions by two different males. Another is at my neck as if holding onto my arms isn't enough to contain me. And Emeric is standing in front of me, so close that I can feel his breath against my lips. So close that he could kiss me or bite me by barely moving an inch.

I hold my breath, not wanting him to scent any of my fear. But I can't contain my wince when I feel the yank of my arms wider against my will. Nails grip my neck like a hot iron being branded into my skin.

"Ambrose will kill you for touching me. I'm not yours. I'm *his*."

Emeric shakes his head. "You're not *his*, not yet. You can't shift. You can't complete the marking ceremony. I'm not even sure if you are his mate."

I frown, searching Emeric's eyes and hoping I'll find something that tells me what the hell happened between the last time I saw him and now. This can't possibly be the same man who trained me. The same man who ripped Ambrose off me when he feared for my life. The same man who is always smiling, playful, and kind. This man is different. There isn't even a shadow of the man I knew before in his eyes.

So, which man is the real Emeric? And what the hell is happening?

"You don't believe that. You know I'm Ambrose's mate. What the hell happened to you? The witches must have cast some sort of spell. You have to fight it, Emeric. This isn't you," I say.

His eyebrow curls up, and then his tongue traces the outline of my lips.

I jerk before remembering that three male wolf shifters are holding my arms and neck, and there is no escaping. Emeric and the rest of the pack can do whatever they want to me.

"You're just a pathetic human. I don't sense any wolf blood in you."

I snarl.

"So feisty, but it won't save you. I see through you. We all do."

"What are you going to do? Kill me so Ambrose will have a new mate?"

Emeric chuckles, and the guys exchange knowing glances. I take the moment to look them all in the eyes. Every single one of the glowing yellow eyes indicates that they are the Moonlight wolves. A pack it's clear now I'll never belong to.

The pack circling the five of us have all shifted into their wolf forms, leaving the four males around me in their human forms.

"As you said, Ambrose will kill us if we kill you. But Ambrose can't see clearly. He can't see what's best for him or for the pack."

He scrapes his teeth over his bottom lip, and I can smell the scent of sex in the air. I glance down for a split second, long enough to see how hard Emeric is in his naked state. The males holding me are the same.

I narrow my eyes at him. "So you're going to rape me? Ambrose will still kill you for it."

Emeric smirks. "He won't when he comes here and sees that you begged for it."

"I'll never beg for sex from any of you."

"By the time we are through with you, Lumi, you will," he says it like it's fact, an inevitability. My heart halts to a stop for a split second. No, I refuse to believe it. I don't care what spell, curse, or dumbass thought process led them to this decision—I will not be seduced by them.

"Do your worst, but you'll regret it when Ambrose is

tearing you apart piece by piece." Because I know he will. The vampires and witches seem to be working with the Moonlight wolves this time. He's not in danger. The entire male pack wouldn't be here if he was. But they are all very much in danger. Because soon enough, he'll get free. And for me, he'll kill them all.

CHAPTER 33

LUMI

For a second, Emeric looks at me like he pities me. It's only a split second, but I see it. And then it's gone as if I imagined it.

Silently, he steps to the side. The entire pack that's been circling us parts, and all eyes face the pathway straight in front of me into the darkness of the forest.

I hold my breath, unsure of what is making its way toward us.

Please, just don't let it be Ambrose. I can't bear for him to watch whatever is about to happen. It's better if he's getting tortured by the vampires than here witnessing my pain.

But who appears is far worse than Ambrose.

"Isolde," I whisper.

She stares at me with a tight-lipped expression. Cold spreads through me as she stares like she's brought winter with her. I'm used to the cold, but this is unusually cold. I know it's her causing it.

"Are you the one who created the runes that are holding Ambrose?"

She smiles sardonically at me.

"Undo them," I command.

She tilts her head, her smile growing larger as her eyes darken.

"I wouldn't be worried about Ambrose if I were you."

I grind my teeth. "Undo the runes, the spell. Let him go." All I can think about is how he's used to being the alpha. Used to being the one saving others. And now he's powerless. He can't break his pack from whatever spell Isolde has put them under. He can't save them. We have to save him first.

She laughs. "You think you're in a position to tell me what to do?"

I growl, knowing that if my wolf doesn't appear now, there is nothing that will make it. My curse has to be that I can find my mate but do nothing about it because I can't shift.

"Who are you working for? Nyx?"

She laughs harder. "Nyx? You think I would work with that abomination?"

"You are working with vampires. Working with Nyx wouldn't be any different."

She shakes her head. "Witches would never work with Nyx or vampires."

I frown, my eyebrows narrowing. "Vampires are currently holding Ambrose hostage. If you aren't working with them, then I suggest you go handle them and free Ambrose before whatever you have planned for me."

The corner of Isolde's mouth lifts. "You really have never been around witches before in your life, have you girl?"

I don't answer, but my silence is enough for her.

"It's a basic enchantment. One to make you think the witches that are holding Ambrose were something else."

My eyes widen, and I look around at the wolves holding onto me and circling me. *How can I tell what's real and what's not if Isolde and the rest of the witches have that kind of power?*

She smirks. "You're way out of your league, girl."

"What do you want?"

"Shhh, enough talking." Isolde raises her hands as her eyes start to glow.

Fuck.

I thrash against the hold the guys have on me. I have no clue what she's about to do, but it can't be good. Their grip on me tightens, leaving no room for me to wiggle free.

Emeric isn't looking at me; he's looking at Isolde. He's my only hope. Whatever spell she cast on him, he's still in there. He's my friend. He's on my side; I know it.

"Fight it, Emeric! Fight whatever hold she has on you!"

Emeric doesn't even glance my way. His eyes are locked on Isolde.

I whip my head back to her just in time to feel the blast of her magic hit my chest with a force so powerful it's like being struck by a cannon. Yet, my body doesn't move.

I scream, but nothing comes out.

I cry, but no tears fall.

I thrash, but my body stays still, trapped in torment.

The blast feels endless, drawing out the agony until I've lost sense of time. Then, in a split second, it's over.

I exhale deeply, trying to purge that energy out. But it's trapped inside my veins. It quickly spreads through my body like a hot fire until I feel it down to the smallest of capillaries in my body.

I stare straight ahead, meeting Isolde's eyes, which have returned to their normal color and are no longer glowing. But her knowing smirk terrifies me. Whatever she did, she's pleased with herself.

"You can release her now."

The second she says the words I'm free. I yank my arms to my sides, but it doesn't matter that I have use of them again. I'm still as trapped as before, with them all surrounding me.

"What did you do to me?" I ask, still feeling the tingling warmth dance through my body.

There's a twinkle in her eyes as she glances at the males around me. They all begin to shift into their human forms one by one until they are all standing bare.

I look for any signs of anyone breaking the hold that Isolde has on them, but they are all watching me so intensely, like they all want to devour me.

Isolde takes a step back as the men take a step closer.

"Emeric?" I say, panicked, even though I don't have a lot of hope that he's broken through the spell on him and can help me. I don't have anyone else here that can help me.

But he's disappeared into the crowd of men circling me.

I take a deep breath, trying to calm myself, when suddenly I get a scent of something—the evergreen, earthy, ancient scent that wraps around me in a familiar embrace and alights an uncontrollable desire in me.

A tsunami of want and lust ripples through me, starting in my core and then spreading out along my veins and capillaries, just like Isolde's spell. My eyes shoot wide as I instantly realize what she did.

"No," I say, barely above a whisper. "No, no, no."

I meet Isolde's gaze behind the circle of guys that all smell like Ambrose. All of them.

The look she gives me is one of pure arrogance.

She won.

I lost.

I still don't understand why she thinks I'm not Ambrose's mate. I'm not sure why she hates me so much and why she wants me gone. But she succeeded. I can feel it as easily as I can feel her magic seeping into every bone in my body. There is no part of me that can escape her, and she knows it.

"Who do you want?" one of the men says to me.

I turn my gaze to the man who spoke. The one with the red hair and sultry grin.

My eyes don't stop at his eyes, though; they quickly sweep down his body, taking in his sculpted chest, rock-hard abs, and not even hesitating to soak in his large cock straining in my direction, more than happy to fulfill any fantasy I have.

I sweep through all of the men. I don't hide my perusal of them. I don't hide that I'm looking at every muscle, sharp line, and intimate part of their bodies. My cheeks don't pinken in embarrassment. Instead, my eyes darken in arousal.

They all see it, all smell it on me.

The air shifts, and I can practically feel them all howling for me to pick them. To want them. To fuck them.

Lust fills every crevice of my body. I pant heavily, and my body tingles with insatiable cravings. The urge is so strong that I know I won't be able to fight it. Short of someone snapping my neck, there is nothing that will stop me.

"I want all of you."

The red-haired man chuckles and licks his lips like he was expecting me to say that.

"Me first."

CHAPTER 34

LUMI

The others growl at the man who called dibs on me first. Surely, they've already agreed he gets to go first.

"Easy, boys. You'll all get a turn." I strip off my leather jacket and shirt, standing in my leather pants and black lace bra. Before I can remove another item of clothing, I feel at least three sets of hands on my bare skin.

No, I should stop this. I don't want this.

I gasp as one of the hands palms my breast over my bra, and another dribbles hot kisses down my neck. My skin tingles, coming more alive with each brush of his lips against my sensitive flesh. Each nip of his teeth against my neck intensifies my arousal until I'm breathless, begging for more.

Stop...

The voice in my head is weaker this time, barely remembering why I shouldn't let them touch me, kiss me, fuck me. All I can think about is how much I want them— all of them.

"Undress me," I purr, needing them to touch every intimate part of my body.

"My pleasure," a deep, growly voice says into the shell of my ear.

In the next breath, my bra is ripped from my chest, and my nipples pebble under the cool air.

I suck in a sharp breath as two hands belonging to two different men palm my breasts. I arch my back, pressing my body into their hands, wanting more of their touch. And yet...

There's a change in the air. Intense feelings wash over me as if someone is watching me from the shadows. An unease stirs in my stomach.

I close my eyes, trying to ignore the feeling. But I can't.

My eyes fly open, and when they do, they meet the glowing yellow eyes of an alpha. Ambrose is watching me from the edge of the circle.

I blink again, assuming it can't be Ambrose. It has to be my imagination; he's bound in a tree right now. But when I open them again, all I see is *him*.

His glowing eyes.

His long, wavy dark hair with flecks of gold.

His larger-than-life muscles.

It's him that I want, not these other guys. *Him—my mate.*

But even as I think it, his name begins to drift out of my mind until it's completely vanished. I know I'm supposed to know him, that he's important to me, but I can't name him. I can't remember who he is to me.

I frown as my head becomes more muddled and my thoughts become clouded.

His eyes are clear, though, as they watch me intently,

and I get a sense that he's waiting for me to do something.

I arch my back as a fingertip brushes against my pebbled nipple. Instinct tells me to close my eyes and enjoy this. It's not every day that you get ravished by an entire pack of hot men. But there is something in me that won't allow me to close my eyes. Something that won't allow me to give in to the sensations happening throughout my body.

His eyes stay locked on mine, and I swear I see his jaw tighten, but it's hard to tell from this angle.

"What do you want?" a male voice says against my ear.

Flaming desire courses through my body, settling between my legs. It's a mix of need and pain that feels like it's about to rip me apart if I don't do something about it soon.

"Pants—" I heave out a breath. "Off."

Before I can get the second word out, my pants have been ripped from my body along with my panties until the only thing left on my body are my boots. There's no chance for a chill to affect my body, as the number of hands touching me is doing more than enough to keep me warm.

I should blush at my sudden nakedness. But the painful desire I feel is too strong to feel anything else.

I exist to feel this desire.

I exist for these men to touch me. To ravish me. To make me come.

My eyes cut back to the alpha. To *him.*

"Don't fuck him. Everyone but him." A female voice I don't recognize floats through my head.

"Why not?" I think back.

"Because he will hurt you. He's not to be trusted."

I frown. He looks like he'd be a good fuck. It's a shame I can't have him.

Before I can think more about him, I feel a hand brushing over the sensitive flesh of my upper thigh.

I gasp at how intense the feeling is. I can't keep track of all the hands, of how many men are touching me, wanting me. The feeling is incredible and overwhelming at the same time.

"More—I want more," my words come out in a throaty voice.

"So do we," another male says.

"Then take it. Take it all from me."

I'm so hot, so needy. I won't survive without a cock inside me much longer. I can't comprehend what all these men could do to me, but I do know I need to be filled. I want to scream my orgasm through the woods until every man within a five-mile radius hears and wants to come to give me another.

Hands grip my thighs, and then suddenly, I'm lifted up into the air. And then it's not just the hands that I feel.

Wetness begins to coat my body as their mouths and tongues brush against my skin. Against my throat, I feel their lips sweeping kisses. Both of my nipples are sucked into two of their fiery mouths. One is taking his time running his tongue gently over the tip of my nipple before sucking gently. While the other is devouring my nipple—sucking, and licking, and nipping at it with his sharp teeth until I yelp at the mix of pleasure and pain that ripples down my body. The sound only makes the man work harder on my breast.

My thighs are spread wider, and I can hear a bit of a scuffle at my feet.

I smirk. They are fighting over who gets to take the space between my legs. But they are taking too long.

I need...need...need...

Fingers dance up my inner thighs on each side of my legs. They tease me, but do not draw close enough to the apex between my thighs.

"Please," I beg them. "Please touch me."

Low growls ripple through every man around me.

I shouldn't be greedy. I should be patient. There are already so many men's hands on my body that I can't keep track of them all. But none of them are touching me where I need them.

My eyes blaze with desire as I look from one face to the next, waiting for any of them to touch me like I need them to. To be the first of them to fuck me. To dampen this uncontrollable desire ripping through me.

They all look at me like they'd be happy to oblige, but there still seems to be a scuffle that I can't see happening past my feet.

A bark rings out, followed by a loud growl that grabs everyone's attention.

I grin, knowing it can only mean one thing. The fight has ended, and one of them has won.

Anticipation races up my body, and I can barely stay still even though I'm being held up in the air by several strong arms. I lick my lip, waiting for the man to come into view—the winner.

It doesn't matter what he looks like. I want them all. I don't care who's first and who's last.

A man steps from the shadows and settles between my legs.

I gasp at the sight of him. He's beautiful with his sweeping blonde hair, long black eyelashes, and crystal blue eyes. But that's not the part of him I care about. My eyes roll down his body, quickly assessing whether he'll be able to do the job or not.

I bite my lip when I see what's hanging between his legs. Hard, long, and ready to impale me—his cock has me drooling.

"Like what you see?" his deep voice asks.

"Let's see if you know how to use it."

He chuckles. "I think you'll be more than pleased." He starts to walk between my legs as the other hands continue to tease and taunt my body. Flicking and rolling my nipple between their fingers, brushing the shell of my ear, dancing up my thighs.

I'm going to combust as soon as this male touches me. I know it. I almost want to tell the others to slow down so I can savor this moment. But I'm too riled up, too needy.

I try to buck my hips, try to strain closer so he will get to me faster. But the man is taking his sweet, sweet time crossing the couple of feet to me.

He's so close.

And then, he kneels.

My jaw slackens. "Wait—" I start, needing him standing so he can fuck me. But then a hot breath blows over my pussy, and his tongue licks up my slit.

I shutter at the heat of his tongue. My thighs begin to squeeze tight before strong hands pull me apart wider, not letting my thighs move an inch together.

The second this man's tongue touches my pussy, he becomes ravenous. It's like he tasted me and now needs to taste every fucking drop of me.

His tongue sweeps up and down my slit, making me squirm and writhe in the men's arms until I'm not sure if they are going to be able to hold me up. The moans slipping from my throat and parted lips are constant. Each lick of his tongue against me has me on the edge of an orgasm that may break the spell I'm under.

I frown as the word spell spills into my head. I don't know why it gives me pause, but it does.

Until his teeth nip at my clit, and then his tongue dips inside me.

"More," I moan, not able to say more. But I need more than this. I need to feel his cock slamming inside me. That's the only thing I can think about. It's my all-consuming thought.

I need your cock. I need you to fuck me. The thoughts float through my head over and over and over again.

But the man isn't listening. His tongue is still torturing my clit and then trying to fill me. His tongue, while incredible, could never replace his cock.

"Fuck me," I finally bark out the order.

I can feel his smile against me at the command. Then I feel the cool breeze against my bare, swollen lips again.

I crane my head, looking down to see if he's finally going to fuck me. But what I see isn't the man. What I see are the most intense glowing golden eyes I've ever seen. All of their eyes are glowing and yellow right now. But this man's are brighter and more intense than anyone else's.

There's something I'm missing, something I've forgotten.

I feel something pressing at my entrance. Something hard and slick and straining. But I don't acknowledge it. I don't want it. Those eyes.

Him.

Alpha.

My mate.

Ambrose.

"Stop!" I yell as everything floods back into my head. The uncontrollable desire I have to fuck every man in sight sputters into nothing. The desire instantly cools in my belly, and I realize in horror what I almost willingly did. I wasn't even fighting it. I was letting it control me.

I don't expect the man to stop. They are all under the same spell I was. They won't stop. They can't stop.

But suddenly, I'm being lowered to the ground until my boots hit the earth below me. The hands leave my body, and a path is made between the men and Ambrose.

Suddenly, I'm very aware that I'm naked. I wrap my arms around my body. My cheeks pinken in embarrassment, but I don't let myself tear my eyes from Ambrose. I'm terrified he'll reject me after what he just witnessed.

I open my mouth to try to explain, but he moves to me in an instant and takes my hand in his, brushing a soft kiss against my palm.

"Welcome to the Moonlight Pack."

CHAPTER 35

LUMI

"What?" I ask, staring at Ambrose in disbelief. My head is still clouded and fuzzy. My heart is still beating so fast and loudly that I'm sure it's the only thing anyone can hear.

Ambrose smiles at me softly, as if he knows the hell I just went through and he's sorry.

"That was the Moonlight pack initiation," he says.

I blink, trying to process the words leaving his mouth. I must still be dreaming. I must still be held captive while one of the pack members fucks me, and this is how I'm coping with it—inventing this fantasy.

Ambrose's smile turns to concern as he watches my reaction. "You passed. It was just a test to see if you are worthy of being part of the Moonlight pack."

"It was all a test? Initiation?" I say the words back like they are a foreign language.

He tucks me under his shoulder, pulling me tight to his body as the rest of the pack hoops and hollers in celebration. But my brain still can't process what happened or why.

The male pack members that seemed under a spell before are smiling at me like I'm their sister, not like they just tried to fuck me. None of them are clothed, though, and some have shifted into their wolf forms as they jog and dance around us, howling into the night sky.

"It was all just an act? They were never spelled?" I ask.

"No, Isolde spelled everyone. The initiation has to be real," Ambrose replies.

"So if I hadn't broken free of her spell…" I can't say the next words out loud, so I use our bond instead. *"They would have all taken turns fucking me. And then what?"*

"Yes, and you wouldn't be able to join the Moonlight pack. At least, not until you proved yourself worthy in a different way."

I chew on my bottom lip, realizing how close I was to that happening. *"And you wouldn't have accepted me as your mate…"*

Ambrose halts, lifting my chin to stare into my watering eyes. *"You will always be my mate. Nothing you do will ever change that. But I had complete faith in you that you would be able to break through Isolde's spell."*

"How? How did you know I could? What if I wasn't strong enough?"

He smiles sweetly, his glowing eyes softening once again. *"Because you're my queen. My mate. You're mine in every way. My equal. I knew you'd be strong enough. I knew you'd break free of her spell. I was never worried."*

I shiver and wrap my arms around myself, still very aware of how naked I am.

"Emeric," Ambrose shouts.

I look over my shoulder to see Emeric jogging up, his large, bright smile on his face."Here you go." He hands

Ambrose my clothes. Ambrose takes my leather jacket from him and wraps it around my shoulders, which I expect is supposed to help with my chill, but it does little to cover my nakedness.

Emeric looks at me but avoids looking anywhere but my eyes. "I'm sorry. I really—"

"I'm sorry, too," I sputter out, partly because I am truly sorry and partly because I can't stand to hear him apologize. I can barely process what happened. I can't cope with the words I should use to describe what almost happened to me, to all of us. I don't know if I'll ever be able to heal from what could have happened.

He frowns. "What do you have to be sorry for?"

"I'm sorry I didn't break free of the spell faster to avoid putting us all through that."

"I've never seen someone break free of a spell so quickly."

My eyebrows furrow. "What do you mean?"

"It's how our initiation works. It always involves a witch casting a spell and having to break free of it. The spell Isolde cast was stronger than any I've ever felt before." Emeric pauses, looking at me in awe. "You're incredible."

I shake my head. "I'm not."

Emeric sighs but turns his attention to Ambrose. "You okay?"

Ambrose nods, his throat bobbing.

I look from Ambrose to Emeric and then back to Emeric before remembering that Emeric feels Ambrose's pain. "What did Isolde do to you?"

Emeric starts to open his mouth to speak, but Ambrose silences him with one look.

"I'm going to kill Isolde," I say.

Ambrose smiles at me gently. "As much as I'd love to see that, we need to finish the initiation."

My eyes widen in fear.

He leans down and kisses my jawline softly. "No more tests. Just magic to officially make you part of the Moonlight pack."

I relax into his side as he wraps his arms around me. "I don't like her."

"She's harmless. Her coven has been working with the Moonlight pack for decades. She plays her part well. We are all trained to hate the witches, but Isolde and her coven are set on helping to break the curse. They are on our side."

He kisses my hair and any ill will I feel toward her melts away. I feel so safe in his arms, so loved.

My heart flutters at that thought. *Is this love? Are we falling in love?*

Those thoughts immediately disappear when I see Isolde approaching us. The others begin circling around us, and despite Ambrose's arms and reassurance that there are no more tests, the fear flutters back into my chest.

Isolde and I stare each other down, much in the same way we did when she had cast a spell over me.

"I wasn't sure if you were strong enough. I'm glad to be proven wrong," Isolde says to me.

I growl. "Don't ever hurt my pack again. Not even for some test."

Isolde raises her eyebrows and smirks as she looks from me to Ambrose. "You found yourself a feisty one. You still sure about her?"

I move to pummel her, but Ambrose holds me tight in his arms, as cool and calm as ever. "More than sure."

Isolde addresses the circle of Moonlight pack members. "Do you find Lumi worthy of joining the Moonlight pack?"

An overwhelming sound of yeses and howling fills the air. And when I look into each of their eyes I see the joy, the hope. They all have hope that I'll be the one to lift the curse.

I will be. I know it.

Isolde just nods, then turns to Ambrose. "And do you, Ambrose, as alpha of the Moonlight pack, accept Lumi into the pack?"

"Yes, she's always been a Moonlight pack member."

And then Isolde turns to me. "Do you, Lumi, wish to join the Moonlight pack?"

I raise an eyebrow as if I'd go through all of that if I didn't wish to join.

"Yes."

Isolde holds out her hands. And just like earlier, I can see and feel the magic she is spinning. I don't know whether I want to hide behind Ambrose or attack her and rip her throat out.

"It's okay. She's just making you part of the Moonlight pack. She won't hurt you. I won't let anyone hurt you," Ambrose says through our bond.

I nod and take a step away from Ambrose, knowing that even though we aren't touching, he's with me.

Isolde smirks at me in her vicious way a second before the blast hits me. I'm not sure what to expect, but it's nothing like the last time. This time, I feel the intensity, but it's like a warm, gentle river flowing through me, slowly finding every vein, nerve, and muscle in my body. The energy is moonlight. It's bright and welcoming.

I smile at the feeling. When I open my eyes and see the entire Moonlight pack smiling at me, my own smile gets brighter.

Rowena and Emeric are the first to run up and congratulate me.

"I'm sorry," Rowena whispers to me with tears in her eyes.

I shake my head. She prepared me as best as she could. I don't know where she appeared from, but I'm glad she's here.

Emeric lifts me up on his shoulders before I protest. I barely grip his hair as he starts running, and before I realize what's happening, he's shifted into his wolf form, and I'm riding on his back next to the entire Moonlight pack.

I've never felt this free or this sense of belonging, even within my own family. A tear rolls down my cheek, though, thinking of my family, of my pack—or former pack.

They are truly all gone. If they weren't, then this initiation might not have worked. My father is dead.

Another tear falls as I think about all I've lost tonight. My father, my family, my pack, and I almost lost...

I shake my head, refusing to think of myself as a victim. I refuse to think of what could have happened and just exist in the hope of my new pack.

Ambrose's large wolf form, practically glowing as bright as the moonlight, jogs up next to us. He tilts his head, motioning for me to jump from Emeric's back to his.

I should be embarrassed that I have to ride on their backs, that I can't shift like everyone else here can. But tonight, I'm not. Tonight, I proved myself. I'll worry about the lack of shifting tomorrow.

So when I climb onto Ambrose's back, I do it proudly. A tiny thrill shoots through me when Ambrose starts running in the opposite direction of the pack.

"I want you to myself tonight."

CHAPTER 36

LUMI

Ambrose slows to a stop, and I slowly climb down from his back. In a second, his golden smile is staring at me, and his fur is replaced with flesh and blood and skin that I long to sink my teeth into. To tear apart and devour in equal measures. To claim and ruin.

He has the audacity to just stand there looking like every fantasy man I've ever imagined with a smug smile.

"My queen, I knew you were the one. I knew it." His eyes light up as he speaks, like everything inside him believes the words he speaks.

I shake my head. "I barely broke free of that spell, and at the very last second. I'm not the one at all." I sigh, letting my head fall while trying not to think about how I would have traumatized us all if I had waited even a few seconds longer to break free of the spell.

He tilts my chin up to look at him. "You're the one."

"The one? What does that mean?"

"It means you will be the one to break the curse."

"I can't."

"You don't get it—"

"No, you don't get it! I can't shift! We can't complete the marking ceremony. I'm weak. I—"

His lips crash down on mine, shutting me up. And for a moment, I didn't realize how much I needed to just be kissed. To stop overthinking and worrying that I'm not enough. When his lips are on mine, I'm more than enough.

The heat of his body presses hard against mine as his hand tangles in my hair, holding me tight against him. I melt into him, loving that we are both naked and that my leather jacket is the only thing clinging to me other than him.

Suddenly, he stops the kiss, leaving me gasping for more.

"You are not weak. You are a Moonlight pack member now. You are my mate. You are my queen. The Moonlight pack's queen. You are more than enough. You proved that tonight. No one has broken through a spell like that before."

"What do you mean?" I cock my head up at him.

"I mean, usually, the initiation takes the pack members far longer to break through the spell. Enduring the worst pain. Their worst nightmares. It takes hours, sometimes days before they break through the spell, if they can break through at all. It never involves someone breaking through the spell that quickly. You are powerful —more powerful than any of us."

I scoff, looking him up and down. "I'm not stronger than you."

"Strength isn't just about physical muscles. And the strength and power you have is like nothing I've ever seen."

I hold my breath, not sure how to respond.

"You can complete the marking ceremony, whether you can shift yet or not. But after tonight, I have no doubt that you'll be able to shift soon. You just have so much power and strength in you. Your body needs to make sure you're ready for the shift first. When you shift, when you tap into that physical strength, you'll be unstoppable."

"You think so?"

He nods, his eyes bearing into my soul. "It's your choice if you want to complete the ceremony before you learn to shift. But you'll survive. I have no doubt about that, just like I had no doubt about tonight."

When he looks at me, there's an undeniable tingling in my body, something so deep and raw.

"But we don't have time, do we?"

His eyes glaze over. "Not really."

I want to know why we don't have time. I want to know all the truths, but I'm not sure I'm ready to ask or hear the answer tonight. Not after everything I've been through.

A part of me just wants to curl up in bed and sleep until I've forgotten this entire nightmare. But the other part...

Before I get a chance to gather the courage to ask, Ambrose's eyes are smiling down at my chest and belly.

I follow his gaze and nearly jump out of my skin. "What is that?"

Ambrose runs his fingers gently over the glowing marks on my chest and belly. "They are runes, magical marks to tell the world you belong to the Moonlight wolves. Everyone in the Moonlight pack has them."

I frown, faintly remembering seeing a hint of a glow

on Ambrose before but that's it. "Why haven't I noticed them before?"

"The curse. The magic isn't as strong as it used to be. Now, only other pack members can see the runes. They'll help protect you and help you fight your individual curse."

I trace my finger over the crested moon surrounded by an intricate design that expands from the middle of my chest across the upper curves of my breasts. I look at him with heavy eyes and see a similar design across his chest. His is darker and twice as large, expanding across his entire chest. I see flickers of lines forming all over his arms and shoulders that begin to dip around to his back. He's covered in the golden marks. *Beautiful.*

"What's my curse?"

He shakes his head. "I'll know when you know."

"How?"

He looks up at the moon and then back at me, like he doesn't want to torture me anymore tonight. And telling me the truth is torture for him. I can't handle any more torture. I can't handle any more pain.

"Kiss me. Fuck me. Make us both forget for the rest of the night." *Forget that I was almost raped by the entire Moonlight pack against all of our wills.*

He opens his mouth to most likely argue with me that I'm not safe with him, but I'm not having it.

"I proved myself more than capable tonight. I'm safe. I trust you," I plead confidently.

His eyes scan mine for any sense of doubt.

I look him dead in the eye, challenging him in the only way I know how.

Ever so slowly, he lowers his lips back to mine, close

enough that they brush against mine but not close enough that he's actually kissing me.

I suck in a deep breath, waiting for him.

"I trust you, too, my queen. I trust that you're strong enough, strong enough to handle me. To truly be my equal."

His kiss lands, and then he's devouring me like he's been waiting for me his whole life. When his lips press against mine, I realize I've been waiting for him, too.

The jacket that was my lifeline protecting what was left of my modesty is tossed to the ground, and I wrap my arms around his neck to keep from immediately grabbing onto other areas of his body that seem far too quick to be touching.

But after Isolde cast that spell on me, I'm horny as hell and desperate for that kind of connection. I'm still not sure Ambrose is going to give me this after denying me so many times before.

"*Your thoughts are loud,*" Ambrose says into my head while smiling against my lips.

I blush. "*I didn't say anything.*"

"*You did, my queen. You did. And don't worry, I'm not stopping until you're completely satisfied tonight.*"

"*Promise? Because we've come close before and—*"

His lips crash in a demanding kiss that has me stumbling backward before he grabs my hips and stops me from tumbling to the ground. All of his body is pressed against me—his lips, his hard chest, and his long, thickening cock is stretched between my legs. His hand roams up and down my body, warming me from the swell of my breast down to my hip bone.

"*I've never wanted anyone more,*" he says while simultaneously kissing me as hard as physically possible. And then he pulls away, leaving me gaping for more. "I've never wanted anyone more. If you want this, then I won't stop it —not anymore. I won't deny either of us what we want. I want you. I've wanted you since the moment I saw you at the offering. It's been torture to deny either of us," he says.

I'm speechless; I don't know what else to say. I'm grinning from ear to ear, not believing that this incredible man, this alpha, is mine. That I can finally have him. Nothing else can come between us, not anymore.

I'm confident that we are mates. I can complete the marking ceremony whether I can shift or not. There is nothing left that can get in our way.

The way Ambrose looks at me is like he's never seen anyone so perfect. Like I'm the thing he's been searching his whole life for, and he can't wait to claim me fully. There might be a marking ceremony later, but tonight is the night we make it official. Tonight is the night that we decide for ourselves that we are mates. We are enough for each other.

"But you might not want me to fuck me once you find out the truth," he says through the bond.

I frown.

"Nothing will make me not want to fuck you," I say out loud instead of silently in his head. He needs me to hear that I want to fuck him as much as I needed to hear him speak the words out loud.

"Ask me."

I narrow my eyebrows at him as he grips me harder, like he's fighting with himself. He's holding onto me desperately like he thinks I'm about to bolt.

But I'm not sure what he wants me to ask.

"Ask me. Ask me the thing you're most curious about.

You already know Emeric and Rowena's curse. Ask me mine."

I swallow hard, and my heart beats rapidly. I'm terrified to ask, but I don't want him to know that. I want him to think that whatever he has to tell me, it will be okay. Because it will be.

I take a deep breath, calming my body in his arms.

"I want you. Whatever your curse is, we will deal with it together. It won't change what I want." I kiss him passionately, sweeping my tongue across the seam of his lips to prove my point.

His expression doesn't change. The fear in his eyes doesn't leave. He hesitates for just a second and then says, "My curse is I can't fall in love. If I do, they die."

CHAPTER 37
LUMI

They die...

His words settle into me like ice, spreading until it's invaded all the comfort I felt seconds before.

I have so many questions. So many things to ask, but I don't know where to start.

"I know because it's happened before. I loved someone, and they died because of it," he says into my head.

I look up at him with wide, sad eyes, still unable to speak.

"When you realize what your curse is, you'll know deep in your soul the truth of it. There is no doubt. You feel it in every bone of your body. So, saying your curse is that you can't shift isn't true. You would have no doubt if it were."

I rake my teeth over my bottom lip, wanting to find the right words.

"I'm sorry."

I frown. *"For what? It's a curse. You didn't ask for this."*

He pauses as if waiting for me to figure out why I

should be angry with him. *"For wanting you. For letting things between us get this far. For letting you in. For giving you hope. For wanting you despite never being able to give you more. For not telling you my curse from the beginning."*

"You still think we are mates?"

He nods.

"I do, too. There was nothing you could do to stop this. Nothing. We were predestined. If I have to die—"

"NO!" he growls aloud. *"No, you won't die. I won't let you."*

"But that means..."

"I'll never let myself love you. I'll never fall fully for you. I can like you. I can fuck you. I can be a good mate. But that's it. I won't allow myself to love you, to kill you. Not until we are successful in breaking the curse."

I hold my breath at his words. *"Can you really do that? Not fall in love with your mate?"*

Moisture fills his eyes. *"I'll have to. The alternate is more than I can bear."*

What is the line between caring about someone and loving them? And how close is Ambrose already to that line?

I can't think about that. I can't think about the fact that this man holds my fate in his hands. That if he can't stop himself from loving me, I die. And if he succeeds, then I spend a lifetime with a man who can never love me, unless we break the curse.

"What happens if I fall in love with you?" I ask quietly out loud.

"Nothing. You'd make me the happiest man on earth, despite the fact that I don't deserve to be loved."

I let out a rattled breath. That was what I was most afraid of, I realize. Not him loving me, but me falling for him.

"Who knows your curse?"

"Just you. No one else knows what my curse is."

My eyes widen at that, but his hand strokes my cheek, touching me for the first time since he started this conversation.

There's a tenderness, a vulnerability in his eyes. *"I should let you go."*

"Impossible," I say.

The corners of his mouth lift. *"Probably, but I should still do it."*

I shake my head. *"We will break the curse. Us being mates and completing the ceremony will break the curse. We won't have to live like this for long."*

"You're incredible, my queen. Even when I can fall in love with you, it won't be what you deserve."

I let my forehead rest against his. *"It will be more."*

And then I catch his lips with mine before he can stop me.

"I'm not afraid of this," I tell him.

He shivers at my words but doesn't stop the kiss. He keeps to his word. He won't be the one to stop this—not anymore. I have all the control. And there is nothing that is going to stop me this time.

I release his lips long enough for us to catch our breaths, when he says. "I'm terrified."

He doesn't speak the words into my head. It's one of the only words he's spoken out loud since he brought me here. I don't know if he speaks them to get me to reconsider, to try and save me, or if he says them simply because they are the truth.

"I'm not," I say, and I mean the words more than I've meant anything I've ever spoken to him. I can't explain the connection I have to this man. I can't explain why my heart beats only for him. I can't explain why I'm not afraid of his curse or my own.

His lips hitch up as he realizes through his wolf senses that I'm telling the truth. I'm not afraid of this, not when I'm with him.

When I reach up, he lowers his head and engulfs me in a kiss that is full of all the heat and passion we've had since the second we laid eyes on each other.

We both moan in unison as if, with this kiss, we are finally giving in. Nothing is going to hold us back anymore.

"I need you, all of you," he whispers into my ear before tracing his tongue over the sensitive flesh there.

I tremble in his arms. "I need all of you now, or I just might die."

There's a twinkle in his eyes at my words. Then he looks around at where we are and frowns.

"What?" I ask.

"I should have brought you back to my house, not the middle of the forest."

I chuckle lightly, stroking his bicep. "I don't care where we are. I don't care if you take me against that tree or on the ground with a stick digging into my back. I just want you."

"We could run back to the house."

I growl. "No, I can't wait. You've made me wait far too long already. And after Isolde did her little spell on me, I'm horny as hell and will curse you myself if you make me wait any longer."

He grabs my hips at that and yanks our bodies flush together until I can feel every bit of him. He's so fucking hard against my softness.

He runs his hand through my hair, pulling it loose from the ponytail it's been in all night. "You're so beautiful, my queen."

I swallow down the lump in my throat as warmth spreads once again throughout my body, just from how he's looking at me.

"Touch me," I whisper.

He laughs. "So demanding, my queen. I'm not going to rush this."

"You couldn't possibly move any slower than you already are."

He smirks, and I feel like I've just issued a challenge that he's more than happy to accept.

"No," I growl, but it comes out as a whimper as he takes the opportunity to kiss my neck. So. Fucking. Slowly. But gods, does it feel good. I melt into his kiss, unable to think whenever his lips are on me.

"I want you spread before me so I can worship every part of your body before, during, and after I fuck you."

I grin. "Yes, please."

Before the words leave my mouth, I find myself on the ground with Ambrose hovering over me with a vicious smile on his lips as his eyes glow bright again. The ground is hard beneath me, the soft moss we are lying on is not doing much to warm or soften the ground. But I could care less where we are or how uncomfortable the ground is. All I want is him. Now.

"Fuck, I can't believe you're mine."

I blush. "Technically, I'm not yours yet. Not until that monster cock of yours enters me."

"So impatient." He kisses me tenderly as our fingers interlink, and he stretches my arms over my head, exposing all of my body to him. Starting at my neck, he kisses down until he reaches the swell of my breasts, where the glowing rune is inked into my flesh.

Shadows swell in his eyes as his body hardens on top of me. His tongue laps over the marks as his hair brushes over my skin. I expect them to be sensitive, like a tattoo fresh on my skin. But the marks aren't a tattoo; they're magic. His tongue sends a rush of hunger over my heated skin.

I bite my lip, trying to stifle my moans as his tongue sweeps down over each nipple. Wetness pools between my legs, and I know he can feel it dripping onto his cock, as it's pushed hard against my opening without entering me.

"Please," I whimper, not sure I'll survive if he doesn't fuck me soon.

He responds by moving his lips lower down my body until his cock moves from the sweet spot where I've been aching all night for him. Our fingers are still linked as he kisses over my mound, and I willingly spread my legs for him.

He breathes over my clit, and I shiver despite not being the least bit cold. And then his tongue licks over the sensitive bundle of nerves. With that simple sweep, I feel like I'm about to combust. Shockwaves shoot through my body.

"Ambrose, I can't…"

"I know."

And then I feel him at my slick entrance, and suddenly, there's a drop of fear. I squeeze my eyes shut, terrified of what's about to happen, as memories of earlier tonight start flashing through my thoughts.

Hands, so many hands are gripping me. I'm not on the forest floor but held in the air. A rougher tongue is licking me. And...

"Look at me, Lumi."

I take a deep breath, and then I open my eyes, hating that he can see the fear that decided to make a reappearance at the worst possible moment.

"I'm sorry—I'm so sorry about what happened to you. I didn't have any control over what your initiation would be, and if I had known, I would have never allowed you to initiate. I hate that you went through that. We don't have to do this—"

"Yes, we do. I want this. I don't know why the thoughts flickered into my head. It's not like anything really happened. I broke free of the spell before anything could."

Concern fills his eyes. "Don't do that. That wasn't nothing. If I could take the memory away, I would."

"You can. Replace it with you. Make everything we went through worth it."

"Are you sure?" He studies me closely, like my body might betray me despite what I say.

"Yes."

"Is this your first time?"

My mouth falls open, shocked that he knows that. I'm twenty-one, and I've never been fucked. Never had a one-night stand. Never had a real lover. But I can't hide that fact from him.

"Yes," I breathe, my voice trembling.

He releases one of my hands long enough to stroke his thumb across my lower lip. "You have nothing to be afraid of. I won't hurt you."

I blush. "I'm not afraid of the pain of fucking a man for the first time. I'm afraid of what it means. What if we realize we aren't mates?" *What if the thoughts of what happened earlier tonight flood my head again?*

His eyes widen in shock. "Not possible. We are mates. Sexual compatibility won't change anything. And even if the first time isn't as magical as I know it will be, we have time to practice and make it better. And I plan on practicing over and over and over until I learn every erotic place on your body."

I smile up at him.

"And trust me, you'll only think of me when I fuck you."

I gasp as I realize he heard my thoughts.

"I'll be gentle. I won't hurt you."

I shake my head. "Don't. Fuck me like you want me. Like you wanted to before you found out I was a virgin."

He doesn't respond. But as his lips press against mine, I feel him entering my body in one hard thrust, giving me exactly what I asked for.

I'm flooded with feeling as I'm stretched so much that I don't know how he fits inside me. The sound that leaves my mouth is a mix of a gasp and moan and scream. My eyes water and then squeeze shut. My body tenses. My nails dig into his back. I can't move.

"Open your eyes, my queen."

I do, obeying him even though I'm terrified he'll see how much pain I'm in and stop. But when I look into his eyes, all the pain I was feeling disappears. The doubt vanishes. All I see is the eyes of the most caring man who's ever wanted me.

His eyes say what his mouth can't. That he'd love me if he could. That he'd give me the universe.

And then suddenly, he's moving inside me. Rocking so

gently as he caresses every muscle in my body until the tension melts away. He angles our bodies together so that his lower abs rub over my clit as he pushes deeper and deeper into my body. But this time, as he goes deeper, I don't tense. I don't feel anything but the pleasure he's giving me.

And then, he changes. Not physically—physically, he's still the gorgeous man that I'm addicted to in every way. But he unleashes a little of the wolf that's inside him.

I bite back a grin, knowing that, in this moment, everything is about to change.

His thrusts change in urgency and need. He becomes ravenous in his kisses as he dips deeper into me.

"You're so beautiful," he says, showing me that he's still in control of himself.

I groan into his mouth, unsure of how he's able to speak as I'm completely ragged and at his mercy.

He grips my waist, and I get a twinkle of warning before he rolls us, and I'm suddenly straddling him. He lifts me up and down on his thick length as he marvels up at me.

He opens his mouth to speak, but it seems he's finally speechless.

"Gods, you feel incredible. You squeeze me so tightly."

I rock down over his cock, letting my instincts take over as my nails sink into his firm chest.

He gasps as I do.

"I'll never get enough of this, Ambrose."

He rolls us again, filling me in such a hard stroke that I'm going to feel it for years.

"Me neither."

His lips capture mine, and all thoughts vanish as he thrusts faster into my body. Faster and faster and faster we rock together on the floor of the forest. I should feel every rock and stick in my back. I should feel the cool breeze. But all I feel is him. His hard cock filling every inch of me. His fingers rubbing on my clit. His other hand wrapped behind my neck as his kisses sweep me into another dimension.

We roll again and again, each taking a turn at riding the other. But I want more. I want it all.

Heat sweeps through me, giving me pause. It's the same heat I felt the last time I was with Ambrose. I'm too hot, but I can't let this end.

Desperation cracks through me. As much as I want to shift, this isn't the moment. I need to finish this with Ambrose as myself.

If he notices the heat overwhelming my body, it doesn't stop him.

"I can't stop." There's a slight panic in his voice.

Well, that answers that question.

"I don't want you to. I don't need you to." I frantically kiss him, afraid my words won't be enough. That he'll find a way to stop this. And that might just kill me.

"Let go." His voice is a gentle caress in my head, sweet and comforting.

"I can't. I'll shift and hurt you."

"You could never hurt me."

"If I shift with you still inside me, I will."

A glint of amusement flickers in his storm-filled eyes. *"Let go, Lumi."*

I squeeze my eyes shut, holding on to the thin line of control I have left as sweat beads across my forehead.

Ambrose doesn't ease up; he thrusts harder as he strokes my clit with his thumb. His lips continue to kiss me in a punishing rhythm. There is no escaping this, no stopping it.

"Let go, Lumi. Trust me. Nothing bad will happen. I've got you."

A power ripples through me, squashing any control I have left, and I do what Ambrose says, I let go.

A beautiful torrent of pleasure cascades through my body in pulsing waves. I scream his name as my body feels like it's being ripped apart in the most wonderful way as he continues to sink into me over and over. I ride my orgasm into blissful aftershocks that do nothing to dampen the heat in my body.

And then, he unravels inside me. I clutch onto his neck, holding on as he spills more and more of himself into me.

Our lips part as we pant into each other. The world stills, and I realize I didn't shift. That the intense feeling wasn't me about to shift; it was me about to come.

"My beautiful queen." He grins down at me as he strokes his fingers through my hair.

"What did you do to me?" I mutter, barely able to speak.

He grins. "Gave you everything I can. For now, at least." There's a hungry promise in those words that he'll find a way to give me so much more.

"It was more than enough."

"Are you okay?" I hear Ambrose's worried voice.

"More than okay." My grin spreads wide across my face as my cheeks heat in a steady blush.

He's my mate. I'm sure of it.

And I can shift; I know it.

Given the right circumstances, I'll be able to shift. I

felt her, my wolf, during that orgasm. She's finally ready. She was just waiting for the other piece of my soul.

I open my mouth to speak, to tell Ambrose about what happened. To tell him everything.

He shakes his head. "Don't—don't tell me. Not yet. Not until I can share the feeling."

CHAPTER 38
LUMI

A loud knocking forces my eyes to fly open, but the warm arm tightening around my waist keeps me in bed.

"Ignore it," Ambrose says in a gruff voice.

I let my eyes fall shut and snuggle into his shoulder again.

But the knocking restarts.

We both groan.

"It's kind of hard to ignore."

"It's just Rowena or Emeric. Both can go the fuck away," Ambrose barks at the door.

"Don't try to alpha command me. It's noon, and as Lumi's best friend, I'm entitled to hear everything about what happened last night. At least prove to me that she's still alive, and I'll go away," Rowena says through the door.

I grin as Ambrose glares at the door. "I'm kicking you out of the pack." But as he says it, Rowena pushes into our room. The second she sees both of us naked in bed together, she squeals and runs over to my side of the bed.

"Oh my gods! It's true! You're a Moonlight pack member, and you two..." She motions between the two of us.

I grin, nodding as my cheeks redden to uncontrollable levels. I can't believe she's bold enough to be in here, acting like Ambrose doesn't even exist.

She squeals again and tosses two coffee cups she's holding onto the nightstand before climbing up on the bed and pulling me into a tight hug.

"I knew it! I knew it! I knew it!"

As she pulls me to her, the covers fall from my body.

"Um, Rowena..."

She stares at my nakedness and rolls her eyes as she straddles my legs. "You really need to get over being ashamed of your body. You're a wolf shifter. We're naked for half our lives. We spend a lot of time naked; get used to it."

I crinkle my eyes. "Well, I'm not going to get used to it while I'm in Ambrose's bed with his ex sitting on top of me."

She scoffs and then reaches over and rustles Ambrose's hair. "We are old news. But you two! Finally, I was so sick of trying to keep the two of you away from each other and these other men away from you."

"Out," Ambrose says pointedly to Rowena.

"I brought coffee." She reaches over and snatches the coffee cups back up off the nightstand and holds them out to us.

"Out," Ambrose says again, snatching a cup from her hand.

She smirks, still holding out my coffee while straddling my thighs. I take the cup from her. "Thanks."

"Shower and get dressed. I want to hear all the details

and introduce you to the rest of the pack." She leans in and takes a good whiff of me. "Although, showering isn't going to wash away your new smell."

"Rowena," Ambrose says in a warning tone. I'm not sure if he actually gives her an alpha command or if she willingly starts to retreat, but a few moments later, Ambrose and I are alone in his bedroom again.

"You don't have to go with her. You don't have to tell her anything. You can stay in bed with me all day," he says with a grin.

I bite my lower lip, trying to hide my excitement at that idea. But then I roll toward him and wince at my soreness.

He frowns but kisses me sweetly on the cheek. "You can also spend the day soaking in the tub while I massage you until your soreness melts away. Then I can try my best to make you deliciously sore all over again."

I stare at the door, considering my options. "She's just going to come back."

"I'll throw her out of the pack." He kisses my neck, and heat floods my body. I'm desperate for him again, even though that's exactly how I spent my entire night— having him over and over and over. We probably only got an hour of sleep.

There's a knock at the door. "Ambrose, you're supposed to be meeting with Isolde to discuss the marking ceremony next week in about an hour," Emeric says through the door.

The desire immediately vanishes from my body. *Well, there goes that idea.*

"I'm going to go meet up with Rowena, unless you want me to go to the meeting with you?"

He shakes his head, pulling me tighter against his naked body. "No, go. You'll have more fun with Rowena."

I kiss him as I begin to move off the bed, but the kiss pulls me back in. I forget what I'm supposed to be doing the second his tongue sweeps into my mouth. He's the only thing I can think about. He consumes everything in me.

Another knock at the door brings us both back to reality.

"You're still up for doing the marking ceremony? Even if you haven't learned to shift yet?"

I nod. "Yes." My eyes blaze as I look at him. And for the first time, I don't doubt that I'll survive the marking. Ambrose will ensure I survive, and I'm strong enough to endure it.

"Stop looking at me like that, or I'm never letting you leave," he warns.

I run my tongue across my bottom lip and watch him nearly come undone. The only thing that stops him is Emeric opening the door.

I freeze, standing completely naked next to the bed, but Emeric doesn't so much as look in my direction. And Ambrose doesn't seem bothered that another man is in the same room as us while I'm naked.

It's so strange to me, but I guess I have to get used to it.

———

"TELL ME EVERYTHING," Rowena says when I've finally showered and dressed. We're walking away from Ambrose's house, and Rowena has promised to introduce me to everyone, but right now, it's me who has to spill.

I blush, and my entire body heats with thoughts of what we did. But I have no idea what to share with her, especially considering how she and Ambrose used to date.

"Oh my gods, look at you! The only part of you that isn't red is your hair."

My cheeks redden even more as we walk. "I'm just not sure I can talk to you about any of this."

"Now I really need to know. How was it? Was it the best sex you ever had? Did you feel the mating bond practically cement between you? Was it rough? Did you shift? He didn't hurt you, did he? Because if he did, I'm going to kick his—"

"He didn't hurt me! It was…" I don't know how to finish my sentence. It was everything I ever imagined. The connection. The intensity. The orgasms. The gentle way he held me. The magic spurring inside me, telling me my wolf was there; she was just waiting for the perfect moment. She wasn't about to ruin my first sexual experience with my mate by making an appearance yet. But she's ready. When I need her, she's ready.

"You love him."

"What?" The pink in my cheeks whitens, and my eyes bulge.

"You love him. I can tell. It's written all over your face."

"I do not. I barely even know him."

She frowns. "Why are you upset about falling for him? He's your mate. It helps things if you two love each other. I'm pretty sure he loves you, too, even if he hasn't said it out loud. And if he didn't before, it seems like the sex cemented the feeling."

My heart races. She can't be talking about Ambrose

falling in love with me. But it confirms that he never told her his curse. I'm the only one who knows.

"It's just..." *How do I get her to stop with all the love talk?*

"Wait..." she halts to a stop, grabs my shoulders, and faces me, staring me down like she can read my mind.

"That was your first time with anyone, wasn't it?"

The blush returns, and I can't look her in the eyes as I answer, "Yes."

"Oh, gods. I'm so sorry. I should have prepared you. Ambrose can be—"

"Please don't finish that sentence." I don't want to think about her and Ambrose together.

"Sorry, I just know that—"

"Nope, I don't want to hear it." I scan the dirt roads and houses, looking for anyone who can save me from this conversation, but the streets are eerily quiet.

"It's just that—"

"Rowena, stop! I really can't hear about it."

She sighs and bites her lip, trying to hold back whatever she was about to say. I need something to distract her.

"Is it strange that no one else seems to be out right now?" It's the middle of the afternoon.

She frowns and looks around, realizing that I'm right. "Come on," she says, yanking me closer to her. We turn around and head back toward Ambrose's house.

She doesn't let go of my arm as we practically run back to the house.

"Maybe you should shift," I say.

She shakes her head. "Then I can't communicate as easily with you. I will as soon as I see a threat."

I nod, remembering that she can shift within a split second.

A question pops into my head I realize I should have asked sooner. It should have been a priority over everything else.

"Why is it so important to break the curse at this full moon? Why can't it wait?"

"Vampires."

"Huh?"

Rowena shifts, and then I see them—Draven, Nikolai, and Vespera. Their gazes are brimming with cold, piercing, lethal intent. Their lips are pressed together as their eyes narrow in on me with a deadly promise—to kill me.

CHAPTER 39

LUMI

They linger in the shadows of the trees. They can't step into the sunlight, but that doesn't mean that they can't do some damage from where they are.

"Who did you hurt?" I ask, terrified they've gone on a killing spree while Ambrose and I were in bed together, completely oblivious to the pain our pack was enduring.

"No one, yet," Draven answers, looking directly at me.

Rowena growls in their direction, putting her body between me and them.

Shift, dammit, shift.

"Call your bodyguard-dog off, Lumi, and no one gets hurt," Draven says.

There is no way I'm going to be able to get Rowena to stop protecting me. I just need to shift; then, we can make a run for it. The vampires might be faster, but not when they can only step into the shadows. We'd have an easy escape.

I close my eyes, relax my body, and try to take myself back to that place I was last night. To the woods with

Ambrose. To that peace. To that connection to my wolf underneath everything else.

I feel her stirring. I feel her wanting to come out. But it's not enough. Nothing changes. I don't shift. I can't bring her to the surface. I don't know how. I might not ever know how, not even to save my own life.

"Rowena, we have to make a run for it. Back to Ambrose's house."

Rowena turns her head back to me and shakes her head no.

I frown, she doesn't think I can make it.

"As long as we stay in the sunlight, they can't touch us. We just have to make it back to the house."

She considers my words and then motions with her head toward her back. She wants me to climb on.

I hate it, but if it's the only way she will run and save herself, then I don't have a choice. I climb onto her back, gripping the gold fur there. She turns, and we are running back toward Ambrose's house.

I can hear the swift movement of the vampires behind us, but they can't reach us. It was stupid of them to try to attack us during the day. There's not enough shade for them.

Faster and faster, Rowena runs. I'm pretty sure she's faster than Ambrose; it's incredible to watch. I can see Ambrose's house on the hill come into view. We are so close.

"Stop!" I scream when I spot her.

But it's too late.

Serenity holds out her hand, and it slams into Rowena's chest.

I scream as we tumble to a stop, with Rowena taking most of the impact to her chest. I fall off her back and hit the ground, bruising my shoulder as I slide against the dirt road we were running on.

I hop up immediately, barely even registering the pain in my shoulder.

Rowena doesn't get up. She's not moving. Her chest doesn't appear to be rising and falling.

"Rowena!" I yell.

She still doesn't move.

I start to run toward her, but before I can move, I'm hit with a blast of Serenity's magic. It's immediately obvious that whatever Isolde did to me during my pack initiation was nothing compared to this. This other-worldly force knocks through my body like a bomb. A pulsing shockwave sends hot flames through me. I succumb to the dizzying rush in my head and heaviness pushing down on my lungs. There is no breaking free of this magic.

"*Vampires, Serenity, Rowena...help,*" is all I can get out to Ambrose before the magic blinds me and controls every aspect of my body to the point that I'm no longer breathing.

———

BREATHING IS A STRUGGLE. Every inhale I take is like pressing against the bars of a cage. I can't take a full breath. Shadows surround me, but the room quickly comes into sharp focus.

I'm lying on a large bed with white silk sheets. Thick, dark shades cover the window, casting the room in darkness. I have no clue if it's daytime or nighttime. My wolf eyesight allows me to see the room clearly, though. The room is simply decorated with abstract paintings on a light gray wall. A dark nightstand and dresser line the walls.

All of a sudden, I get a pit in my stomach as I feel eyes on me, watching me.

I pop up and see them—the vampires and Serenity.

"You're a tough little thing, I'll give you that," Nikolai says.

I frown. "Where is Rowena?"

"I think you should be more concerned about yourself," Verspera says.

"Where is Rowena?" I repeat.

"Dead, alive? Who knows? We left her where she fell after I hit her with my spell. She was weak," Serenity says.

They all step closer to me, watching me closely. I'm not bound. And the magic Serenity used on me seems to have almost disappeared from my body. They aren't afraid of me running or shifting. They know.

"I told you," Nikolai says.

"She can't shift, not even to save herself," Vespera spits out in disgust.

"I can shift," it's not a lie. I know I can. I just haven't, not yet.

"Don't lie to us!" Serenity roars. "We are tired of waiting, child. Shift, prove to us that you can break the curse. We only have a week left. We are running out of time. Shift."

I glare at her. "I'm not a dog. I don't just shift because you command it."

"You don't shift because you can't. You couldn't to save your friend. You can't to save yourself," Serenity says.

"I don't have to prove anything until the marking ceremony. But it doesn't matter if I can shift or not; I can break the curse. I'm strong enough. I've already proven that."

Serenity laughs. "Fool, no one can survive if they haven't come into their full powers yet. Not that we care if you survive or not, but you have to survive long enough to actually break the curse. You won't be able to. You're weak. Too fucking weak for an alpha's mate. I don't know why he chose you or what his plan is, but you aren't a match. We can smell how unlike mates you two are."

"You're wrong. We're mates. I can shift if I want to. And even if I can't, I'll survive. I'll break the curse."

"Why should we believe you?" Serenity asks.

I open my mouth, considering telling them the truth. I doubt they would believe me, and I doubt it would be enough even if they did. There is nothing I can do to save myself except shift. And I don't know how to do that on command.

"That's what I thought. You can't shift. That means you die, so the universe will give Ambrose a new mate. Kill her," Serenity says to her vampire friends.

They move before she's even finished speaking, and at once, I feel three sets of fangs sink into my neck and wrists.

This is how I die.

CHAPTER 40

AMBROSE

"Has she shifted yet?" Isolde asks from where she sits across the desk in my office.

Emeric is sitting next to her, his face dropping into a snarl at her question.

"What?" She shrugs. "I have to ask. That was why you wanted her initiated into the Moonlight wolves, after all."

"It's only been a few hours. Give her some time," Emeric says.

Isolde ignores him, raising her fair-colored eyebrow as she looks at me, waiting for my answer.

"No, she hasn't," I answer.

She purses her lips as she leans back in her chair and folds her hands together in her lap. "I see."

"What the hell is that supposed to mean? She still has a week; that's plenty of time," Emeric comes to Lumi's defense.

But I study Isolde. There's something she's not telling me.

"What is it?" I ask her.

She looks up at me. "You know I've put all of my

coven's hopes on you breaking the curse."

"I'm aware," I say in a low voice, unsure of where she's going with this. But I don't like to be threatened.

"Then you should know what will happen if you fail—"

"I won't fail. Lumi is the one—the one the prophecy states will break the curse. She's my mate—"

"And she can't shift," Isolde says with tired eyes.

"It doesn't matter if she can shift. She's strong."

"Not strong enough to survive if she can't shift."

Isolde's words stop my heart.

"How do you know? How do you know she won't survive if she can't shift?"

"Our coven's seer has seen it. If she doesn't learn to shift, she'll die. And our hope of the curse breaking this month will die with it."

My throat closes up, and there is heaviness pressing down on my chest. "How do I help her?"

"Well, I don't think spending what little time you have left fucking her is going to help," she snarls.

I grind my teeth together and growl, making it clear what I will do if she continues to speak about my relationship with Lumi.

But Isolde has known me for too long a time to back down. "I could use my magic to free her wolf. But then, I'd always have control of when and how she shifts. She'd lose that power forever."

"No."

Isolde and I stare at each other, neither of us backing down. Emeric glares at Isolde, ready to attack her if I give him the signal.

"Then you know what you have to do..."

I do, but it's not something I want to think about. I

still think she can do this. She can shift, she has to. One week—that's all we have left. Less than that really because she needs practice to be able to do it on command.

"Vampires, Serenity, Rowena...help," Lumi's voice floats into my head so softly I'm not sure it was real or if I imagined it.

"Lumi, what's happened?" I send back, concentrating hard so that she can hear me clearly.

But our connection I'm used to feeling is empty, like I'm shouting my words into a deep void.

"Lumi? Talk to me, Lumi."

My stomach hollows out, and I know. I know deep down that she's not going to respond to me. She can't respond to me.

"Where are you?"

I jump from behind my desk, not bothering to tell Isolde or Emeric what's happening. I know Emeric can feel the shift in me and that he will be hot on my heels.

I'm careful not to think too hard about what it means that the vampires most likely have her. I take deep, calming breaths as I step out of my office, listening carefully to see if Lumi or anyone else is in my house. The house is empty except for Emeric and Isolde.

Lumi mentioned Rowena.

"Rowena?"

I open the door and start running, unsure of what I'm going to find as I shift into my wolf form.

But I realize immediately that it was a mistake. It's harder to control my feelings in this form. Harder to remember that my feelings for Lumi have to be dampened. I can't care about her too much. I can't dare to cross close to the line from like to love.

Mate, mate, mate. You have to protect her. Save her. She's your mate.

The feelings begin to flood me in an uncontrollable way. I have to find a way to stop this, or I'm going to kill her even if the vampires don't.

Blood, I smell blood. But it isn't Lumi's blood.

Still, I run toward the scent, my only clue as to where she might have been taken.

Rowena.

Her body is lying on the dirt road. She's not breathing, and a pool of blood is surrounding her.

A hollow ache hits me hard in the gut as a primal fear takes hold of me. I hold onto that feeling, only letting myself think of Rowena and not Lumi. As long as my feelings stay with Rowena, I can't think too much about Lumi. My feelings for her won't have room to grow.

I collapse next to Rowena's body, not sure if I can save her or not.

"Go," Emeric says suddenly next to me. "I'll make sure Rowena is okay. Go!"

Where?

But then I get a whiff of their scent on Rowena, and I know exactly where they've taken her—to Draven's house.

I look back at Rowena one more time, and I see one of her fingers twitch. She's going to be okay. Emeric will take care of her.

———

I RUN up the steps of Draven's house near the edge of San Fransisco. It should have taken me days to get here, but it only took me hours as I ran faster than I ever have in my wolf form. Halfway here I got word from Emeric that Rowena is awake and they are traveling fast behind me. They will be here soon. But I don't have time to wait for them.

I don't take in any of the details of the house. I barely take in the concrete steps I'm climbing in my human form or the solid black door until I'm upon it. The only reason I even know this house is Draven's is because when my father was alpha, he brought me here with him. My father thought he could find a way to break the curse if he talked to all supernatural creatures. He thought that we all had missing pieces of the puzzle and that together, we would be able to break the curse.

Draven thought my father was insane for trying to bring us all together. But deep down, I know he respected him. It was the only reason he allowed us to leave without attacking us.

Now everything has changed.

I expect to be greeted by one of them as I approach the house, possibly attacked before I can even get a word out. But as I turn the door handle and push inside the house, I realize their focus isn't on intruders.

I've never run so fast in my life as I climb the stairs and throw open the bedroom door. I try to clear my mind and keep my feelings neutral as my eyes adjust to the scene in front of me.

My heart thunders in my chest, and a guttural growl builds deep in my chest until it rumbles out of me. Their fangs are plunged deep into Lumi's neck and wrists. Her blood spills from their mouths in puddles on the floor. They aren't feeding off of her; their only intention is to kill her.

"Enough," I say.

CHAPTER 41
LUMI

My pulse starts off fast, trying to keep up with what's happening, pumping adrenaline through my body like that's going to save me. The only thing that is going to save me is shifting, but even that might not be enough. Sweat drips down my brow and into my eyes, until I can barely see as the sharp fangs dig deeper into my veins. I can't move as my skin changes from warm to cool. My head begins to spin, and my breath begins to weaken.

How much blood have they taken? How much longer until this pain ends?

It can't take three vampires very long to drain me completely. My head feels lighter, and the room starts to spin. It won't be long now.

"Enough," a deep male's voice rings through the room.

To my shock, the pain in my neck and wrists lessons. But the room is spinning so fast that I can barely register who's in it. I feel weak, so weak that I can barely hold my own head up. They must still be holding onto me, or I'd fall to the floor.

Whoever spoke saved me, but just barely. Another second, and I would have drifted off to the other side. I'd be dead.

"Kill me, not her," the voice says again. So familiar, the voice.

Mine—the voice belongs to me.

What?

I question my own thoughts. *What the hell does that mean?*

"Hold on, Rowena and Emeric are on their way. Just hold on," the voice says in my head.

Rowena?

Emeric?

Who are they?

Think, think...

I try to make sense of anything. I try to lift my head. To open my eyes. But everything inside me is screaming that I should die, let go—that would be the best for everyone.

"Hold on, don't you dare die," that voice says in my head again.

But then why is my heart begging to stop beating? Why is it telling me to let go, that my death will save him?

Mine, he's mine. I love him. Save him.

The words flood my head.

I love him. He's your mate. Save him. Save him by dying.

My eyes fly open, and I see Ambrose standing on the other side of the room. He looks incredibly calm, but he's all alone. There are no other pack members with him. Serenity is holding out her hand, holding him with her magic. I don't know who's stronger—her or him.

Ambrose doesn't seem concerned. He's looking directly at me with such intense focus.

"*No,*" I try to send the single word to him to not make this trade. If he gets the message, he doesn't react or send me a message back.

"Done," Serenity says.

With the single word, the vampires toss me to the floor and attack Ambrose with the same viciousness they were just attacking me.

"No," I say in barely a whisper as I watch in horror as all three sink their teeth into his flesh. He doesn't so much as flinch as their fangs find his veins.

I hit the floor with a hard thump a second before my head bounces against it. My head feels unbearably heavy, like it's being weighed down by the vampire's mind control. In reality, I'm just so weak my neck struggles to lift my head. Inch by inch, I find the strength to lift my head up. I have to find a way to stop this before it's too late.

He loves you. That's why he traded his life for yours. If he doesn't die, then you will.

I shake my head. It doesn't matter. He can't die.

Mouthfuls of Ambrose's blood leaves his body as the vampire's sloppy drinking spills so much of his blood from their mouths onto the floor around him. Ambrose's eyes meet mine. He looks at peace, like this is how he always thought he'd meet his end.

Tears streak down my eyes. "*Save yourself. Please.*"

The corners of his lips twitch upward, and then he starts to say the words into my head. Words he would only speak if he thought he was truly dying. "*It's true. I lo—*"

"NO!" I growl. I won't let us end like this. We barely

even started. We have a whole lifetime together. We have a pack to save. This will not be how we end.

Pain, as I've never felt before, shoots through my body. I break my gaze from Ambrose, assuming that Serenity must have broken her promise to let me go and is now torturing me with her magic. But her focus is completely on Ambrose.

My head whips back to Ambrose, and for a split second, I see his eyes widen in awe before the pain overwhelms me to the point that I can't see anything but the darkness once again.

Heat, overwhelming heat burns through my body to the point that I think I'm on fire. Bones begin to twist, muscles grow, and veins, arteries, and nerves restructure. My entire body shifts, and even my brain can't think clearly.

The pain rips through me over and over and over. It will never end. I'm trapped in this body that's spiraling in unending pain. It consumes me to the point that I forget about saving Ambrose. All I want is to die to make the pain stop.

And then, suddenly, it's over.

My eyes are still squeezed shut. I'm terrified to open them. Ambrose is most likely dead. I was too late. I let the pain get the best of me.

Slowly, I open my eyes. Ambrose is still standing, still breathing. But he's so pale I doubt there is more than a couple of drops of his blood left in his body.

I don't think I just leap.

My muscles are new, but they're strong. Even though they are untested, I know what they are capable of. And if I'm wrong, then I'll die trying to save him.

I go for Draven, who is at Ambrose's neck first, and sink my own teeth into his neck.

"Stop. Release me," Draven says firmly. I feel the magic in his command dig like a knife into my brain. It feels like he's torturing me from the inside out, but it only makes me more determined.

I clamp down harder, tasting his cold, hollow flesh.

Save him, save him, save him.

The words I sing to my wolf are the only commands she listens to.

Kill Draven; save our mate.

"Release me!" Draven tries again.

I snarl against the magic that feels like a thousand stabs to my head. I release him, but only long enough to swipe at him with my massive white paws speckled with a golden hue of moonlight.

I'm Ambrose's mate. The color of my fur confirms it. His fur is black with gold flecks; mine is white with gold —a perfect match.

I don't know how to use my new body, but my wolf knows exactly what to do. The swipe of my paw hits Draven in the cheek. My claws dig into his skin, ripping a deep gash into his cheek.

He stumbles back. He's weak, weaker than I expected from a vampire who has recently been feeding on us. But I won't stop until he's dead.

My hind legs squat before I leap into the air, launching the full weight of my wolf form onto him. My front paws hit his chest, knocking him to the ground before my teeth tear apart his neck piece by piece.

I go for his arm next, clamping my teeth down onto his bicep. My head swings hard, ripping his arm from its socket. His second arm comes off even easier than his first.

Draven is lifeless on the floor, but from what I know about vampires, he won't truly be dead until a stake pierces his heart.

I'm tempted to shift back into my human form to finish the job when I see Ambrose lying still on the floor.

The other vampires and Serenity have fled—the cowards. I run to his side and watch as his chest rises and falls. He's still alive.

"*Ambrose!*" I yell through our bond, the connection coming even easier than before now that I'm in my wolf form.

He doesn't respond, doesn't so much as twitch a muscle. He doesn't have much time. He needs blood and a doctor.

I let out a soft whine as I circle him, trying to figure out how to pick him up without shifting into my human form. My wolf strength and speed is the only chance he has at surviving.

I nudge my snout under his body and toss him up in the air just enough to get my neck under his heavy body. Even in this form, he feels heavy to me. My muscles strain as I gently shift him from my neck and onto my back.

"*Hold on,*" I tell him, hoping some part of him will listen. Somehow, his fingers tighten ever so slightly into my thick fur.

And then I run.

The stairs are tricky to manage without bouncing him off, but I somehow manage to get downstairs. Thankfully, the front door is open, and I burst through the doorway. My muscles scream at me to slow down and take it easy. They are brand new, after all. But the wolf, she knows—

she knows we can't stop. She knows we have to save our mate. And she knows exactly where to run.

Ambrose told me Rowena and Emeric were coming. We just have to make it to them.

They don't appear for hours. Ambrose must have been far ahead of them when he came to rescue me. But despite my heavy breathing and aching muscles, I've managed to keep running the entire time, until I finally spot Rowena running toward us as she darts between the trees.

"Help! Ambrose lost a lot of blood!" I scream at Rowena before remembering I'm in my wolf form, and she can't hear anything other than a growl from me.

She's at my side within seconds, seeing Ambrose's limp body on my back.

Emeric appears on my other side but barely standing. He looks like he's on death's door, which means… Ambrose. Emeric feels Ambrose's pain. *Did I make it in time?*

Rowena shifts into her human form before gently rolling Ambrose off my back. His body hits the ground with a loud thud. She immediately starts chanting something over him.

"What happened?" Emeric asks, looking at me in awe.

"Vampires," I say the word before I remember he can't hear me.

But Emeric nods, like he completely understands.

"I don't know how to shift back," I say, but of course, Emeric doesn't understand me.

Rowena's body is blocking my view of Ambrose, but I can see Emeric's color returning to his face, his pain receding.

"He's going to be fine," Emeric says.

He's going to be okay. He's going to be okay.

But am I going to be okay?

Suddenly, I feel very weak. The world starts to spin around me as the pain returns in harsh waves and heats my body. The burn is fast this time, like wildfire burning away the fur and leaving human flesh in its wake.

Emeric screams as he takes in my human form. "Rowena! Lumi lost a lot of blood. I'm not sure she's going to—"

Darkness engulfs me, and I'm pretty sure I saved Ambrose only for his curse to kill me.

He loves me...

CHAPTER 42

LUMI

"*I don't love you. I don't love you. I don't love you. I don't love you. I don't love you.*" The words repeat over and over in my head, growing louder and louder and louder. "*Please, please. I didn't mean it. I don't love you, Lumi.*"

"I know you don't. I'm alive," I whisper with a smile on my lips. I expect to be lying on the ground in the forest, but when I open my eyes, I'm lying in Ambrose's bed at his house. Rowena and Emeric are here, along with another woman I recognize but don't know her name.

Before I can say anything else, Ambrose engulfs me in a bone-crushing hug. "You're alive. Oh my gods, you're alive!"

"It appears that way," I laugh uneasily as Ambrose continues to hold onto me, as if he thinks I might slip away at any moment. My body feels like it's been through hell and back. Everything is sore, and my head quickly begins to spin.

"How are you feeling?" the woman asks me.

"Lightheaded, dizzy, sore, tired."

She nods. "That's to be expected after everything you went through. I'm Serenai. Can I examine you?"

I nod, and Ambrose gently helps me lay back in bed while she does a quick examination. All the while, Ambrose never lets go of my hand.

She frowns a few minutes later.

"What's wrong?" I ask.

"Nothing. Within a couple of days of rest you'll be back to yourself. Your body went through a lot. You lost almost every drop of blood in your body. Shifting into your wolf form saved your life, but it also took an incredible toll on you. We tried giving you a blood transfusion earlier, but your body rejected it. So, unfortunately, there isn't much to do but wait for your body to heal itself." She looks to Ambrose. "There is nothing more to do but wait."

She squeezes his shoulder and then walks out of the room.

Silence stretches between the four of us remaining. There's something I'm missing. None of them should be this quiet about taking a couple of days for me to heal.

"What aren't you telling me?" I ask.

Rowena steps forward. "You've been out for almost a week."

"What?" *That can't be possible.*

She's almost in tears, so is Emeric.

A week. I've been unconscious for a week. *How did I not die? Does Ambrose really love me, and I'm never actually going to recover? Is my body going to continue to slowly decline until I finally die?*

I turn to Ambrose, knowing if anyone is going to tell me the truth, it's going to be him.

"Tell me," I say.

He opens his mouth but then closes it.

"Tell me," I demand into his mind.

"Tonight is the full moon," he finally says.

It takes me a second to process what he's saying. Tonight is the full moon. Tonight is the marking ceremony—our only chance for another month to cement our bond as mates. To break the curse.

And I see it in all of their faces. They don't think I'm strong enough.

"I can do it. I proved that I can shift. I—"

"We know that you can, but you don't understand how close to death you were and still are. It's suicide if you try to complete the marking ceremony in this state. You need to be at your strongest," Ambrose says.

I frown. "I thought I just had to be able to shift. I'm sure I can..." but that pull to the wolf inside me is weak, just like my pulse. I close my eyes, trying to connect to her —that part of me deep inside that saved me, that part that I barely know. But the connection feels severed, like it was never there in the first place.

When I open my eyes, I see them all looking at me with pity.

"I can still do this whether I can shift tonight or not. That was the plan all along anyway."

"That was when you were at full strength. In this state, you won't survive. I know things are rough between the packs, vampires, and witches, but we can all survive another month. Just postpone one month. You shouldn't die breaking the curse," Rowena says.

I look from her to Ambrose, then Emeric. Emeric looks away, and I know he knows what Ambrose's curse is. How could he not when his own curse ties him so closely to Ambrose's feelings? Rowena is the only one that doesn't know the cost. That I'll die either way. If I can't survive the marking ceremony, I'll die. But if we wait a month, Ambrose's growing feelings will ensure that I die from his curse. My only chance is to try to break the curse tonight.

"I know you're worried about me, Rowena, but I can do this. I have to."

She shakes her head with tears in her eyes. "You don't."

"I do." I try to make her believe me, but her eyes widen in disbelief.

"Are you two not going to say anything? She shouldn't do this. It will kill her!" Rowena shrieks.

"It has to be Lumi's decision," Emeric says.

Ambrose looks white as a ghost, and I'm not sure how much he's recovered from losing so much blood. But it's our only chance. He knows it. I know it. Emeric knows it.

"How much time do I have?" I ask Emeric, who seems like the only one who might answer me at the moment.

He glances out the window. "The sun will set in the next hour. The packs and witches have already gathered. The vampires weren't invited after what happened last week. Isolde has gathered the witches that will lend their power to the ceremony. It seems like everyone truly believes this will work tonight. Isolde has been studying any texts she can find about the curse and how to break it. It seems this ceremony will be more in-depth than initially thought."

"Great," I mutter under my breath, focusing on Ambrose and how healthy he is or isn't. I have to do this. For him. For me. For Kael—Nyx will kill him if I don't. And for the rest of the wolf packs. They don't deserve to live another month with their curses.

"Don't do this," Rowena says again. "It doesn't matter

that everyone has gathered. We will protect you for another month."

I look at her with a serious expression. "And how many Moonlight wolves will die trying to protect me? I'm not willing to let anyone die for me. Not when I can end this tonight." I turn to Emeric. "Tell everyone the ceremony goes on as planned. Ambrose and I have made a full recovery, and we're ready."

He nods and then leaves the room.

Rowena grinds her teeth together.

"I know you think I shouldn't do this, but like Emeric said, it's my decision to make," I tell her.

"I'm not going to watch you die," Rowena says with tears in her eyes.

"I'm not asking you to."

"Aren't you?"A heavy exhale heaves from her chest as she casts her eyes downward in defeat. "I'll go see if Emeric needs any help."

"Thank you," I say, choking back my own tears as she leaves.

Ambrose looks over at me. "You don't have to do this. We'll find another way. A way to protect the pack for another month. You and I will spend the month apart. That way there is no way I'll fall in love with you."

Our eyes connect, and he feels it just like I do—it doesn't matter if we spent the entire month apart or not; his feelings would only grow. I don't know if he has to actually confess the words out loud for the curse to trigger or just feel them, but either way, I'm not taking a chance with the curse.

And he doesn't know the other reason I have to break the curse tonight. He doesn't know about the deal I made with Nyx. I have to break the curse for Kael, too.

"Just hold me until we have to go. Just rest and recover with me. Give us both the best chances of surviving."

He frowns as he climbs into bed with me. "We'll survive. We're both strong, even if we aren't at our strongest. You're my mate."

"And you're mine."

He kisses my temple as he wraps his arms tightly around me, promising to never let me go. "You're my queen. And you shifted! I'm so fucking proud of you, so incredibly..." his words drift off as he realizes talking about what happened might trigger his feelings for me.

But I don't need to hear the words to know how proud he is. How strong he believes to me. And how close he is to loving me.

I close my eyes as he begins to speak into my mind. Words to settle me. Words to join us. Words that relax me and words that terrify me. But his words only cement my choice even more.

We have to break the curse tonight.

CHAPTER 43

AMBROSE

"Is she here?" I ask Emeric as I leave the bedroom where Lumi is sound asleep.

"Yes," Emeric says, looking me up and down like he's afraid I'm going to collapse again at any second.

I listen carefully, trying to discern where she is, but my powers are drained. I need rest, but there is no time, not until I talk to the seer.

"She's in your office," Emeric says.

"Protect Lumi with your life." I don't need his promise, but I hear it as I walk away.

"I will."

The door to my office is cracked open, and finally, I can hear the seer witch as I approach. Her heartbeat is slow and rhythmic, and so is her breathing. She's not afraid to be here.

"Are you going to come in or keep spying on me out there, wasting my time?" she snaps.

I open the door and step inside, not used to being disrespected like this, but I don't say anything. I need her. I can't piss her off.

My eyes widen when I see her. She's not at all what I expected. For one, she can't be more than twenty years old, standing before me in jeans and a cream-colored sweater. Her long red hair frizzes at the edges, and freckles splatter across her nose and cheeks. Her green eyes narrow in on me.

She's not like any of the other witches from around here who prefer to live in the woods and wear flowing gowns, reminding them of their ancestors and their otherworldliness. This woman looks human in every way possible.

Did Emeric get it right? Or is she just a human he unwittingly kidnapped?

"Stop looking so surprised. You are the one who summoned me after all," she sits in my chair and props her feet up on my desk.

"I don't know who I summoned, but I'm sure it wasn't you."

She shakes her head. "Always so arrogant. It will get you killed someday if you don't change."

"Is that a prophecy?"

"No, just a premonition."

"How is that different?"

She tilts her head as she stares at me. "Are you going to get on with it and ask your question? I have a calculus test to take soon."

"A calculus test? Are you sure you're a seer? Are you even a witch?"

"Unlike most of my coven, I prefer to live my life among the humans. I don't see them as less than. I find them fascinating. And as male humans are our only choices to procreate with, I prefer actually spending time with them instead of just randomly spelling a man into my bed. College is a great way to scope out an intelligent, good-looking man to become my sperm donor."

"Who are you?" I stand over her, looking as intimidating as possible. I don't trust her. I don't know who she is, but I'm convinced Emeric got it wrong.

She rolls her eyes, and with a nonchalant wave of her hand, she launches me into the corner office chair.

"I'm Thalia, the most powerful seer in the world. But if you don't believe me or want my help, I'll be on my way."

My body shakes with the power she just blasted at me. Even if I was at my full strength, I've never seen a power like hers, and she knows it.

"Will Lumi survive if we try to break the curse tonight? Does she have to shift into her wolf form to survive the marking ceremony?"

Her lips curl in a vicious smile. "A snow wolf will be marked by the moonlight. Once marked, the curse can be broken. But the marking will awaken a great darkness that will threaten you both."

"How do I prevent her from dying? Does she need to shift into her wolf form? The Moonfire coven's seer said she needed to shift into her wolf form."

"That's another question."

I growl. "It's a follow-up to your vague prophecy. Don't you want the curse broken? Lumi is the only one who can break the curse. You just said so yourself—she's the snow wolf. Help us break the curse."

She looks up at me slyly. "Who said I wanted to break the curse?"

"All creatures want to break the curse."

She shakes her head solemnly. "The Moonfire seer said, if she doesn't learn to shift, she'll die. Lumi has learned to shift. The Moonfire seer never said that she had to shift during the marking ceremony to survive.

"But someone will die tonight. There is always a great price to pay when magic is involved, and breaking the curse will involve tremendous magic."

"Who? Will Lumi die?"

"Shifting could keep her alive, but so could staying in her human form."

"So she'll live?"

"As long as you don't fall in love with her, then yes, she'll live."

Fuck, I can do that. My heart pounds in my chest, calling me a liar.

"You said once marked, the curse can be broken. *Can* —does that mean it will be? What does *can* mean?"

"I can't answer that."

I grind my teeth together, and my claws spring from my fingertips as I stand, towering over her.

"It's not because I refuse to give you an answer but because I can't see anything beyond the marking ceremony. The snow wolf's future is blurred."

I frown, retracting my claws. "Then how do you know that she'll break the curse?"

"I don't. I just know she has the ability to."

"Why? Why her?"

"Now, that's a good question, isn't it?" She rises from behind the desk.

"But not one you're going to answer," I snap.

"It's not a question you need the answer to yet."

"You're wrong. We need all the answers when it comes to breaking the curse. There are too many lives at stake. Try—try again to see more."

Thalia shakes her head. "I'm cursed, the same as you.

The curse prevents me from seeing more of the prophecy. I'm sorry."

"So am I." I turn and walk out the door without a goodbye or a thank you. Her answers weren't nearly enough, but I did get the one answer to the question I care most about. Lumi will live if we try to complete the marking ceremony tonight as long as I don't fall in love with her.

"You love her," Rowena says.

I freeze, not realizing that Rowena had been standing outside my office listening in.

"Don't—don't do this," I say, closing my eyes tightly. My heart is beating out of my chest, trying to find the strength to deny my feelings once again.

"You do; I can see it. Tell me it's true, I need to know. It's not fair to Lumi to put her through tonight if you don't love her."

I open my eyes, my stare boring into Rowena's soul, begging her to stop this line of questioning. Rowena could be the one to prevent the curse from being broken. With one question, she could end Lumi's life.

I hear footsteps, and I know what I must do.

"I don't," I say with as much truth in my voice as I can muster.

Rowena searches my eyes. "Liar."

My heart thrums fast, a warmth sinking into my chest, and I know I'm seconds away from killing her. I have to stop this. I have to, no matter the cost. I have to prevent Lumi's death.

I grab Rowena's waist, clearing my mind completely as I pull her hard to me and press my lips against hers, kissing her with everything I have. Rowena tries to pull away for a split second, but I press my tongue against the seam of her lips, and she opens, allowing me access.

I don't think as my tongue sweeps in her mouth, eliciting a soft, shocked moan.

Her hands push hard against my chest, breaking the kiss as quickly as it started, and Rowena looks wide-eyed at the person behind me.

"Lumi," Rowena says in one breathless word.

CHAPTER 44

LUMI

Their lips touch, and it's seared into my brain forever. I'll never stop seeing them kiss. Not when I close my eyes. Not when I sleep. I'll never be able to look at Rowena again without seeing her kiss Ambrose.

Mine—he's fucking mine! My entire body screams for me to claim him loudly and viciously so that she, nor anyone else, ever dares to touch him again. Ambrose is my mate. If I didn't believe it before, I believe it now. This coiled feeling of intense possession confirms it.

But I don't scream or shout.

I don't say any of the words to let out the pain bleeding from my damaged heart.

I don't pull Rowena away from him.

I don't attack either of them for what they did.

My reaction is blank and laser-focused on why I'm here.

I know why he kissed Rowena. He's trying to deny his feelings for me, to try and prove to the gods that he doesn't love me. He did it to save me, to buy us a few more minutes of time to break the curse before his curse ends me.

Ambrose's back is to me, but he feels my presence. I'm thankful he doesn't turn to look at me, because I don't want to see the expression on his face. Whatever is there will devastate me. I'm strong, but not strong enough to face that. So I build up my shields in my head, blocking him out so that he can't speak to me or accidentally send me any of the emotions he's feeling.

But Rowena's misty eyes don't stray from mine.

"Lumi...I'm so sorry. I didn't mean—" she says barely above a whisper.

"Don't," I should say more. I should tell her not to apologize. I understand why it had to be done. But I can't say any of those words. If I start, I'll break. I'll probably end up killing her and then regretting it after.

She opens her mouth to say more, but I turn to the office door.

"I need to speak with the seer." I don't wait for them to respond. I don't want an apology or an explanation. I just want to forget what I saw, because I'll die if I think about it too long.

I force my legs to walk through the door, turning my attention to the woman inside. I stutter when I see her. She isn't what I expected at all. She's my age for one, and two, there are no ridiculous flowing white robes in sight.

The red-haired woman smirks at me from the chair she sits in behind Ambrose's desk. "Not what you were expecting?"

I swallow. "Not exactly."

"You are exactly what I was expecting." Her words sound as if that's a bad thing. Apparently, she sees me as nothing more than a weak human who struggles to shift and isn't strong enough to break the curse.

I grind my teeth together, my anger palpably adjusting the air from cold to warm. But I take a seat across from her, knowing I don't have the strength to stand for much longer. My head is still light-headed, and my body feels like a light breeze could knock me over.

Her lips curl up. "That wasn't meant to be disrespectful. As a seer, I've seen you coming for years. It's nice to finally meet you in person."

"Oh," I almost say sorry, but then, after what just happened, I'm not in the mood to apologize to anyone anytime soon.

"My name is Thalia; I belong to the Starlight coven."

"I'm Lumi—"

"I know exactly who you are." Her eyes beam into mine as if to say she knows what pack I belong to or used to belong to. She knows I'm from the Wintermoon pack.

I pause, hoping she doesn't call me out in a house full of eavesdropping shifters.

"I've spelled this room. No one can hear our conversation."

I raise my eyebrows in surprise. *Can she read my thoughts?* Whether she spelled the room or not, I get the impression that I shouldn't trust her implicitly.

"I assume you're here to ask what prophecy I told Ambrose?"

"You don't know why I'm here?"

She rakes her teeth over her bottom lip. "I don't see everything, only what the prophecies say."

I take a deep breath, smelling Ambrose's scent as I do. The rage returns as his familiar scent infiltrates the shields I've put up. I love him, and he kissed her. He kissed another woman like I was nothing. He—

I hold my breath, pushing the pain down into my gut, knowing that it will brew there until I explode later. But not right now.

"No," I know he'll tell me what she told him. It would be a waste of time to ask her what prophecy she told him.

"How do the prophecies work? Who can see them?"

Her green eyes widen at my questions. "Those with the gift of a seer are the only ones who can see a prophecy. The seers are the most powerful witches in each coven. But the curse has prevented any one witch from seeing an entire prophecy. We only get small parts now. Parts that can be easily misconstrued and lead us to inaccurate conclusions." She frowns as if it pains her.

"So if I saw something in a dream, what does that mean?"

Her eyes snap to me. "No wolf shifters have the gift. Anything you saw was just a dream, not a prophecy."

I sigh, knowing she's telling the truth. I have no special gift. There is nothing special about me that helps me see the future or have any additional knowledge about how to break the curse.

"Don't you want to know if you're the one that's destined to break the curse?"

Do I want to know? No, because it terrifies me if I'm the only one who can break it. I'd much rather know that many could break it. The pressure is too great.

She doesn't wait for me to answer. "A snow wolf is destined to be the key to breaking the curse."

I suck in a breath, knowing that a snow wolf is me. My name means snow. But then, in my heart, I've always known I was the one—the one everyone has been waiting for.

"But you should know, you aren't the first the prophecy has said would break the curse. You're just the current destined one."

"What happened to others?" I ask.

"They died trying to break the curse."

CHAPTER 45

LUMI

Ambrose and I stand at the top of the hill with our fingers intertwined. We look down at the crowd that has gathered on the side of a hill overlooking the stage where I was presented as an offering last month. This time, I'm here because it's my choice. And this time, I know exactly who my mate is.

I'm dressed in a long, curve-hugging, black lace dress next to Ambrose and his black suit. Golden crowns adorn both our heads. I've never felt so powerful, even if I've never physically been weaker. The blood flowing through my veins is just enough to keep me standing, to keep me walking. Ambrose, despite putting on a brave front, hasn't fully recovered yet, either. But he squeezes my hand as if he has enough strength for both of us.

When we reach the top of the hill, silence falls through the crowd as all eyes track us. Together, we start to descend the stairs hand in hand.

I was sure the crowns were too much, but as we walk, several pack members and even nonpack members bow to us. They seem to understand and respect the sacrifice we are about to make.

I spot Isolde at the bottom of the stairs where the stage is and stumble. I knew she was the witch that would conduct the ceremony, but I still don't like her.

"I've got you. You're safe. I won't let Isolde hurt you," Ambrose says in my head.

"I know. I trust you."

His lips curl up just a touch, and the warmth and assurance in his eyes tell me any doubt from earlier is long gone. He truly believes that we can do this. I know we can.

We only briefly discussed what Thalia said to us about the prophecy. But it was enough to give us both confidence that we can break the curse and survive. We avoid speaking about his kiss with Rowena.

Once we hit the stage, Ambrose turns to face the crowd. "Tonight, my mate and I will complete the marking ceremony confirming that we are mates. We will break the curse. And my queen and I will take our places as alphas of the Moonlight wolves."

Cheers break out, but Ambrose and I just stare everyone down. I scan every one of their faces until I find who I'm looking for. Nyx is standing next to Kael in the front row. Nyx raises his eyebrow at me as if to call my bluff. But I'm not backing down. I quickly scan Kael. He doesn't seem hurt, but I can't read much about his condition beyond any obvious outward injuries. There is nothing I can do to help him at the moment, even if he is injured.

So, for now, I push Kael out of my mind and then sweep my attention to Emeric and Rowena, who are on the other side of the aisle in the front row. Emeric is grinning wildly at us with all the faith in the world that we are going to do this. Rowena, however, looks like she's chewed her nails completely off at this point and doesn't know what to do with her hands now.

"It's going to be okay. We can do this," I mouth to her as much for my own sake.

She nods but doesn't look too assured. Shame still marks her face. She tried to speak with me before the ceremony, but I brushed her off. When we break the curse, and everything can be spoken about, then we'll talk.

Ambrose and I both turn to face Isolde. Ambrose warned me that this ceremony will probably be a bit different than what we saw before. He said Isolde has been doing a lot of research, but he didn't tell me more than that. It's probably because, based on how fast his heart is beating next to me, he doesn't know what Isolde has planned either.

"As Ambrose has said, we are gathered here to conduct the marking ceremony and break the curse. Thank you to everyone who came to ensure that the ceremony goes off smoothly. I know how desperate we all are to end this." She flicks her hand in a signal, and suddenly, the stage is surrounded by witches.

The crowd gasps.

Ambrose and I are both stone-faced. We expected this, but it's still shocking to see an entire coven of witches surrounding us. There is no turning back now.

They all hold their hands up at the same time, and I watch as golden threads flow from their fingers up toward the sky. The threads begin to weave together in an intricate pattern that I would call beautiful if it wasn't for the fact that it was forming a cage around us.

Ambrose and I continue to hold hands while keeping our expressions neutral. We are either leaving this cage as true mates, having broken the curse, or we die.

Isolde turns to us with a calculated smirk and a cold, piercing stare that screams she'll be happy either way.

"She better hope we die. I plan on killing her after we break the curse."

Ambrose chuckles under his breath. *"Nothing less than what she deserves, my queen."*

My queen—I love it when he calls me that. It has nothing to do with the crown on my head or the role he expects me to play. He calls me that because of how he feels about me.

"The moon will soon be at its peak. It's time to start." Isolde holds up her hands. "Do you, Lumi, accept Ambrose as your mate?"

"Yes."

"Do you, Ambrose, accept Lumi as your mate?"

"Yes."

"Very well, we shall see if you both chose correctly. There are two parts to the ceremony. Part one is to join as your human selves. Part two is to shift into your wolf forms and for Ambrose to mark Lumi's upper shoulder. If you both survive, then the mating bond should make itself known."

I'm listening, but still focused on the first part. *"What does she mean about joining as our human selves?"*

"I'm not—"

But then an ivory altar with gold etchings up the side similar to the runes marking our bodies appears in the center of the stage. There is a single pillow and very thin looking mattress that makes the altar look like a bed and it becomes perfectly clear what she means.

"Sex, she means sex."

"We don't have—"

"We do. We will. Whatever it takes. I trust you."

"I'll help you kill her the second this is over," he growls in my head.

"No, she's mine."

"We have restraints if you need to use them to get the job done, Ambrose," Isolde says with a cruelty in her voice that leaves an unsettled feeling in my stomach.

A raw, primal growl pours out of Ambrose as he uses his body like a shield, blocking me from her. "That won't be necessary," he says through clenched teeth.

"I'll make this fast and keep you as covered as I can. I'll—" he says in a panicked voice in my head.

"I know. I trust you. I don't care who sees our bond. We are doing this, not just because we have to but because we want to. You're my mate, Ambrose. I want the world to know."

His jaw twitches, but he takes me by the hand and leads me gently to the altar-like bed.

"Just focus on me." His eyes lock on mine and mine on his as we both take a slow, deep breath. His fingers gently brush against my cheek before her cradles my neck with the palm of his hand, and his lips brush over mine. Once, twice before he quickly sweeps his tongue through the seam of my mouth and gently lifts me onto the hard altar.

Heat weaves through me with every purposeful kiss until I'm quickly burning up. A fervent longing beats hard in my chest as my core begs for him inside me to quench the ache between my thighs.

"It's just us."

"Just us."

That's all the preparation I'll get—anything more would be too intimate and take too long. It would expose my body to the rest of the world. There are no blankets, nothing to cover our bodies with. He kissed me just enough to turn me on, just enough to make this pleasurable for me, to prepare my body, but nothing more.

Ambrose gently spreads my legs and takes up the space between them, hiking my dress up my thighs until it's bunched around my waist. His thumb circles my clit over my panties once before he realizes how soaked the material is. I'm ready for him; I'm always ready for him. He carefully pushes my panties to one side.

"I want you so much." His voice is desperate, as is the look in his golden eyes.

I don't look away as I hear the zipper of his pants. *"Me too."*

I feel the tip of his length brush against my clit, and then he takes me in one hard thrust, burying himself to the hilt. My eyes squeeze shut as the quick shot of pain overwhelms me. I thought I was more than ready for him, but his large size compared to the heaviness of the moment is more than I was prepared for.

Despite my best efforts, a wretched moan squeaks out before I can contain it. I quickly bite my lip, refusing for anyone to see or hear that I'm in any pain—especially Isolde.

Ambrose is focused, though. He fucks me fast to get this over as quickly as possible. His lips dance over mine again, soothing my agony.

"I'm sorry—"

"Don't. I'm okay," I reassure him.

Both of our voices are strangled, pushing through the torment we feel in this moment.

His lips brush against mine again and again, and the

heat returns to my body, quickly overshadowing the burning and stretching I felt before.

I don't dare open my eyes, too terrified I'll lock eyes with anyone in the crowd. Instead, I focus on feeling Ambrose inside me. But my mind is rushing through all the possibilities of what could happen. *What if we can't break the curse? What if...?*

The bruised, burning feeling when he first took me is gone, but my mind won't allow me to settle into the moment with him like I usually would. I'm too panicked. Thrust after thrust, he expertly fucks me. It's pleasurable but nothing like when we've had sex before. It's as if he doesn't want to share that part of us with the world. This feels methodical, mechanical. He's going through the motions but not really revealing much of our relationship to the world.

Panic sneaks up my chest as I realize it's going to take forever for me to come.

"Please don't let me having an orgasm be required for our joining as humans to be complete."

"It's not. Just me. You coming undone is only for me. I won't share that with anyone else in the world."

"Good. I don't want to share it either."

"I promise to make you come all night long as soon as this is over."

"I can't wait." I bite my lower lip to keep another moan from leaving my lips as my back drives into the hard altar with one of Ambrose's thrusts.

"So close, my queen," Ambrose pants in a tormented whisper.

"Finish this," I demand.

And then I feel his seed spilling inside me in warm

ribbons as if he was waiting for me to give him permission.

I take a deep, long breath as Ambrose pulls out of me, pulling my dress down my thighs to ensure no one gets a view of my body. He quickly helps me into a sitting position with my legs dangling over the side of the altar. Stars twinkle in my vision instead of the crowd surrounding us.

"You okay?"

"Yes." I blink, and my vision returns to normal as I look at him. He looks as perfect as when we first walked here, not at all like he just fucked me in front of a hillside of supernatural creatures. Even the crown atop his head hasn't tilted.

He takes a deep breath that washes over me like a warm blanket, instantly calming me. And then adjusts my crown sitting on my curled white hair.

I'm composed, but I still refuse to look out at the crowd. I was barely exposed. No one saw anything, but it was still embarrassing, still too much.

Ambrose holds me tight to his body as he looks at Isolde. "Move on to part two."

She nods. "Shift."

"We are doing part two without shifting," he says.

She smirks like she knew that's what we'd say. "That's not your choice. I know she can shift now."

With a wave of her hand, magic burns into me hard and fast like lightning striking my body. Violent tremors wreck me as I try to maintain control. An explosive force of heat infiltrates every nerve, muscle, and flesh of my skin.

I consider shifting just to make the pain stop. But I remember Serenai's warning—shifting when I'm this weak could kill me. Besides, I can barely feel my connection to my wolf inside me. And she's made it clear time and time again that she won't make an appearance to save my life. The only thing strong enough to bring her out is needing to save my mate.

"Ah!" a scream is pulled from my body as the witches in Moonfire's coven begin to pour their magic into me one by one until all twelve are attacking me at once. They are going to force me to shift, giving them the ability to control my wolf for the rest of time.

I'm going to die. I'm too weak, and my wolf can't appear when I'm this fragile.

"Lumi!" Ambrose screams, but his voice feels like it's miles away from me. "Stop this, Isolde! She can shift on her own. Just give her a minute."

"We don't have a minute. The moon is cresting. It has to be now," Isolde says.

"Lumi, hold on," Ambrose says in a terrified voice that echoes in my head, but I can't focus through the intense pain seizing my body.

I don't know how long the magic pours through me. Time feels endless and meaningless. Fire burns through my body in the way it does before I shift. But it's too intense. It's too much. I feel my body give out as I collapse to the floor.

As soon as I hit the ground, the witches stop. It's quiet, so quiet that I can hear every breath and heartbeat of every mortal and immortal creature within a mile radius.

I stand, ignoring the ache in every crevice of my body. With a heavy breath, I look Isolde straight in the eyes, and I say, "I will complete the ceremony in my human form."

"You'll never survive," she says with a hint of pleasure in her tone.

"Watch me," I growl with unrestrained fury.

I turn to Ambrose. "Shift."

He watches me closely, waiting for me to second-guess myself. But I don't. I won't.

A second later, Ambrose's large black wolf with golden streaks and glowing eyes is standing in front of me. His frame is still scary as hell, as are his sharp teeth that are about to tear into my human flesh. But I don't feel any of that fear when I look at him now. I know what has to be done, and I know I'm strong enough.

"Do it," I say.

He growls low in warning.

"Do it," I give my own alpha command, unsure if it will work. "Mark me as your mate."

Ambrose bares his sharp canines at me, reminding me of the pain I'm about to endure.

I swallow the lump in my throat, preparing my body for the pain. It doesn't matter how painful it is; I'll survive. Not because I'm stronger than anyone else here, but because he's my mate. My soulmate. My lover. *Mine.* The connection between us will ensure I survive.

Ambrose stalks toward me. I take a deep breath and brush my snowy-white hair off my shoulder, giving him easy access. My eyes blaze at his a second longer before he opens his massive jaw, and I wait for the pain. The pain that will make everything worth it. The pain that will break the curse.

His teeth brush against my skin in warning before his canines begin to pierce my sensitive flesh. I grind my teeth together but will not allow myself to show any outward pain. I will survive this. I will—

"Stop! I'm your mate, not Ambrose," a deep voice says, halting Ambrose as if he's been commanded.

I blink, unsure of who spoke, but the pain in my neck has lessened as a drop of blood rolls down my neck, stopping at my clavicle. I don't know why Ambrose even listened to him, but when I look at Ambrose, I see that magic is holding him frozen a few feet away from me.

My heart thunders as I turn toward the voice—Nyx.

"You're not my mate. Ambrose is," I say clearly.

"I'm calling in my favor," Nyx says. My eyes widen as I realize he says it in my head.

What the hell?

"I think you got it wrong. I think I'm your mate, not Ambrose. I want to challenge him to be your mate." Nyx stalks toward us.

"You're not my mate," I say again and more clearly.

"You let me do this, or our deal is over, and Kael is dead."

I look over to Kael and see two vampires surrounding him.

"Kael!" I scream, trying to warn him, but it's too late. He's held tightly by the two vampires at his side.

I glare at Nyx. "Let him go."

Ambrose still hasn't moved. He's completely frozen. And I have no clue what to do.

I look to Rowena and Emeric. Both look ready to leap into action at my command. The entire Moonlight pack is behind them and ready.

"Release Ambrose, and let us continue the ceremony. The moon will crest soon," I say to Isolde.

"Afraid I can't do that," she says.

"Can you break free? What do we do?" I ask Ambrose.

But he doesn't respond. I doubt he even got my message with the magic surrounding him and stopping me from talking to him.

I look at Rowena and give her the slightest nod. We're going to have to fight our way out of this.

Then I shift.

With Ambrose in danger, my wolf makes an easy appearance. The world goes black as blinding pain rips through me. At the same time, I hear the chaos break out around us.

I focus all my energy to shift faster, but I can't make my body change any faster. And I can't help unless I shift. So I'm trapped in my body as every muscle painstakingly slowly shifts from my thin ribbons into thick bands, giving me the bulk and strength my wolf form needs.

Hands engulf my body, and I feel myself being carried, but I have no idea by whom. No idea if it's Ambrose or...

Nyx.

I can smell him. A distinct metallic scent invades my nostrils. He smells like blood.

My eyes burn open as my shift completes, but it's too late. I flail in his arms, but his grip doesn't loosen on me. I don't know how Nyx is strong enough to carry me when I'm in my wolf form, and he's still in his human body. But his grip doesn't loosen as he carries me off the stage and into the forest behind it. I look behind us, trying to find Ambrose, Emeric, or...Rowena.

I gasp as I spot her lifeless body lying on the ground in a puddle of blood.

"She's dead," Nyx says.

"NO! Put me down!" I scream in my head, but I'm not sure if he can hear me. I fight harder to get free. She can't be dead, she can't be.

"You can't save her. You can save Kael. You can save Ambrose. You can save the rest of your pathetic pack, but you can't save her," he says aloud.

I sob, but it comes out a howl in my wolf form.

Nyx doesn't release his hold on me as I scream and scream, each scream tearing through my body like a hurricane. I sob, and scream, and flail as heartbreak spills through my body. With each sob, I feel myself shrinking, getting smaller and smaller, my senses lessening until I begin to shiver from the cool air hitting my human skin once again.

Nyx cradles my naked body against his chest as he runs effortlessly through the forest. I don't know where he's taking me, and I don't have the strength to fight him. Time once again escapes me. I don't know how long he runs, just that time stretches infinitely as he does. Eventually, he stops and puts me down on the ground.

I shiver as more cold air hits my naked skin.

"You killed Rowena, didn't you?" I ask, my throat scratchy and my eyes stained with tears as I stare at the ground.

"It doesn't matter who killed her."

I look up at him, finally seeing who he really is. His mouth is covered in blood, and his fangs are sharper than any other wolf shifter. He's not just a wolf shifter...

"You're a vampire."

He nods.

"How? How are you part vampire, part shifter?"

"The same way your mate is part shifter, part witch."

"What?"

He chuckles. "You really are a fool. I'm almost not sure it was worth rescuing you."

"You didn't rescue me."

"I sure as hell did. If I had let you continue with that little ceremony of yours, you'd be dead by now."

"No, I would have broken the curse."

He scoffs. "No, you wouldn't have. But we'll have to agree to disagree. For now, I want you to start telling me the truth. What do you really know about breaking the curse?"

"What are you talking about?"

"I know who you are, Lumi. I know you're part of the Wintermoon wolves. I know you're the snow wolf that the seers talk about. And I know you spoke with Thalia. I know you have more pieces of the prophecy than you've let on. I have a feeling it's a lot more complicated, and there are a lot more stipulations than what the ceremony was about. So if you want me to keep being nice to you, then start talking."

Through tear-stained eyes, I look at him directly. I know Thalia said that only seers receive parts of the prophecy. That my dreams can't be prophecy, but maybe she's wrong. That those who are part of the prophecy also receive pieces. The way that Nyx is looking at me, I know he believes it's possible.

He's a vampire and a wolf shifter. If what he speaks is true, Ambrose is a wolf shifter and witch. There is nothing that isn't impossible.

"Yes, I have pieces of the prophecy that no one else knows. But I'll never tell you."

He smirks, his eyes darkening. "We'll see about that. I think you'll change your mind when you've been mine for a few months."

"I'll never be yours."

"You already are," he says as he plunges his fangs over the spot on my neck where Ambrose started to mark me.

———

THANK you for reading Marked by Moonlight! You can continue the story in Bitten by Bloodmoon.

One-click Bitten by Bloodmoon Here

"A snow wolf will be the one to break the curse," the seer's voice plays over and over in my head as I watch Lumi and Ambrose descend down the stairs.

Click here to read the prologue of Bitten by Bloodmoon from Nyx's perspective.

ALSO BY ELLA MILES

TRUTH OR LIES:

Taken by Lies #1

Betrayed by Truths #2

Trapped by Lies #3

Stolen by Truths #4

Possessed by Lies #5

Consumed by Truths #6

SINFUL TRUTHS:

Sinful Truth #1

Twisted Vow #2

Reckless Fall #3

Tangled Promise #4

Fallen Love #5

Broken Anchor #6

LIES SERIES:

Lies We Share: A Prologue #0.5

Vicious Lies #1

Desperate Lies #2

Fated Lies #3

Cruel Lies #4

Dangerous Lies #5

Endless Lies #6

RETRIBUTION GAMES SERIES:

Mistaken Hero #1

Forbidden Princess #2

Tempted Hero #3

Fatal Princess #4

Tortured Hero #5

Dangerous Princess #6

RETRIBUTION KINGS SERIES:

Lennox #1

PRETEND SERIES:

Pretend I'm Yours

Pretend We're Over

Pretend: The Complete Series

DIRTY SERIES:

Dirty Obsession

Dirty Addiction

Dirty Revenge

Dirty: The Complete Series

ALIGNED SERIES:

Aligned: Volume 1

Aligned: Volume 2

Aligned: Volume 3

Aligned: Volume 4

Aligned: The Complete Series Boxset

UNFORGIVABLE SERIES:

Heart of a Thief

Heart of a Liar

Heart of a Prick

Unforgivable: The Complete Series Boxset

MAYBE, DEFINITELY SERIES:

Maybe Yes

Maybe Never

Maybe Always

Maybe: The Complete Series

Definitely Yes

Definitely No

Definitely Forever

Definitely: The Complete Series

STANDALONES:

Finding Perfect

Savage Love

Too Much

Not Sorry

Hate Me or Love Me: An Enemies to Lovers Romance Collection

About the Author

Ella Miles writes steamy romance, including everything from dark suspense romance that will leave you on the edge of your seat to contemporary romance that will leave you laughing out loud or crying. Most importantly, she wants you to feel everything her characters feel as you read.

Ella is currently living her own happily ever after near the Rocky Mountains with her high school sweetheart husband. Her heart is also taken by her goofy five year old black lab who is scared of everything, including her own shadow.

Ella is a USA Today Bestselling Author & Top 50 Bestselling Author.

Stalk Ella at:
www.ellamiles.com
ella@ellamiles.com

www.ingramcontent.com/pod-product-compliance
Lightning Source LLC
Chambersburg PA
CBHW021242190726
48289CB00005B/1453